A PLUME BOOK

THE KING'S GOLD

ARTURO PÉREZ-REVERTE is a former war journalist. His novels *The Flanders Panel*, *The Club Dumas*, *The Fencing Master*, *The Seville Communion*, *The Nautical Chart*, and *The Queen of the South* have been translated into twenty-nine languages and published in more than fifty countries. He lives in Madrid.

Praise for *The King's Gold*

"[The] series recalls the great adventure novels of Dumas and Scott . . . [Pérez-Reverte] brings Seville to life as if he were animating a painting by Velázquez." —*The New York Times*

Praise for Arturo Pérez-Reverte and the Adventures of Captain Alatriste

"Hardboiled, mordantly funny, unapologetically entertaining." —*Time*

"Wonderful, stirring entertainment." —*The New York Times Book Review*

"It's great fun in the tradition of historical swashbucklers such as *The Three Musketeers* or *The Scarlet Pimpernel*." —*The Boston Globe*

"Few contemporary writers conjure up derring-do as well as Arturo Pérez-Reverte, a Spanish literary maestro. The true thrill lies in Pérez-Reverte's deft plotting and thread-the-needle resolutions." —*The Christian Science Monitor*

"Thrilling." —*Detroit Free Press*

"Grabs the reader from the get-go with its moody evocation of a lost time." —*USA Today*

"A feast of dark historical detail and believable danger in which celebrated historical figures, such as poet Francisco de Quevedo and painter Velázquez, are mixed in for authentic flavor." —*The Denver Post*

"Intrigue and double-dealing . . . Pérez-Reverte is a master at evoking . . . els, taverns, torero arenas, and dar . . . mes

THE KING'S GOLD

Arturo Pérez-Reverte

TRANSLATED FROM THE SPANISH BY
Margaret Jull Costa

A PLUME BOOK

PLUME
Published by the Penguin Group
Penguin Group (USA) Inc., 375 Hudson Street, New York, New York 10014, USA • Penguin Group
(Canada), 90 Eglinton Avenue East, Suite 700, Toronto, Ontario, Canada M4P 2Y3 (a division of
Pearson Canada Inc.) • Penguin Books Ltd., 80 Strand, London WC2R 0RL, England • Penguin
Ireland, 25 St. Stephen's Green, Dublin 2, Ireland (a division of Penguin Books Ltd.) • Penguin
Group (Australia), 250 Camberwell Road, Camberwell, Victoria 3124, Australia (a division of Pearson
Australia Group Pty. Ltd.) • Penguin Books India Pvt. Ltd., 11 Community Centre, Panchsheel Park,
New Delhi – 110 017, India • Penguin Group (NZ), 67 Apollo Drive, Rosedale, North Shore 0632,
New Zealand (a division of Pearson New Zealand Ltd.) • Penguin Books (South Africa) (Pty.) Ltd.,
24 Sturdee Avenue, Rosebank, Johannesburg 2196, South Africa

Penguin Books Ltd., Registered Offices: 80 Strand, London WC2R 0RL, England

Published by Plume, a member of Penguin group (USA) Inc. Previously published in a Putnam edition.

First Plume Printing, September 2009
1   3   5   7   9   10   8   6   4   2

 REGISTERED TRADEMARK MARCA—REGISTRADA

The Library of Congress has catalogued the Putnam edition as follows:

Pérez-Reverte, Arturo.
[Oro del, rey. English]
The king's gold / Arturo Pérez-Reverte ; translated from the Spanish by Margaret Jull Costa.
p.   cm.
ISBN 978-0-399-15510-9 (hc.)
ISBN 978-0-452-29542-1 (pbk.)
I. Costa, Margaret Jull.   II. Title.
PQ6666.E76507613   2008   2008016578
863'.64—dc22

Printed in the United States of America
Original hardcover design by Marysarah Quinn

To Antonio Cardenal,

for ten years of friendship, movies, and fencing

What do we gain from it all? A little glory?
Some rich rewards, or merely boredom?
You'll find out if you read our story.

GARCILASO DE LA VEGA ·

THE KING'S GOLD

1. THE HANGED MEN OF CÁDIZ

*The reason we are brought so low is that those who
should honor us instead conspire against us. Once, it
was enough merely to brandish the word "Spaniard"
for all to tremble; now, for our sins, that reputation is
almost lost.*

I closed the book and looked where everyone else was
looking. After several hours without a breath of wind, the
Jesús Nazareno was finally heading into the bay, driven by
the westerly breeze now filling the creaking mainsail.
Grouped along the deck of the galleon, in the shadow of
the great sails, soldiers and sailors alike were pointing at
the corpses of the English, which either adorned the walls
of Santa Catalina castle or hung from gallows erected on
the shore, along the edge of the vineyards that face out to

sea. They resembled bunches of grapes ripe for harvesting, except that these grapes had been harvested already.

"Curs," growled Curro Garrote, spitting into the sea.

He had greasy, grimy skin, as did we all: soap and water were in scarce supply on board, and after the five-week voyage from Dunkirk via Lisbon, bringing home the soldiers from the war in Flanders, the lice were the size of chickpeas. Garrote bitterly stroked his left arm, rendered almost useless by the English at Terheyden, and gazed in satisfaction at the San Sebastián sandbank, where, opposite the chapel built next to the lighthouse, lay the smoking remains of a ship that the Earl of Leicester himself had ordered to be burned, with as many of his own dead on board as he could find, before reembarking on another ship and fleeing with those who had survived.

"They paid a heavy price," someone said.

"And would have paid a still heavier one," said Garrote, "if we'd gotten here in time."

He would gladly have strung up some of those bunches of grapes himself. The English and the Dutch, as arrogant and full of themselves as ever, had attacked Cádiz the week before, with one hundred fifty warships and ten thousand men, determined to sack the city, set fire to our ships in the bay, and seize the treasure fleet that was due to arrive from Brazil and New Spain. In his play *The Girl with the Pitcher*, the great Lope de Vega began his famous sonnet thus:

The Englishman bold, armed only with trickery,
Thinking the lion of Spain asleep in his lair . . .

And that was precisely how the Earl of Leicester had arrived, the typical cunning, cruel, piratical Englishman—however much the people of that nation may hide behind privileges and hypocrisy. He disembarked a great many soldiers and succeeded in taking the Fort of Puntal. At the time, neither the young Charles I nor his minister Buckingham had forgiven the rebuff received when the former had wanted to marry a Spanish infanta, who kept him waiting around in Madrid for so long that he finally lost patience and returned to London with his tail between his legs. I'm referring to the episode, which I'm sure you'll remember, when Captain Alatriste and Gualterio Malatesta came within an ace of putting a hole in the young king's doublet. However, unlike the day thirty years before when Cádiz was plundered by the Earl of Essex, God chose otherwise this time: our men were armed and ready, the defense was hard-fought, and the soldiers of the Duque de Fernandina were joined by the inhabitants of Chiclana, Medina Sidonia, and Vejer, as well as by any infantrymen, horses, and old soldiers who happened to be at hand, and thus we Spanish gave the English a sound drubbing, and the English hindered our efforts only by spilling a great deal of their own blood. After much suffering and having advanced not one inch, Leicester hurriedly reembarked when he realized that what he could see hoving into view was not the treasure fleet but our galleons, six large ships and a few smaller vessels, Spanish and Portuguese—for, at the time, thanks to the great King Philip's inheritance from his mother, Spain and Portugal shared both empire and enemies—each one equipped with good artillery, and carrying veterans coming home on leave and infantrymen from now disbanded regiments, all of them battle-hardened men from the war in Flanders. When our admiral was given the news in Lisbon, he had set off for Cádiz under full sail.

The heretics' sails, however, were now nothing but tiny white dots on the horizon. We had passed them at a distance the previous evening, limping home after their failed attempt to repeat their good fortune of 1596, when all Cádiz burned and when they had plundered even the libraries. It's amusing really how the English make such a fuss about the defeat of what they, with heavy irony, refer to as our Invincible Armada, and about Essex and so on, but they never mention the occasions on which they came off worst. Poor Spain may have been an empire in decline, with more than enough enemies eager to dip their bread in the sauce and mop up the gravy, but the old lion still had teeth and claws enough to go down fighting before its lifeless body was shared out amongst the crows and the merchants, whose Lutheran and Anglican duplicity—Devil take them—never seemed to have any problem combining their worship of a very indulgent God with piracy and profit, for, amongst heretics, being a thief had become one of the respected liberal arts. If one were to believe their chroniclers, we Spaniards made war and enslaved people purely out of pride, greed, and fanaticism, while those who murmured about us behind our backs, they, of course, plundered and trafficked and exterminated in the name of liberty, justice, and progress. But that, alas, is the way of the world. What the English left behind them on this occasion were thirty ships lost at Cádiz, many colors brought low, and a large number of dead on land—about a thousand, not counting the stragglers and drunks whom our men mercilessly hanged from the city walls and from the gallows erected in the vineyards. This time their plan blew up in their faces, the whoresons.

Beyond the forts and the vineyards we could see the city with its white houses and turrets tall as watchtowers. As we rounded the bastion of San Felipe, when the port finally came into view, we could already scent the earth of Spain the way donkeys can scent grass. A few salvos of cannon greeted us, and the bronze mouths protruding from our gunports offered a loud response. At the prow of the *Jesús*

Nazareno, the sailors were preparing to drop anchor. And only when the men had scrambled up the yardarms to take in the sails, and the canvas was already flapping loose on the spars, did I put away my copy of *Guzmán de Alfarache*—bought by Captain Alatriste in Antwerp as reading matter for the voyage—and go to rejoin my master and his comrades on the forecastle. Almost everyone was excited and glad to be once more within reach of land, knowing that all the troubles of the voyage would soon be over: the danger of being hurled onto rocks by contrary winds, the stench of life belowdecks, the vomiting, the damp, the meager daily ration of rank water, the dried beans, and the worm-eaten ship's biscuits. A soldier's lot may be a wretched one on land, but it is far worse at sea. If God had intended man to live there, he would have given him fins, not hands and feet.

When I reached Diego Alatriste's side, he gave a slight smile and placed one hand on my shoulder. He looked thoughtful, his clear green eyes studying the scene before him, and I remember thinking that his was not the expression one would expect on the face of someone arriving home.

"Well, here we are again, my boy."

He said this in a strange, resigned tone, as if being there were no different from being anywhere else. I, meanwhile, was gazing ahead at Cádiz, fascinated by the play of light on its white houses and the majesty of its vast blue-green expanse of bay, a light so very different from that of my birthplace, Oñate, and yet which I also felt to be mine.

"Spain," murmured Curro Garrote.

He sneered as he said this, pronouncing the word as if he were spitting it out.

"The ungrateful old bitch," he added.

He touched his shattered arm again as if in response to a sudden pang of pain, or as if he were trying to remember why it was that he had been prepared to risk both limb and life at Terheyden. He was about to say something else, but Alatriste shot him a stern glance with those piercing eyes of his, which, along with his aquiline nose and bristling mustache, gave him the threatening air of a cruel, dangerous falcon. He looked at him briefly, then at me, and again turned cold eyes on Garrote, who said nothing more.

The sailors had dropped anchor, and our ship stood motionless in the bay. Black smoke from the Fort of Puntal still hung over the strip of sand that joins Cádiz to the mainland, but the city had otherwise barely been touched by the battle. People had gathered near the royal warehouses and the customhouse and were standing on the shore, waving, while feluccas and other smaller boats gathered around us, their crews cheering as if we had been the ones to drive the English from Cádiz. Later, I learned that they had mistaken us for the advance party of the Indies fleet, whose yearly arrival we, like the soundly beaten Earl of Leicester and his Anglican pirates, had anticipated by a matter of days.

And God knows, our voyage, too, had been long and full of incident, especially as far as I was concerned, for this was my first experience of those cold northern seas. From Dunkirk, in a convoy of seven galleons—with various merchant ships and Basque and Flemish privateers bringing our numbers up to seventeen—we broke through the Dutch blockade as we headed north, where no one was expecting us, and fell upon the Dutch herring fleet, of whom we made short work, before continuing around Scotland and Ireland and returning south across the ocean. The merchant ships and one of the galleons left us—at Vigo and at Lisbon, respectively—and the other larger ships sailed on down to Cádiz. As for the privateers, they stayed in the north, prowling the English coast and doing an excellent job of plundering, burning, and generally disrupting the enemy's maritime activities, just as they regularly did to us in the Antilles and wherever else they could. God, sometimes, is well served, and it's true what they say: As ye sow, so shall ye reap.

It was on this voyage that I witnessed my first naval battle. We had sailed through the channel between Scotland and the Shetland Islands, a few leagues west of an island called Foul, a black, inhospitable place, like all those gray-skied isles, when we came upon a large flotilla of those herring boats that the Dutch call *buizen,* under escort by four Lutheran men-of-war, amongst them an *urca,* a large, impressive storeship. The merchant vessels with us stood aside, keeping well to windward, while the Basque and Flemish privateers fell like vultures on the fishing boats, and our flagship, the *Virgen de Azogue,* led the rest of us into battle against the Dutch men-of-war. As usual, the heretics made excellent use of their artillery, firing on us from a distance with their forty-pound cannon and their culverins, all thanks to the skillful maneuverings of their crews, so much better adapted to the sea than the Spanish, a skill in which—as the disaster of the Great Armada demonstrated—the English and the Dutch always had the advantage, for their sovereigns and their governments encouraged the nautical sciences, took good care of their sailors, and paid them well, whereas Spain, whose vast empire depended on the sea, merely turned her back on the problem, accustomed as she was to giving more importance to the soldier than to the sailor, so much so that even at a time when common port prostitutes boasted aristocratic names like Guzmán and Mendoza, the army still felt that it had something of the nobility about it, while the navy continued to be considered one of the lowlier professions. The result was that while the enemy had plenty of good artillerymen, skilled crews, and captains experienced at sea and at war, we—despite our excellent admirals and pilots and even better ships—had only valiant infantrymen. At the time, though, we Spaniards were greatly feared when it came to hand-to-hand fighting, and for that reason, during naval battles, the Dutch and the English usually tried to keep us at a distance, to dismast our ships with cannon shot, and to batter us into submission by slaughtering as many men on deck as possible, while we struggled hard to get close enough to board, for that was where the Spanish infantry was at its best and had proved itself to be both ruthless and unbeatable.

So it was during the battle near the isle of Foul, with us, as usual, trying to edge in closer, and the enemy, as was their way, trying to prevent us from doing so with their almost continuous fire. The *Azogue,* however, despite this onslaught—which brought down half the rigging and left the deck awash with blood—managed valiantly to get in amongst the heretics, so close to the Dutch flagship that we actually rammed their forecastle with our spritsail. From there, grappling irons were thrown, and a horde of Spanish infantrymen boarded, amidst much musket fire and brandishing of pikes and axes. Not long afterward, we on the *Jesús Nazareno,* now sailing to leeward and firing on the enemy with our harquebuses, saw that our fellow Spaniards had reached the quarterdeck of the Dutch flagship and were brutally repaying the enemy for what they had hurled at us from afar. I need only say that the most fortunate among the heretics were those who jumped into the icy water to avoid having their throats cut. Thus we captured two *urcas* and sank a third; a fourth, badly damaged, managed to escape, while the privateers—for our Catholic Flemings from Dunkirk did not hold back— gleefully plundered and burned twenty-two herring boats, which desperately tacked this way and that, like chickens when a fox sneaks into the chicken run. And at nightfall, which, in those latitudes, arrives when it is still only midafternoon in Spain, we headed southwest, leaving behind us, on the horizon, a scene of fires, shipwrecks, and desolation.

There were no further incidents apart from the discomforts of the voyage itself, and if we discount the three days of storm halfway between Ireland and Cape Finisterre, which flung us about belowdecks and had us all saying our Paternosters and our Ave Marias—indeed, before it could be resecured, a loose cannon rammed several men against the bulkhead, crushing them like bedbugs— leaving the galleon *San Lorenzo* so much the worse for wear that in the end she limped off to seek shelter at Vigo. Then came the alarming news that the English were once again attacking Cádiz, something we learned only in Lisbon. And so, while some escort ships detailed to the Indies

route headed off for the Azores in order to warn the treasure fleet and provide it with reinforcements, we set sail at
once for Cádiz, just in time, as I said, to see the backs of the
English.

I made use of the voyage to read, with great delight and
profit, Mateo Alemán's *Guzmán de Alfarache,* and other
books that Captain Alatriste had either brought with him
or acquired on board; these were, if I remember rightly,
The Life of the Squire, Marcos de Obregón, a volume of
Suetonius, and the second part of *The Ingenious Gentleman
Don Quijote de la Mancha.* There was also, as far as I was
concerned, a practical aspect to the voyage that would, in
time, prove extremely useful, for after my experiences in
Flanders, where I had acquired all the skills of war, Captain Alatriste and his colleagues took it upon themselves to
train me in swordplay. I was rapidly approaching the age
of sixteen; my body had filled out, and the hardships endured in Flanders had strengthened my limbs, tested my
mettle, and toughened my resolve. Diego Alatriste knew
better than anyone that a steel blade can place the most
humble man on the same footing as a monarch, and that
when all the cards are stacked against you, knowing how
to handle a fine piece of Toledo steel provides a more than
decent way of earning one's daily bread—or, indeed, of
defending it. To complete my education, which had had its
harsh beginnings in Flanders, he had decided to teach me

the secrets of fencing, and to this end, every day, we would seek out an empty part of the deck, where our comrades would make room for us or even form a circle to watch with expert eye, proffering opinions and advice and larding these comments with accounts of feats and exploits sometimes more imagined than real. In that world of connoisseurs and experts—for, as I once said, there is no better fencing master than the man who has felt cold steel in his own flesh—Captain Alatriste and I practiced thrusts, feints, attacks, and retreats, strikes performed with the palm up and with the palm down, wounds inflicted with the point of the sword and with the edge of the blade, and various other techniques at the disposal of the professional swordsman. Thus I learned all the tricks of the trade: how to grab my opponent's sword and then drive my blade into his chest; how to draw my blade back, slashing his face as I did so; how to slice and to thrust with both sword and dagger; how to use a lantern to dazzle, or even the light of the sun; how to make unashamed use of feet and elbows, or of the many ways of wrapping my cloak around my opponent's blade and then finishing him off in a trice. In short, I learned everything that goes into making the skilled swordsman. And although we could not know it at the time, I would soon be presented with an opportunity to put all this into practice, for a letter awaited us in Cádiz, along with a friend in Seville and an extraordinary ad-

venture that would take place at the mouth of the
Guadalquivir River. But all of this I will unfold in the full-
ness of time.

Dear Captain Alatriste,

*You will perhaps be surprised to receive this
letter, which serves, first and foremost, to welcome
you on your return to Spain, which I hope has been
happily concluded.*

*Thanks to the news you sent me from Antwerp—
where your face, bold Spaniard, doubtless made
even the River Scheldt grow pale—I have been able
to follow your steps, and I hope that, despite cruel
Neptune's traps, you continue safe and well, as, too,
our dear Íñigo. If so, you have arrived at precisely
the right moment. For if, upon your arrival in
Cádiz, the Indies fleet has still not arrived, I must
ask you to come at once to Seville by whatever
means possible. The king is currently in this city of
Betis, on a visit to Andalusia with Her Majesty the
queen, and since I am, thankfully, still in favor with
Philip IV and with his Atlas, the Conde-Duque de
Olivares (although, of course, yesterday is gone,
tomorrow has not yet come, and one untimely
sonnet or epigram could easily cost me another
period of exile in my personal Enxine Sea—*

*Torre de Juan Abad), I am here in his illustrious
company, doing a little of everything, and,
apparently, a great deal of nothing, at least
officially. As to the unofficial, I will tell you about
that in detail when I have the pleasure of once more
embracing you in Seville. I can say no more until
then, only to remark that since the matter requires
your participation, it is (naturally) a matter
requiring swords.*

*I send you my very warmest regards, and
greetings also from the Conde de Guadalmedina,
who is here with me, looking as handsome as ever
and busily seducing all the ladies of Seville.*

Your friend, always,

Francisco de Quevedo Villegas

Diego Alatriste put the letter away in his doublet and
climbed into the skiff beside me amongst the bundles containing our luggage. The boatmen's voices rang out as they
leaned upon the oars, which splashed in the water, and we
gradually left behind us the *Jesús Nazareno*, where it lay
motionless in the still water, along with the other galleons,
so imposing with their high, pitch-black sides, their red
paint and gilt glinting in the daylight, the spars and the
tangled rigging rising up into the sky. Shortly afterward,
we were back on land, feeling the ground sway beneath our

uncertain feet. After weeks confined to the deck of a ship, we found it bewildering to be amongst so many people and with so much space in which to move about. We delighted in the food on display outside the shops: oranges, lemons, raisins, plums, salt meat, and fish, the white bread in the bakeries, the pungent smell of spices, and the familiar voices touting all kinds of unusual goods and merchandise: paper from Genoa, wax from Barbary, wines from Sanlúcar, Jerez, and El Puerto de Santa María, sugar from Motril . . . The captain stopped at a barber's, who shaved him and trimmed his hair and mustache, and I remained at his side, gazing happily about me. In those days, Cádiz had not yet displaced Seville in importance as regards the route to and from the Indies, and the city was still small, with only four or five inns and taverns, but its streets, frequented by people from Genoa and Portugal, and by black slaves and Moors, were bathed in a dazzling light, the air was transparent, and everything was bright and cheerful and a world away from Flanders. There was barely a trace of the recent battle, although everywhere one saw soldiers and armed civilians, and the Cathedral square, our next stop after the barber's, was packed with people going to church to give thanks to God that the city had been saved from being plundered and burned. A messenger, a freed black slave sent by don Francisco de Quevedo, was waiting for us there as arranged, and while we took a cool drink at an inn and ate a few slices of tuna with white bread and green beans drizzled with olive oil, he explained the situation. After the alarm provoked by the English attack, every horse in town had been requisitioned, and the safest way, therefore, to reach Seville was to cross over to El Puerto de Santa María, where the king's galleys were anchored, and there board a galley that was preparing to sail up the Guadalquivir to Seville. He had, he said, arranged for a small boat with a skipper and four sailors to take us to El Puerto, and so we returned to the port and, on the way, were given documents signed by the Duque de Fernandina—a passport granting free passage and embarkation as far as Seville "to Diego Alatriste y Tenorio, one of the king's soldiers on leave from Flanders, and to his servant Íñigo Balboa Aguirre."

In the port, where bundles of soldiers' luggage and equipment were being piled high, we bade farewell to the few comrades still lingering there—as caught up in their card games as they were with the local whores, who, in their distinctive half-capes, were taking full advantage of the recent disembarkation to seize what booty they could. When we said our goodbyes, Curro Garrote was already back on dry land, crouched beside a gaming table that guaranteed more tricks and surprises than spring itself, and playing cards as if his life depended on it, his doublet open and his one good hand resting, just in case, on the pommel of his dagger, while his other hand traveled back and forth between his mug of wine and his cards, which came and went accompanied by curses, oaths, and blasphemies, as he saw half the contents of his purse disappearing into someone else's. The Malagueño nevertheless interrupted his activities to wish us luck, adding that he would see us again somewhere, here or there.

"And if not there," he concluded, "then in Hell."

Next, we said goodbye to Sebastián Copons, who, as you will remember, was an old soldier from Huesca, small, thin, and wiry, and even less given to talking than Captain Alatriste. Copons said that he was thinking of spending a few days' leave in Cádiz and would then, like us, travel up to Seville. He was fifty, with many campaigns behind him and far too many scars on his body—the latest, earned at the Ruyter mill, had traced a line from his forehead to his ear—and it was, he said, perhaps time to be thinking about going back to Cillas de Ansó, the little village where he'd been born. A young wife and a bit of land of his own would suit him fine, if, that is, he could get used to driving a spade into the earth rather than a sword into the guts of Lutherans. My master and he arranged to meet up again in Seville, at Becerra's. And when they said goodbye, I noticed that they embraced in silence, with no fuss, but with a stoicism typical of both.

I was sorry to leave Copons and Garrote, even though,

despite all we'd been through together, I had never warmed to the latter, with his curly hair, his gold earring, and his disreputable air, but they were the only two comrades from our company in Breda who had traveled back to Cádiz with us. All the others had, in one way or another, been left behind: Llop from Mallorca and Rivas from Galicia were lying six feet under the Flemish earth, one at the Ruyter mill and the other in the barracks at Terheyden. Mendieta from Vizcaya—always assuming he was alive to tell the tale—would be lying in a gloomy military hospital in Brussels, prostrated by the black vomit, and the Olivares brothers, taking with them as page my friend Jaime Correas, had reenlisted for a new campaign in the regiment led by don Francisco de Medina, when our Cartagena regiment, which had suffered so much during the long siege of Breda, was temporarily disbanded. The war in Flanders had been going on for a long time, and it was said that after all the money and lives the last few years had cost, the Conde-Duque de Olivares, minister and favorite of our King Philip IV, had decided to place our army there on a defensive footing only, in order to cut expenses, reducing the fighting force to an indispensable minimum. The fact is that six thousand soldiers had been discharged either voluntarily or by force, which is why the *Jesús Nazareno* was returning to Spain full of veterans, some of them old and infirm, some having been paid off, either because they'd completed the regulation period of service or because they were being posted on to different regiments and units in Spain itself or around the Mediterranean. Many of them were weary of war and its perils, and might well have agreed with that character in a Lope de Vega play:

> *What have the Lutherans*
> *ever done to me?*
> *The Lord Jesus made them,*
> *And He can slay them—*
> *If He so chooses—*
> *Far more easily than we.*

The freed slave sent by don Francisco de Quevedo also took his leave of us in Cádiz, having first shown us to our boat. We climbed aboard and were rowed away from the shore, and after we had again passed our imposing galleons—it was strange to see them from so low down— the skipper, judging that the wind was right, gave orders for the sail to be raised. Thus we crossed the bay, heading for the mouth of the Guadalete, and at evening we joined the *Levantina,* an elegant galley anchored along with many others in the middle of the river—all with their lateen yards and spars tied up on deck—opposite the great salt mountains that rose like heaps of snow on the left bank. The city, white and tawny, stretched away to the right, with

the tall castle tower protecting the mouth of the anchor-
age. El Puerto de Santa María was the main base for the
king's galleys, and my master knew it from the time when
he set sail against the Turks and the Berbers. As for the galleys, those war machines propelled by human blood and
muscle, he knew far more about them than most would
care to. That is why, after presenting ourselves to the captain of the *Levantina*, who glanced at our passport and
gave us permission to stay on board, Alatriste found us a
comfortable place near a crossbow embrasure—having first
greased the palm of the galleymaster in charge of the rabble with a silver piece of eight—and remained awake all
night, his back resting against our luggage and his dagger
at the ready. As he explained in a whisper, a faint smile on
his lips, it would take at least three hundred years in Purgatory before even the most honest of galley slaves—from
the captain down to the last forced man—was given his discharge papers and allowed into Heaven.

I slept wrapped in my blanket, untroubled by the cock-
roaches and lice scampering over me, for they were hardly
a novelty after my experiences on our long voyage on the
Jesús Nazareno. Any ship or vessel is home to gallant le-
gions of rats, bedbugs, fleas, and all manner of creeping
things who were quite capable of eating a cabin boy alive

and who observed neither Fridays nor Lent. And whenever I woke to scratch myself, I would see close by me Diego Alatriste's wide eyes, as pale as if they were made of the same light as the moon moving slowly above our heads and above the masts. I thought of his joke about galley slaves being discharged from Purgatory.

The truth is I'd never heard him give a reason why he had asked Captain Bragado for us to be discharged after the Breda campaign, and I couldn't get a word out of him either then or afterward; however, I sensed that I might have had something to do with the decision. Only years later did I learn that, at one point, Alatriste had considered the possibility, one among many, of traveling with me to the Indies. As I have told you before, the captain had, in his fashion, looked after me ever since my father's death in battle at Jülich in the year 1621, and had apparently now reached the conclusion that, after my experience with the army in Flanders, useful for a lad born into that particular period and with my particular talents—as long as I did not leave behind me there health, life, and conscience—it was time to prepare for my education and my future by returning to Spain. Alatriste did not believe that a career as soldier was the best choice for the son of his friend Lope Balboa, although I proved him wrong about that, when— after Nördlingen, the defense of Fuenterrabía, and the wars of Portugal and Catalonia—I was made ensign at Rocroi and, after leading a company of two hundred men, was appointed lieutenant of the Royal Mail and, later, captain of the Spanish guard of King Philip IV.

However, such a record only shows how right Diego Alatriste was, for although I fought honorably on many a battlefield, like the good Catholic, Spaniard, and Basque that I am, I gained but little reward, and what advantages and promotions I was given were due less to the military life itself and more to the favor of the king, to my relationship with Angélica de Alquézar, and to the good fortune that has always accompanied me. For Spain, rarely a mother and more often a wicked stepmother, always pays very little for the blood of those who spill it in her service, and others with more merit than I were left to rot in the anterooms of indifferent functionaries, in homes for the old and frail, or in convents, just as they had been abandoned to their fate in many a battle and left to rot in the trenches. I was the exception in enjoying good fortune, for in Alatriste's and my profession, the normal end to a life spent watching bullets rain down on armor was this:

> *Broken, scarred and crippled,*
> *Carrying, if you're lucky, a letter,*
> *To present at the door of hospitals*
> *Where no one ever gets better.*

Not even asking for a reward, a benefice, the captaincy of a company, or even bread for your children, but merely a little charity for having lost your arm in Lepanto, in Flanders, or in Hell itself, and, instead, seeing the door slammed shut in your face with the words:

So you served His Majesty
And lost your arm?
Bad luck, we say!
But why, pray, should we pay
For Flanders' harm?

And then, of course, Captain Alatriste was growing older. Not old in years, you understand, for at the time—the end of the first quarter of the century—he must have been a little over forty. I mean that he had grown old inside, as was the case with other men like him, who had been fighting for the true religion ever since they were boys, receiving nothing in exchange but scars, travails, and misfortunes. The Breda campaign, in which Alatriste had placed some hopes for himself and for me, had proved hard and unrewarding, with unfair officers, cruel commanders, much sacrifice, and little benefit, and we were all as poor as when we had started two years before, apart from what we had managed to ransack from Oudkerk and from other pillaging expeditions, and not counting the discharge pay—my master's, that is, for we servants were unpaid—which, in the form of a few silver escudos, would at least allow us to survive for a few months. Despite all this, the captain would go on to fight again, when life obliged us to serve once more under the Spanish flag, until I saw him die as I had seen him live: standing, his hair and mustache now grizzled, sword in hand, his eyes calm and indifferent, at the Battle of Rocroi, on the day when the best infantry in the world allowed themselves to be defeated merely in order to remain faithful to their king, and to their own legend and glory. And thus, exactly as I had always known him, in good times, of which there were few, and in bad, of which there were many, Captain Alatriste died true to himself and to his own silences. Like a soldier.

But let us not anticipate stories or events. Long before that, as I was saying, something was already dying inside the man who was then my master. Something indefinable, but of which I first became truly aware on the voyage that brought us back from Flanders. For all my youthful lucidity, however, I still did not quite understand what that something was, and could only watch as a part of Diego Alatriste slowly died. Later, I decided it was a kind of faith, or the remnants of a faith, perhaps a faith in the human condition, or in what heretical unbelievers call fate and what decent men call God. Or perhaps it was the painful certainty that our poor Spain, and Alatriste with her, was sliding down into a bottomless pit, with no hope of anyone getting her or us out of it, not for a long time, not for centuries. And I still wonder if my presence at his side, my youth, and the adoring way I looked at him—for I worshipped him then—did not force him to maintain his composure, a composure that, in other circumstances, might have drowned like mosquitoes in wine, in those mugs of wine of which he occasionally drank far too many, or might else have found resolution in the black, definitive barrel of his pistol.

2. A MATTER
REQUIRING SWORDS

"There'll be some killing involved," warned don Francisco
de Quevedo. "Possibly a lot."

"I only have two hands," responded Alatriste.

"Four," I said.

The captain kept his eyes trained on his mug of wine.
Don Francisco adjusted his spectacles on his nose and studied my face for a moment before turning to a man seated
at another table at the far end of the room in a discreet corner of the inn. He had been there when we arrived, and our
friend the poet had referred to him as Master Olmedilla,
with no further introduction or explanation, except that,
later, he added the word "accountant": the accountant
Olmedilla. He was a small, thin man, bald and very pale. He
appeared timid and mouselike, despite his black clothes and
the little curled mustache that set off a short, sparse beard.

He had ink-stained fingers and the look of a pettifogging lawyer or a government official who lives by candlelight, surrounded by files and papers. He gave a prudent nod to the silent question Don Francisco was asking him.

"There are two parts to the task," Quevedo told the captain. "The first will involve you helping that gentleman over there carry out certain, shall we say, negotiations," and he indicated the little man, who remained entirely impassive beneath our scrutiny. "For the second part, you can recruit as many men as you think necessary."

"They'll require some payment in advance."

"God will provide."

"Since when have you involved God in these matters, don Francisco?"

"You're right, but with or without him, there will be no shortage of gold."

He lowered his voice, whether at the mention of God or gold I'm not sure. The two long years that had passed since our encounter with the Inquisition—when don Francisco de Quevedo had plucked me from an auto-da-fé by dint of some very fast riding—had placed two more furrows in his forehead. He seemed somewhat weary as he toyed with his inevitable mug of wine, on this occasion a good white wine from Fuente del Maestre. The sunshine coming in through the window simultaneously caught the golden pommel of his sword and my hand resting on the table, and traced a line of light around Captain Alatriste's profile. Enrique Becerra's inn, famous for its lamb in honey sauce and stewed pork jowls, was near the public bawdy house in Compás de la Laguna, next to the Puerta del Arenal, and from the top floor, beyond the walls and the flat roof where the whores hung their linen out to dry, could be seen the masts and pennants of ships moored in Triana, on the far side of the river.

"As you see, Captain," added the poet, "once again, there's nothing for it but to fight, although this time I will not be coming with you."

Now he was smiling in a friendly, reassuring fashion, with that singular affection he always reserved for us.

"Well," muttered Alatriste, "we each have our own fate to follow."

The captain was dressed entirely in brown, with a suede doublet, a flat Walloon collar, canvas breeches, and military-style gaiters. He had left his last pair of boots, their soles full of holes, on board the *Levantina*, having swapped them with the sub-galleymaster for some dried mullet roe, some boiled beans, and a wineskin to sustain us on the journey upriver. For that and other reasons, my master did not seem particularly upset to find that the first thing he should meet with when setting foot again on Spanish soil was an invitation to return to his old profession. Perhaps because the commission came from a friend or perhaps because, according to that friend, the commission came from much higher up, but mainly, I suspect, because the money purse we had brought back with us from Flanders made not a sound when shaken. From time to time, the captain would regard me thoughtfully, as if wondering just where my nearly sixteen years and the skills he himself had taught me fit in with all this. I didn't wear a sword, of course, and only a *misericordia,* a dagger of mercy, hung from my belt at my back, but I had been tried and tested in the fire of war; I was bright, quick, and brave and very useful when called upon to serve. The question Alatriste was asking himself, I suppose, was whether to include me or to exclude me. Although, given the way things were, he could no longer make that decision alone; for good or ill, our lives were intertwined. And as he himself had just remarked, each man has his own fate to follow. As for don Francisco, to judge by the way he was looking at me, astonished at how I'd shot up and at the fuzz of hair on my upper lip and cheeks, I guessed that he was thinking exactly the same: I had reached the age when a lad is just as capable of dealing out sword thrusts as receiving them.

"And Íñigo goes too," Queredo said.

I knew my master well enough to know when to keep silent, which is precisely what I did, following his example and staring into my mug of wine on the table before me—for as regards wine, too, I had grown up. Don Francisco's comment was not a question, merely an affirmation of an obvious fact, and after a silence, Alatriste nodded slowly and resignedly. He did so without even looking at me, and I felt an inner surge of joy, bright and strong, which I concealed by putting the mug of wine to my lips. The wine tasted to me of glory, maturity, adventure.

"So let's drink to Íñigo," said Quevedo.

We drank, and the accountant Olmedilla, that small, pale fellow, all in black, joined us not by raising his glass but with another brief nod of the head. As for the captain, don Francisco, and myself, this was not the first toast of the day, since the three of us had embraced at the pontoon bridge connecting Triana and El Arenal, after we had disembarked from the *Levantina*. The captain and I had sailed along the coast from El Puerto de Santa María, past Rota, before crossing the bar at Sanlúcar and continuing on to Seville, passing first the great pinewoods growing along the sandy banks and then, farther upriver, the dense groves of trees, orchards, and forests on the shores of what the Arabs called Uad el Quevir, the great river. In contrast, what I remember most about that journey is the stink of dirt and sweat, the galleymaster's whistle marking time, the labored breathing of the galley slaves, and the clink of their chains as the oars entered and left the water with rhythmic precision, driving the galley forward against the current. The galleymaster, sub-galleymaster, and constable walked up and down the gangway, keeping a watchful eye on their parishioners, and every now and then the whip would come down hard on the bare back of some idler and weave him a doublet of lashes. It was painful to watch the oarsmen, one hundred and twenty men seated on twenty-four benches, five to each oar, with their shaved heads and heavily bearded faces, their torsos shining with sweat as they rose and fell and worked the long oars. There were Moorish slaves, former Turkish pirates, and renegades, as well as Christians serving sentences meted out by a justice they had not had gold enough to buy.

Alatriste said to me, "Never let them get you onto one of these ships alive."

His cold, pale, inscrutable eyes were watching the poor unfortunates row. As I said, my master knew this world well, for he had served as a soldier on the galleys of the Naples regiment during the Battle of La Goleta and in attacks on the Kerkennah Islands; and after fighting Venetians and Berbers, he himself, in 1613, came very close to being forced to serve on a Turkish galley. Later, when I was one of the king's soldiers, I, too, sailed the Mediterranean on these ships, and I can assure you that few seaborne inventions bear a closer resemblance to Hell. To give a measure of the harshness of a galley slave's life, suffice it to say that even for the very worst crimes, the term meted out was never more than ten years on the galleys, for they calculated this to be the maximum length of time any man could survive without losing health, reason, and life to hardship and the lash:

Take off the man's shirt,
To wash his soft flesh,
See what's written by the lash,
Bold and bloody 'neath the dirt.

Thus, by dint of whistle and oar, we had traveled up the Guadalquivir and arrived in the most fascinating city, trading port, and marketplace in the world, a gold and silver galleon anchored between glory and misery, opulence and profligacy, capital of the Ocean Sea and of all the wealth brought by the annual treasure fleet from the Indies; a city populated by nobles, merchants, clerics, rogues, and alluring women; a city so rich, powerful, and beautiful that neither Tyre nor Alexandria in their day could have equaled it. Homeland and home to all who came to her, a place of inexhaustible marvels, a mother to orphans and a cloak for sinners, just like the Spain of those wretched and magnificent times, a place where poverty was everywhere, and yet a place where no one capable of scraping a living need ever be poor. Where everything was wealth, but where it took but a moment's inattention to lose it all—as easily as one could lose one's life.

We spent a long time at the inn, talking but without exchanging one word with the accountant Olmedilla; however, as soon as Olmedilla stood up to leave, Quevedo instructed us to go after him, following at a distance. It would be a good thing, he explained, for Captain Alatriste to familiarize himself with the man. We walked along Calle de Tintores, astonished at the number of foreigners frequenting the inns there, then we set off for Plaza de San Francisco and the Cathedral, and from there, through Calle del Aceite, we reached the Mint, near the Torre del Oro, where Olmedilla had some business to attend to. As you can imagine, I, wide-eyed, was busily taking everything in: the newly swept doorways where women were emptying out their washbowls or planting up pots with flowers; the shops selling soap, spices, jewels, and swords; the boxes of fruit outside the fruiterer's; the gleaming basins that hung above the door of every barber; the street sellers; the ladies accompanied by their duennas; the men haggling; the grave-faced canons mounted on their mules; the black and Moorish slaves; the houses painted in red ocher and whitewash; the churches with their glazed tile roofs; the palaces; the orange and lemon trees; the crosses placed at the corners of streets to commemorate some violent death or simply to discourage passersby from relieving themselves . . . And even though it was still winter, everything glittered beneath a splendid sun that caused

my master and don Francisco to fold up their cloaks and
wear them slung crosswise over chest and shoulder or else
to throw back their capes and undo the loops and buttons
on their doublets. The knowledge that the king and queen
were both in Seville only added to the natural beauty of the
place, and that celebrated city and its more than one
hundred thousand inhabitants bubbled with excitement
and celebration. Unusually that year, King Philip IV was
preparing to honor with his august presence the arrival of
the treasure fleet, which would be bringing with it a fortune in gold and silver to be distributed—unfortunately,
rather than fortunately, for us—to the rest of Europe and
the world. The overseas empire that had been created a
century before by Cortés, Pizarro, and other adventurers
with few scruples and a great deal of pluck, with nothing
to lose but their lives and with everything to gain, now
provided a constant flow of wealth that allowed Spain to
pay for the wars in which it was embroiled with half the
known world, wars waged in defense of our military hege-
mony and of the one true religion, money that was even
more necessary, were that possible in a country like ours,
where—as I have said before—absolutely everyone gave
himself airs, where work was frowned upon and commerce
held in low esteem, and where the dream of every
scoundrel was to be granted letters patent of nobility and
thus live a life free from taxes and from work. Young men,

understandably, preferred to try their fortune in the Indies or in Flanders rather than languish in Spain's barren fields, at the mercy of an idle clergy, an ignorant, decadent aristocracy, and a corrupt government bureaucracy eager to suck the blood and the life out of them. It is said, and it is very true, that the moment when vice becomes the custom marks the death of a republic, for the dissolute person ceases to be considered loathsome, and all baseness becomes normal. It was thanks to the rich deposits in the Americas that Spain was able, for so long, to maintain an empire based on that abundance of gold and silver and on the quality of its coinage, which served both to pay the armies—when indeed they were paid—and to import foreign goods and products; for although we could send flour, oil, vinegar, and wine to the Indies, everything else came from abroad. This obliged us to go elsewhere for supplies, and our much-valued gold doubloons and our famous silver pieces of eight played a major role. We survived thanks to the vast quantities of coins and bars of gold that traveled from Mexico and Peru to Seville, whence they were immediately scattered throughout all the other countries of Europe and even the Orient, ending up as far away as India and China. The truth is that all this wealth benefitted everyone except the Spanish: since the Crown was always in debt, the money was spent before it even arrived; as soon as it was disembarked, the gold left Spain to be squandered in those lands where we were at war, vanished into the Genoese and Portuguese banks that were our creditors, and even into the hands of our enemies. To quote don Francisco de Quevedo:

In the Indies he was born an honest man,
When all the world admired his purity,
But in Spain, he spent both substance and security
And, losing life and interest, died a Genoan.
But anyone who claims to be his kinsman,
Howe'er sour-faced, becomes as sweet as honey,
For he remains a powerful gentleman,
Does our Sir Money.

The umbilical cord that kept our poor—and paradoxically rich—Spain breathing was the treasure fleet, which sailed the seas as much at risk from hurricanes as from pirates. This was why its arrival in Seville provoked indescribable celebration, for as well as the gold and silver destined for the king and for certain private individuals, it brought with it, too, cochineal, indigo, logwood, brazilwood, wool, cotton, hides, sugar, tobacco, and spices, not forgetting chili, ginger, and Chinese silk brought from the Philippines via Acapulco. To this end our galleons sailed in convoy from New Spain and Tierra Firme as far as Cuba, where they formed one gigantic fleet. And it has to be said that during all that time, despite deprivation, disaster, and difficulty, the Spanish sailors carried out their work with great pride. Even at the very worst moments—when, for example, the Dutch captured an entire fleet—our ships continued to cross the sea at the cost of great effort and sacrifice, and except on certain unfortunate occasions, always managed to keep at bay the threat from the French, Dutch, and English pirates, in a struggle in which Spain fought alone against those three powerful nations, all set on having a share of the spoils.

"Not many bluebottles about," commented Alatriste laconically.

This was true. The fleet was about to arrive, the king in person was honoring Seville with his presence, religious ceremonies and public celebrations were being organized, and yet there was hardly a catchpole or a constable to be seen in the streets. The few we passed were in groups, armed to the teeth, with more steel on them than a Basque foundry, and fearful even of their own shadow.

"There was an incident four days ago," Quevedo told us. "The law officers tried to arrest a soldier on one of the galleys moored in Triana, but the other soldiers and conscripts went to his aid, and people were being knifed left, right, and center. In the end, the catchpoles managed to drag him off to jail, but the soldiers surrounded the place and threatened to set fire to it if they didn't give them back their comrade."

"And how did the matter end?"

"Since the prisoner had killed a constable, they hanged him from the railings before handing him back." The poet chuckled as he described what had happened. "So now the soldiers are on the hunt for constables, and the constables only dare go about in gangs, and even then only very cautiously."

"And what does the king have to say about it all?"

While the accountant Olmedilla was sorting out his business at the Mint, we stood in the shadow of the gateway known as the Postigo del Carbón, immediately below the Torre de la Plata. Quevedo pointed to the walls of the ancient Moorish castle that extended as far as the Cathedral's immensely tall bell tower. The red-and-yellow uniforms of the Spanish guard stood out brightly against the battlements emblazoned with the king's coat of arms, and little did we imagine that, many years later, I myself would wear that uniform. More sentinels bearing halberds and harquebuses kept watch at the main gate.

"His Sacred, Catholic, Royal Majesty knows what he's told, nothing more," said Quevedo. "The great Philip is staying at the Alcázar and only leaves there to go hunting or to a party or for a nighttime visit to some convent. Our friend Guadalmedina, by the way, is acting as escort. They have become close friends."

The word "convent," spoken in that tone of voice, brought back grim memories, and I couldn't help but shudder when I remembered poor Elvira de la Cruz and how close I, too, had come to being burnt at the stake. Don Francisco de Quevedo had meanwhile been distracted by the sight of a rather attractive lady. She was accompanied by her duenna and a Morisco slave girl laden with baskets and packages, and when she lifted the hem of her dress to avoid the trail of dung caking the street, she revealed fashionable cork-soled clogs. When the lady passed us on her way to the mule-drawn coach waiting a little farther on, the poet adjusted his spectacles on his nose and very courteously doffed his hat. "Lisi," he murmured with a melancholy smile. The lady reciprocated with a slight nod before drawing her cloak more closely about her. Behind her, the aging duenna, clothed in deepest mourning, wearing a crow-black wimple and clutching a rosary, shot him a withering look. Quevedo stuck his tongue out at her. As he watched them depart, he smiled sadly and turned back to us without a word of explanation. He himself was dressed as soberly as ever: black silk stockings and shoes with silver buckles, a somber gray costume, a hat of the same color with a white feather, and the cross of St. James embroidered in red beneath the short cape caught back on his shoulder.

"Convents are his specialty," he added after that brief, pensive pause, his eyes still fixed on the lady and her companions.

"Guadalmedina's or the king's?" Now it was Alatriste who was smiling beneath his soldierly mustache.

Quevedo took a while to respond, then, sighing deeply, said, "Both."

I positioned myself next to the poet and, with eyes downcast, asked, "And the queen?"

I asked this in a casual, respectful, irreproachable tone, as if it were the mere curiosity of a boy. Don Francisco turned a penetrating eye on me.

"As lovely as ever," he answered. "She now speaks the language of Spain a little better than she did." He glanced at Alatriste and then back at me, his eyes glinting merrily behind the lenses of his spectacles. "She practices with her ladies-in-waiting and her mistress of the robes, and with her maids of honor."

My heart was beating so hard I was afraid it might give me away. "Did they all accompany her on the journey?"

"They did."

The street was spinning. *She* was in this fascinating city. I gazed around me: at the empty, sandy area known as El Arenal, one of the most picturesque parts of Seville, which stretched from the city walls down to the Guadalquivir, with Triana on the farther shore; at the sails on the sardine boats and the shrimpers, and at all the other little boats coming and going; at the king's galleys moored over by Triana, which was crammed with vessels as far as the pontoon; at El Altozano and the sinister castle that was the seat of the Inquisition; at the crowd of great ships on the nearer shore: a forest of masts, spars, lateen yards, sails, and flags; at the swarms of people, the tradesmen's stalls, the bundles of merchandise; I could hear the hammering of ship's carpenters, see the smoke from the caulkers' tar barrels, and the pulleys on the great naval crane at the mouth of the Tagarete that was used to careen the ships' bottoms.

The Basques in the north send us wood,
And cloth and iron and ships true and good,
And the sailor brings from the brave new world
Ambergris, pearls, silver and gold,
And skins and strange exotic dyes,
And everything else that money buys.

Lope de Vega's play *El Arenal de Sevilla,* from which these lines came, had remained engraved on my memory ever since I first saw it with Captain Alatriste at the open-air theater of El Príncipe when I was a mere boy, on the famous day when Buckingham and the Prince of Wales fought alongside him. And suddenly, that place, that city that was, in itself, so splendid, was made magical and marvelous. Angélica de Alquézar was there, and I might perhaps see her. I gave a sideways glance at my master, fearful that my inner turbulence might be visible from without. Fortunately, Diego Alatriste had more worrying things on his mind. He was studying the accountant Olmedilla, who had finished his business and was walking toward us, eyeing us about as cordially as if we had come to administer the last rites. Grave-faced and dressed entirely in black, apart from his white ruff, and wearing a narrow-brimmed black hat unadorned by any feather, and with that curious sparse beard that only accentuated his gray, mouselike appearance, he had the pinched air of one plagued by acid humors and bad digestion.

"What do we need with this fool?" muttered the captain, as he watched him approach.

Quevedo shrugged. "He's been given a mission to fulfill. The count-duke himself is pulling the strings. And Master Olmedilla's work will discomfit quite a number of people."

Olmedilla greeted us with a curt nod, and we followed him to the Triana gate. Alatriste was speaking to Quevedo in a low voice: "What exactly does he do?"

The poet responded equally softly: "As I said, he's an accountant, an expert at balancing books. A man who knows everything there is to know about figures, about customs duties and suchlike. Why, he could outshine the mathematician Juan de Leganés."

"Has someone been stealing more than he should?"

"There is always someone stealing more than he should."

The broad brim of Alatriste's hat cast a mask of shadow over his face, a mask that only emphasized the paleness of his eyes, with the light and the landscape of El Arenal reflected in them. "And where exactly do *we* fit in with all of this?" he asked.

"I'm only acting as intermediary. I am currently much in favor at court. The king requires me to be witty, and the queen laughs at my jokes. As for the count-duke, I do him the occasional small favor, and he repays me in kind."

"I'm glad to see that Fortune is finally smiling on you."

"Don't speak too loudly. Fortune has played so many tricks on me in the past, I view her very warily indeed."

Alatriste observed the poet, amused. "Nevertheless, don Francisco, you certainly look every inch the courtier."

"Oh, please, Captain!" Quevedo was tugging at his ruff where it irritated his skin. "Being an artist and enjoying regular hot meals are two activities that are rarely compatible. I am simply having a run of good luck at the moment: I'm popular and my poetry is being read everywhere. As usual, I even have attributed to me poems I did not write, including some monstrosities by that bugger, that Babylonian, that sodomite Góngora, whose grandparents spurned bacon and worked as cobblers in Córdoba, and

whose 'letters patent' you'll find hanging from the Cathedral ceiling, along with the names of other Jews. Indeed,
I have just hailed his latest published work with a delicate
little poem of my own, which ends thus:

"Be not flatulent,
Vilest of sewers,
Through which Parnassus
Purges its excrement!

"But to return to more serious matters. As I was saying,
it's convenient to the count-duke to have me on his side. He
flatters me and uses me. As for your involvement in the
matter, Captain, that is a mere caprice on the part of
the count-duke himself. For some reason, he remembers
you. Given that we're talking about Olivares, that, of
course, could be a good thing or a bad. Perhaps, in this in-
stance, it's good. Besides, you did once offer him the services of your sword if he would help save Íñigo."

Alatriste darted a glance at me, and then nodded slowly
and pensively. "He has a damnably good memory, the
count-duke," he said.

"Yes—when it suits him."

My master again turned his attention to the accountant
Olmedilla, who was walking a few paces ahead through the
hustle and bustle of the harbor, his hands behind his back

and a sour look on his face. "He's not much of a talker," he commented.

"No," said Quevedo, laughing. "In that respect, you and he should get along famously."

"Is he a man of consequence?"

"As I said, he is merely an official, but he was put in charge of collating all the evidence when don Rodrigo Calderón was put on trial for embezzlement. Now are you convinced?"

He fell silent to allow the captain to absorb all the implications of this statement. Alatriste whistled through his teeth. The public execution a few years ago of a powerful figure like Calderón had shaken all of Spain.

"And whose trail is he on now?"

The poet declined to answer at first and, for a while, said nothing. Then, at last, he said, "Someone will tell you all about that tonight. As for Olmedilla's mission and, indirectly, yours, shall we just say that the commission comes from the count-duke, but the impulse behind it comes from the king himself."

Alatriste shook his head incredulously. "You are joking, aren't you, don Francisco?"

"On my faith, I am not. Devil take me if I am, or may that little humpbacked playwright Ruiz de Alarcón suck all the talent from my brain."

"God's blood!"

"That's exactly what I said when they asked me to be a third party in the matter. On the positive side, if things turn out well, you'll have a few escudos to spend."

"And if things turn out badly?"

"Then I'm afraid you'll wish you were back in the trenches at Breda." Quevedo sighed and looked around him like someone hoping to change the subject. "I'm just sorry that, for the moment, I can tell you no more."

"I don't need to know much more," said my master, a mixture of irony and resignation dancing in his gray-green eyes. "I just want to know from which side to expect an attack."

Quevedo shrugged. "From every side, as per usual," he replied, still gazing indifferently about him. "You're not in Flanders now, Captain Alatriste. This is Spain."

They arranged to meet again that night, at Becerra's. The accountant Olmedilla, still looking glummer than a butcher's shop in Lent, withdrew to an inn in Calle de Tintores where he had his lodgings and where there was also a room reserved for us. My master spent the afternoon sorting out his affairs, getting his military license certified, and buying new linen and supplies—as well as a new pair of boots—with the money don Francisco had advanced him for the work ahead. As for me, I was free for a few hours, and went for a stroll into the heart of the city, enjoying the walks around the walls and the atmosphere in the narrow streets, with their low arches, coats of arms, crosses, and *retablos* depicting Christs, virgins, and saints— streets far too narrow for the carriages and horses that jammed them; a place at once dirty and opulent, seething with life, with knots of people at the doors of taverns and tenements, and women—whom I eyed with new interest since my experiences in Flanders—dark-skinned, neat, and self-assured, who spoke with an accent that lent a special sweetness to their conversation. I saw mansions with magnificent courtyard gardens glimpsed through wrought-iron gates, with chains on the door to show they were immune from ordinary justice, and I sensed that while the Castilian nobility, in their determination not to work, took their stoicism to the point of ruin, the Seville aristocracy had a more relaxed approach and often allowed the words "hidalgo" and "merchant" to be conjoined. Thus the aristocrat did not scorn commerce if it brought him money, and the merchant was prepared to spend a fortune in order to be considered an hidalgo—even tailors required purity of blood from the members of their guild. On the one hand, this gave rise to the spectacle of debased noblemen using their influence and privileges to prosper by underhanded means, and on the other, it meant that the work and commerce so vital to the nation continued to be frowned upon and, consequently, fell into the hands of foreigners. Thus, most of the Seville nobility were rich plebeians who had bought their way into a higher stratum of society through money and advantageous marriages and now felt ashamed of their former trades. A generation of merchants spawned, in turn, a generation of "noble," entirely parasitic heirs, who denied the origins of their fortune and squandered it without a qualm, thus proving the truth of that old Spanish saying *From tradesman to gentleman to gambler to beggar in four generations.*

I also visited the Alcaicería, the old silk market, an area full of shops selling rich merchandise and jewels. I was wearing black breeches and soldiers' gaiters, a leather belt with a dagger stuck in it at the back, a military-style jerkin over my much-darned shirt, and on my head a very elegant cap of Flemish velvet—the spoils of war from what were fast becoming "the old days." That and my youth both favored me, I think, and adopting the air of a battle-hardened veteran, I idled along past the swordsmiths' shops in Calle de la Mar and Calle de Vizcaínos, or past the braggarts, doxies, and pimps in Calle de las Sierpes, opposite the famous prison behind whose black walls Mateo Alemán had languished and where good don Miguel de Cervantes had also spent some time. I swaggered past the legendary steps of the Cathedral—that cathedral of villainy—teeming with sellers, idlers, and beggars with signs hanging around their necks and displaying wounds and deformities, each one falser than a Judas kiss, as well as people who had been crippled on the rack but claimed to have been wounded in Flanders and who sported real or fake amputations, which they attributed to days spent fighting in Antwerp or Mamora but which could as easily have been acquired at Roncesvalles or at Numantia, for one had only to look them in the face, these men—who claimed to have won their scars for the sake of the true religion, king, and country—to know that the closest they had come to a heretic or a Turk was from the safety of the audience at the local playhouse.

I ended up outside the Reales Alcázares, staring up at the Hapsburg flag flying above the battlements, and at the imposing soldiers of the king's guard armed with halberds and standing at attention at the great gate. I wandered around there for a while, amongst the citizens eager to catch a glimpse of the king or queen, should they chance to enter or leave. And when the crowd, and I with them, happened to move too close to the entrance, a sergeant in the Spanish guard came over to tell us very rudely to leave. The other onlookers obeyed at once, but I, being my father's son, was piqued by the soldier's bad manners, and so I dawdled and lingered with a haughty look on my face that clearly nettled him. He gave me a shove, and I—for my youth and my recent experience in Flanders had made me prickly on such matters—thought this the act of a scoundrel, and so I rounded on him like a fierce young hound, my hand on the hilt of my dagger. The sergeant, a burly, mustachioed type, roared with laughter.

"Oh, so you fancy yourself a swashbuckler, do you?" he said, looking me up and down. "Aren't you a little young for that, boy?"

I held his gaze, shamelessly unashamed and with the scorn of a veteran, which despite my youth, I was. This fat fool had spent the last two years eating hot food and strolling about royal palaces and fortresses in his red-and-yellow-checkered uniform, while I had been fighting alongside Captain Alatriste and watching my comrades die in Oudkerk, at the Ruyter mill, in Terheyden, and in the prison cells of Breda, or else foraging for food in enemy territory with the Dutch cavalry at my back. How very unfair it was, I thought, that human beings did not carry their service record written on their face. Then I remembered Captain Alatriste, and I said to myself, by way of consolation, that some people did. Perhaps one day, I thought, people will know or guess what I have done simply by looking at me, and then all these sergeants, fat or thin, whose lives have never depended on their sword, would have to swallow their sarcasm.

"I may be young, but my dagger isn't," I said resolutely.

The other man blinked; he had not expected such a riposte. I saw that he was taking a closer look at me. This time he noticed that I had my hand behind me, resting on the damasked hilt of my knife. Then he gazed dumbly into my eyes, incapable of reading what was in them.

"A pox on't, why I'll . . . "

The sergeant was fuming, and it certainly wasn't incense issuing forth from him. He raised his hand to slap me, which is the most unacceptable of offenses—in the olden days, one could only slap a man who wasn't dressed in the knightly uniform of helmet and coat of mail—and I said to myself, "I'm done for. Avenging every little slight can all too swiftly lead to death. Here I am in a situation from which there is no escape, and all because my name is Íñigo Balboa Aguirre and I'm from Oñate, and more to the point, because I have just returned from Flanders and my master is Captain Alatriste, and I cannot consider any market too dear where one buys one's honor with one's life. Whether I like it or not, every path is blocked, and so when I grasp my dagger, I will have no option but to stab this fat pig in the belly—one thrust and it's done—and then run like a deer and get myself a hiding place, and just hope that nobody finds me." In short—as don Francisco de Quevedo would have said—there was, as usual, nothing for it but to fight. And so I held my breath and with the fatalistic resigna-tion of the veteran—a recently acquired characteristic—prepared myself for what would follow. It seems, however, that God spends his spare moments protecting arrogant

young men, because just then a bugle sounded, the palace
gates were flung wide, and there came the sound of wheels
and hooves on gravel. The sergeant, mindful of his duty, immediately forgot all about me and ran to marshal his men,
and I stayed where I was, greatly relieved, and thinking
that I'd had a very lucky escape.

Carriages were leaving the palace, and when I saw
the insignia on the coach and saw the cavalry escort, I
realized that it was our queen, accompanied by her ladies-
in-waiting and her mistress of the robes. And my heart,
which, during the episode with the sergeant, had remained
steady and firm, suddenly bolted as if it had been given its
head. Everything around me was spinning. The carriages
rolled past to the sound of cheering and hallooing from
the crowd, which rushed forward to greet them, and one
pale royal hand, lovely and bejeweled, waved elegantly at
one of the windows, in genteel response to this tribute
from the people. I, though, had other interests, and in each
of the carriages that passed, I eagerly sought the source of
my unease. As I did so, I took off my cap and drew myself
up, standing hatless and motionless before the fleeting vision of lace, satin, and furbelows, of female heads with
coiffed and ringleted hair, of faces covered by fans, and of
hands waving. In the last coach I glimpsed a fair head and
a pair of blue eyes that saw me as they passed, recognizing
me with startled intensity, before the vision moved off, and
I was left there, overwhelmed, watching the hunched back

of the footman at the rear of the carriage and the dust covering the rumps of the guards' horses.

Then behind me I heard a whistle, one that I would have recognized in Hell itself. *Ti-ri-tu, ta-ta*. And when I turned, I found myself face to face with a ghost.

"You've grown, boy."

Gualterio Malatesta was looking straight into my eyes, and I was sure that he could read my every thought. He was, as ever, all dressed in black, and wearing a black hat with a very broad brim and, hanging from his leather baldric, the usual threatening sword with the long cross-guard. He was still very tall and thin, with that face of his devastated by pockmarks and scars, which gave him such a cadaverous, tortured appearance that even the smile he directed at me, far from softening that appearance, only emphasized it.

"You've grown," he said again. He seemed about to add "since the last time," but he did not. The "last time" had been on the road to Toledo, when he drove me in a closed carriage to the dungeons of the Inquisition. For very different reasons, the memory of that adventure was as unpalatable to him as it was to me.

"And how is Captain Alatriste?"

I didn't answer, I merely held his gaze, which was as dark and fixed as that of a snake. When he spoke the name of my master, the smile beneath his fine, Italian-style mustache grew more dangerous.

"You remain a boy of few words, I see."

He was resting his left hand, gloved in black, on the guard of his sword, and he kept turning this way and that, as if distracted. I heard him utter a soft sigh, almost of annoyance.

"So, in Seville too," he said, and then he fell silent before I could fathom what it was he meant. After a while, with a glance and a lift of his chin, he indicated the sergeant of the Spanish guard, who was some way off, occupied with organizing his men by the palace gate.

"I saw what happened between you and him. I was watching from the crowd." He was studying me thoughtfully, as if assessing the changes that had taken place in me since the last time we had met. "I see you are as punctilious as ever in matters of honor."

"I've been in Flanders," I blurted out. "With the captain."

He nodded. I noticed that there were a few gray hairs now in his mustache and in the side-whiskers visible beneath the black brim of his hat, as well as a few new lines or scars on his face. The years pass for everyone, I thought. Even for hired swordsmen with no heart.

"I know," he said, "but regardless of whether you've been in Flanders or not, you would do well to remember one thing: honor is a very complicated thing to acquire, difficult to preserve, and dangerous to sustain. Ask your friend Alatriste."

I stood up to him with all the firmness I could muster. "Ask him yourself, if you've got the spunk."

My sarcasm elicited not a flicker of response from his impassive face. "I know the answer already," he replied, unmoved. "I have other less rhetorical matters pending with him."

He was still looking pensively in the direction of the guards at the gate. Then he chuckled to himself, as if at a joke he preferred not to share with anyone else. "Some fools never learn," he said suddenly. "Like that imbecile who raised his hand to you without a thought for what you might do with yours." The hard black snake eyes fixed on me again. "If it had been me, I would never even have given you the chance to take that dagger out."

I turned to observe the sergeant. He was strutting about, keeping an eye on his soldiers while they closed the palace gates. And it was true: he was completely unaware how close he had come to having a span of steel in his guts and how close I had come to being hanged for his sake.

"Remember that next time," said the Italian.

When I turned back, Gualterio Malatesta was no longer there. He had disappeared into the crowd, and all I could see was a black hat moving off past the orange trees, beneath the bell tower of the Cathedral.

3. CONSTABLES AND CATCHPOLES

That night would prove to be a long and busy one, but first there was time for supper and some interesting talk. There was also the unexpected arrival of a friend. Don Francisco de Quevedo had not told Captain Alatriste that the person he would be sharing supper with was none other than Álvaro de la Marca, the Conde de Guadalmedina. To Alatriste's surprise, and to mine, the count appeared at Becerra's inn just after sunset, as cordial and self-assured as ever. He embraced the captain, patted me affectionately on the cheek, and called loudly for good wine, a decent meal, and a comfortable room in which he could converse with his companions.

"Now tell me all about Breda."

Apart from the buff coat he was wearing, he was dressed very much in the style favored by our king. His clothes were otherwise expensive but discreet, with no embroidery and no gold; he wore military boots, pale amber gloves, a hat, and a long cloak; and tucked in his belt, as well as a sword and a dagger, were a pair of pistols. Don Álvaro's night would doubtless last long beyond his conversation with us, and, toward dawn, some husband or abbess would have good reason to keep one eye open as he or she slept. I remembered what Quevedo had said about the count's role as companion to the king on the latter's nocturnal sorties.

"You look very well, Alatriste."

"So do you, Count."

"Oh, I take good care of myself, but make no mistake, my friend, at court not working is very hard work indeed."

He was still the same: handsome, elegant, and with exquisite manners that were not in the least at odds with the easy, slightly rough, almost soldierly spontaneity with which he had always treated my master ever since the latter had saved his life during a disastrous Spanish attack on the Kerkennah Islands. He toasted Breda, Alatriste, and even me; he argued with don Francisco about the syllables in a sonnet, dispatched with an excellent appetite the lamb in honey sauce served up in good Triana earthenware, called for a clay pipe and tobacco, and sat back in his chair, wreathed in pipe smoke, with his buff coat unfastened and a contented look on his face.

"Now let's get down to serious matters," he said.

Then, in between drawing on his pipe and taking sips of Aracena wine, he studied me for a moment as if calculating whether or not I should be listening to what he was about to say, and then, at last, he laid the facts before us. He began by explaining that the system of fleets to transport the gold and silver, Seville's commercial monopoly, the strict controls imposed on who could and could not travel to the Indies had all been devised to prevent foreign interference and smuggling and to ensure the smooth running of the vast machinery of taxes, duties, and tariffs on which the monarchy and its many parasites depended. That was the reason for the *almojarifazgo*: the customs cordon around Seville, Cádiz, and its bay, which was the only port from which ships could embark for the Indies and disembark on their return. The royal coffers drew a large income from this, although it should be noted that in a corrupt administration like Spain's, it was in the crown's interest to let agents and other people in authority pay a fixed rate for their positions and then surreptitiously line their own pockets, stealing money hand over fist. In lean times, however, there was nothing to prevent the king from occasionally imposing an exemplary fine or ordering the seizure of goods from private individuals who were traveling with the fleets.

"The problem," said the count, taking a couple of puffs on his pipe, "is that all these taxes, which are intended to pay for the defense of our trade with the Indies, devour the very thing they're supposed to defend. A lot of gold and silver goes toward paying not only for the war in Flanders but also for the widespread corruption and general apathy. And so merchants have to choose between two evils: being bled dry by the Royal Treasury or else indulging in a little contraband, all of which breeds a thriving criminal class." He looked at Quevedo, smiling, soliciting his agreement. "Isn't that so, don Francisco?"

"Oh, yes," agreed the poet. "Here, even the fools are clever."

"Or busily putting gold in their purses."

"Very true." Quevedo took a long drink of wine, then wiped his mouth with the back of his hand. "He remains a powerful gentleman, does our Sir Money."

Guadalmedina looked at him, surprised. "Very well put. You should write a poem about it."

"I have."

"Really? Well, I'm pleased."

"In the Indies he was born an honest man . . ." don Francisco began, taking another sip of wine and reciting in a resonant voice.

"Oh, that," said the count, winking at Alatriste. "I thought that was by Góngora."

The poet choked on his wine. "God's teeth and blood!"

"All right, my friend, all right . . ."

"No, Devil take it, it's not all right. Not even a Lutheran could come up with a worse insult. What have I to do with poetasters and versifiers like him who, in one bound, go from being Jews or Moors to playing at being shepherds?"

"It was only a joke."

"I've had duels before now over jokes like that, Count."

"Well, don't even consider such a possibility with me," said the count, smiling, conciliatory and good-natured, stroking his curled mustache and his goatee. "I still remember the fencing lesson you gave to Pacheco de Narváez." He gracefully raised his right hand and very politely doffed an imaginary hat. "My apologies, don Francisco."

"Hm."

"What do you mean, 'Hm'? I'm a grandee of Spain, damn it! At least be so kind as to acknowledge my gesture."

"Hm."

Once the poet's wounded feelings had, despite all, been soothed, Guadalmedina continued to provide more details, to which Captain Alatriste listened intently, his mug of wine in his hand, and his reddish profile half lit by the flames of the candles on the table. War is at least clean, he had said once, some time ago. And at that moment, I understood precisely what he meant. Foreigners, Guadalmedina was saying, get around the monopoly by using local intermediaries and third parties—they were called "dodgers," a word that said it all—thus diverting the merchandise, the gold and the silver, which they would never have been able to obtain directly. More to the point, the idea that the galleons left Seville and returned there was a legal fiction; they almost always remained moored in Cádiz, in El Puerto de Santa María or Barra de Sanlúcar, where the cargo was loaded onto another ship. This encouraged many merchants to move into that area, where it was easier to elude the guards.

"They've even built ships with an official declared tonnage but whose real tonnage is quite different. Everyone knows that while they happily own up to carrying five tons, in fact they can carry ten. Bribery and corruption, however, keep people's mouths shut and their willingness to cooperate open. A great many people have made their fortune that way." He studied the bowl of his pipe, as if its contents merited his particular attention. "And that includes certain high royal officials."

Guadalmedina continued his account. Made lethargic by the benefits of overseas trade, Seville, like the rest of Spain, had become incapable of sustaining any industry of its own. Many people from other lands had managed to set up businesses there, and thanks to hard work and tenacity, had made themselves indispensable. This put them in a privileged position as intermediaries between Spain and the parts of Europe with which we were at war. The paradox was that while we were locked in battle with England, France, and Denmark, as well as with the Turk and the rebel provinces, we were, at the same time, through those intermediaries, buying all kinds of merchandise from them: rigging, tar, sails, and other goods that were essential both in the Peninsula and across the Atlantic. Thus the gold from the Indies slipped away to finance the armies and navies that were fighting us. It was an open secret, but no one put a stop to this traffic because everyone was profiting from it. Including the king.

"The result is obvious: Spain is going to the dogs. Everyone steals, cheats, and lies and no one pays his debts."

"They even boast about it," added Quevedo.

"They do."

The smuggling of gold and silver, Guadalmedina went on, was crucial to this state of affairs. With the frequent connivance of customs officers and officials at the Casa de Contratación, only half the real value of any treasure imported by individuals was declared. Each fleet brought with it a fortune that disappeared into private pockets or ended up in London, Amsterdam, Paris, or Genoa. This smuggling was enthusiastically embraced by foreigners and Spaniards alike, by merchants, government officials, captains of fleets, admirals, passengers, sailors, soldiers, and clerics. An example of the last was the scandal surrounding Bishop Pérez de Espinosa, who, when he died in

Seville a couple of years earlier, had left five hundred thousand *reales* and sixty-two gold ingots, which were immediately seized by the Crown when it was discovered that all this wealth had come from the Indies without having passed through customs.

"It's estimated," Guadalmedina went on, "that, taking into account the king's treasure and that brought by private individuals, the treasure fleet which is about to arrive is carrying—along with sundry other merchandise—twenty million silver *reales* from Zacatecas and Potosí, as well as eighty quintals of gold in bars."

"And that's only the official amount," said Quevedo.

"Exactly. They reckon that, of the silver, a quarter more is arriving as contraband. As for the gold, it almost all belongs to the Royal Treasury, but one of the galleons is carrying a secret cargo of ingots, a cargo no one has declared."

The count paused and took a long drink so as to allow Captain Alatriste to absorb these facts. Quevedo had taken out a small box containing powdered tobacco. He took a pinch and, after sneezing discreetly, wiped his nose on the crumpled handkerchief he kept up his sleeve.

"The ship is called the *Virgen de Regla*," Guadalmedina continued at last. "It's a sixteen-cannon galleon, the property of the Duque de Medina Sidonia, and hired by a Genoese merchant based in Seville called Jerónimo Garaffa. On the voyage out, it transports a variety of goods, from Almadén mercury for the silver mines to papal bulls, and on the return voyage it carries everything and anything it can. And it can carry a great deal, because while its official capacity is nine hundred barrels of twenty-seven arrobas each, in reality it has been so built that its actual capacity is one thousand four hundred barrels."

The *Virgen de Regla*, he went on, was traveling with the treasure fleet, and its declared cargo included liquid amber, cochineal, wool, and skins intended for the merchants of Cádiz and Seville. There were also five million silver *reales*—two-thirds of which were the property of private individuals—and one thousand five hundred gold ingots destined for the Royal Treasury.

"A fine booty for pirates," commented Quevedo.

"Especially when you consider that this year's fleet comprises another four ships with similar cargo." Guadalmedina studied the captain through his pipe smoke. "Now do you understand why the English were so interested in Cádiz?"

"And how did the English know?"

"Damn it, Alatriste. We know, don't we? If you can buy the salvation of your soul with money, imagine what else you can buy. You seem a touch ingenuous tonight. Where have you spent the last few years? In Flanders or in Limbo?"

Alatriste poured himself more wine and said nothing.

His eyes rested on Quevedo, who gave a faint smile and shrugged. That's the way it is, said the gesture. And always has been.

"At any rate," Guadalmedina was saying, "it doesn't much matter what they claim the official cargo to be. We know that the galleon is carrying contraband silver too, at an estimated value of one million *reales*. The silver, however, is the least of it. The *Virgen de Regla* is carrying in its hold another two thousand gold bars—undeclared." The count pointed with the stem of his pipe at the captain. "Do you know how much that secret cargo is worth, at the very lowest estimate?"

"I haven't the slightest idea."

"Well, it's worth two hundred thousand gold escudos."

The captain was studying his hands, which lay motionless on the table. He was silently calculating.

"That's one hundred million *maravedís*," he murmured.

"Exactly." Guadalmedina was laughing. "Everyone knows how much an escudo is worth."

Alatriste looked up and stared hard at the count. "You're mistaken there," he said. "Not everyone knows it as well as I do."

Guadalmedina opened his mouth, doubtless intending to make some new joke, but the icy expression on my master's face immediately dissuaded him. We knew that Captain Alatriste had killed men for a tiny fraction of that amount. He was doubtless imagining, as was I, how many armies could be bought for such a sum. How many harquebuses, how many lives and how many deaths. How many minds and how many consciences.

Quevedo cleared his throat and then recited in a low voice:

> *"Life and stealing are the same,*
> *Thieving is no deadly vice,*
> *All that's worldly has a price,*
> *So take it, filch it, that's the game.*
> *None is ever stripped and whipped*
> *For stealing silver, gold, or cash;*
> *The poor, alone, deserve the lash."*

This was followed by an awkward silence. The count was studying his pipe. Finally, he put it down on the table.

"In order to carry those forty quintals of extra gold, as well as the undeclared silver," he went on, "the captain of the *Virgen de Regla* has removed eight of the galleon's cannon. They say that even so, she's still very heavily laden."

"Who does the gold belong to?"

"That's a delicate matter. On the one hand, there's the Duque de Medina Sidonia, who is organizing the whole operation, providing the ship, and creaming off the largest profits. There's also a banker in Lisbon and another in Antwerp, and a few people at court. One of them, it seems, is the royal secretary Luis de Alquézar."

The captain shot me a glance. I had, of course, told him of my encounter with Gualterio Malatesta outside the royal palace, although I had made no mention of the carriage and the blue eyes I thought I had glimpsed in the queen's retinue. Guadalmedina and Quevedo, who were, in turn, studying the captain, exchanged a look.

"The plan," said the count, "is this: Before unloading officially in Cádiz or Seville, the *Virgen de Regla* will anchor at Barra de Sanlúcar. The captain and the admiral of the fleet have both been bribed to anchor the ships there for at least one night on the pretext of bad weather or the English or whatever. Then the contraband gold will be transferred to another galleon waiting there—the *Niklaasbergen*, a Flemish *urca* from Ostend, with an irreproachably Catholic captain, crew, and owner, which is free to come and go between Spain and Flanders under the protection of our king's flag."

"Where will the gold be taken?"

"Medina Sidonia's share and that of the others will go to Lisbon, where the Portuguese banker will keep it in a safe place. The rest will be sent straight to the rebel provinces."

"That's treason," said Alatriste. His voice was quite

calm, and the hand that raised his mug to his lips, wetting his mustache with wine, remained perfectly steady, but I saw his pale eyes grow strangely dark.

"Treason," he said again.

The tone in which he said the word revived recent memories. The ranks of the Spanish infantry standing undaunted on the plain surrounding the Ruyter mill, with the drums beating at our backs, awakening a nostalgia for Spain in those about to die. The good Gallego Rivas and the ensign Chacón, who had died trying to save the blue-and-white-checkered flag beside the Terheyden redoubt. The cry from a hundred men as they emerged at dawn from the canals for the assault on Oudkerk. The men whose eyes were gritty with dirt after fighting hand-to-hand in the narrow mining and antimining tunnels. Suddenly, I, too, felt a desire to drink, and I emptied my mug of wine in one gulp.

Quevedo and Guadalmedina exchanged another look.

"That's how Spain is, Captain Alatriste," said don Francisco. "You seem to have forgotten during your time in Flanders."

"It's a purely commercial matter," explained Guadalmedina. "And this certainly isn't the first time it's happened. The only difference now is that the king and, even more so, Olivares both distrust Medina Sidonia. The welcome they received two years ago on his estate in Doña Ana, and the lavish hospitality bestowed on them during this present visit, make it clear that don Manuel de Guzmán, the eighth duke, has become a little king of Andalusia. From Huelva to Málaga to Seville, his word is law, and that, with the Moor just across the water, and with Catalonia and Portugal held together with pins, makes for a highly dangerous situation. Olivares fears that Medina Sidonia and his son Gaspar, the Conde de Niebla, are preparing a move that will give the Crown a real fright. Normally, these things would be resolved by holding a trial in keeping with their social status and then slitting their throats. The Medina Sidonia family, however, is very high up the scale indeed, and Olivares—who, despite being a relative of theirs, loathes them—would never dare involve their name in a public scandal without solid proof."

"And what about Alquézar?"

"Not even the royal secretary is easy prey now. He has prospered at court, he has the support of the Inquisitor Bocanegra and of the Council of Aragon. Besides, Olivares, with his dangerous taste for double-dealing, considers him to be useful." Guadalmedina gave a scornful shrug. "And so he has opted for a discreet and effective solution that will please everyone."

"He is to be taught a lesson," said Quevedo.

"Exactly. This includes snatching the contraband gold from underneath Medina Sidonia's nose and placing it instead in the royal coffers. Olivares himself has planned it all with the approval of the king, and that is the reason behind this royal visit to Seville. Our fourth Philip wishes to see the show himself, and then, with his usual impassivity, to bid farewell to the old duke by folding him in an embrace, tight enough for him to be able to hear the duke's teeth grinding. The problem is that the plan Olivares has come up with has two parts, one semiofficial and somewhat delicate, and the other official and more . . . difficult."

"The precise word is 'dangerous,'" said Quevedo, always exact when it came to language.

Guadalmedina leaned across the table toward the captain.

"As you will have gathered, the accountant Olmedilla is involved in the first part."

My master nodded slowly. Now all the pieces were slotting into place.

"And I," he said, "am involved in the second."

Guadalmedina calmly stroked his mustache. He was smiling. "That's what I like about you, Alatriste, there's never any need to explain things twice."

It was already dark when we set off along the narrow, ill-lit streets. The waning moon filled the hallways of the houses with a lovely milky light, bright enough for us to be able to see one another silhouetted beneath the eaves and the shady tops of the orange trees. Occasionally, we passed dark shapes, which scurried away when they saw us, for at that hour of night, Seville was as dangerous as any other city. As we emerged into a small square, a figure swathed in a cloak and leaning at a window, whispering, suddenly drew back and the window slammed shut, and as well as that black, male shadow, we saw a precautionary glint of steel. Guadalmedina gave a reassuring laugh and bade the motionless figure good night, and we continued on our way. The sound of our footsteps preceded us down alleyways and along the paths around the city walls. Now and then, the light from an oil lamp could be seen through the shutters behind the grilles at windows, and candles or cheap tin lanterns burned at the corners of certain streets, beneath an image, made from glazed tiles, of Our Lady, or of Christ in torment.

As we walked, Guadalmedina explained that the accountant Olmedilla might be a mere faceless official, a creature of figures and files, but he had a real talent for his job. He enjoyed the complete confidence of the Conde-Duque de Olivares, whom he advised on all accounting matters. And just so that we could get an idea of his character, he added that Olmedilla had acted not only in the investigation that had led Rodrigo Calderón to the scaffold, but also in the cases brought against the Duques de Lerma and Osuna. More than that, he was held to be an honest man, something almost unheard of in his profession. His sole passions were addition, subtraction, multiplication, and division, and the one goal of his life was to make the books balance. All the information they had received about the contraband gold came from reports compiled by the count-duke's spies, and these had been confirmed by several months of patient research by Olmedilla in the relevant offices, cabinets, and archives.

"All that remains for us now is to ascertain the final details," concluded the count. "The fleet has been sighted, and so we do not have much time. Everything has to be resolved tomorrow during a visit that Olmedilla will pay Garaffa, the man who chartered the galleon, so that he can clarify certain points concerning the transfer of the gold to the *Niklaasbergen*. The visit, of course, is an unofficial one, and Olmedilla has no document or letter of authority." Guadalmedina raised his eyebrows ironically. "So Garaffa will probably refuse to talk."

We passed a tavern. The window was lit and from inside came the strumming of a guitar. A gust of laughter and singing emerged as the door opened. On the threshold, a man vomited loudly before staggering homeward to sleep off the wine he had drunk. Between retches, we heard his hoarse cries invoking God, although not exactly prayerfully.

"Why don't you just arrest this Garaffa?" asked Alatriste. "A dungeon, a scribe, and a bit of strappado can work wonders. All you have to do is call on the king's authority."

"It's not that easy. There's a dispute over who holds sway in Seville, whether the Audiencia Real or the Cabildo, and the archbishop has a finger in every pie. Garaffa is well connected with the Church and with Medina Sidonia. There would be a huge scandal, and meanwhile the gold would have vanished. No, everything must be done as discreetly as possible. And once Garaffa has told us what he knows, he will have to disappear for a few days. He lives alone with just the one servant, so no one would mind very much if he disappeared forever." He paused significantly. "Not even the king."

After saying this, Guadalmedina walked a little way in silence. Quevedo was lagging slightly behind me, limping along in dignified fashion, one hand on my shoulder as if, in a way, he was trying to keep me out of the whole business.

"In short, Alatriste, it's up to you how you play the cards."

I couldn't see the captain's face, only his dark silhouette ahead of me, his hat, and the tip of his sword, which glinted in the rectangles of moonlight that slipped through the gaps between the eaves. After a moment, I heard him say, "Getting rid of the Genoese gentleman is easy enough, but as for the other business . . ."

He paused, then stood still. We caught up with him.

He had his head slightly bowed, and when he looked up, his pale eyes glittered in the darkness.

"I don't like torturing people."

He said this quite simply, bluntly, and undramatically. It was an objective fact spoken out loud. He didn't like sour wine either, or stew with too much salt in it, or men who were incapable of sticking to the rules, even if those rules were personal, individual, and apparently unimportant. There was a silence, and Quevedo removed his hand from my shoulder. Guadalmedina gave an awkward little cough.

"That's not my business," he said at last, somewhat embarrassed. "Nor do I wish to know anything about it. How you get the information we need is a matter for Olmedilla and for you. He does his job and you get paid for helping him."

"Besides, dealing with Garaffa is the easy part," said Quevedo, in a placatory tone.

"It is," agreed Guadalmedina, "because once Garaffa has given us the final details of the plan, there is another minor matter, Alatriste."

He was standing opposite the captain, and any awkwardness he may have felt before had vanished. I couldn't see his face clearly, but I'm sure he was smiling.

"The accountant Olmedilla will provide you with money to recruit a select group of men, old friends and so on—professional swordsmen, to put it bluntly. The best you can find."

There came the singsong voice of a beggar standing at the end of the street, an oil lamp in his hand, calling on us to pray for the souls in Purgatory. "Remember the dead," he was saying. "Remember." Guadalmedina watched the light from the lamp until it was swallowed up by the darkness, and then he turned again to my master.

"Then you will have to board that wretched Flemish ship."

Still talking, we reached the part of the city wall near El Arenal, by the little archway known as El Golpe, with its image of the Virgin of Atocha on the whitewashed wall above. El Golpe provided access to the famous Compás de la Laguna bawdy house. When the gates of Triana and El Arenal were closed, that archway and the bawdy house were the easiest way to slip out of the city. And as he hinted to us, Guadalmedina had an important appointment in Triana, at La Gamarra tavern, on the other side of the pontoon bridge that linked the two banks of the river. La Gamarra stood next to a convent whose nuns had all reputedly been sent there against their will. The Sunday-morning mass attracted even larger crowds than the latest play at the playhouse; it positively seethed with people; there were wimples and white hands on one side of the grille and young men sighing on the other. And, or so they said, such was the fervor of certain gentlemen from the best society—including distinguished strangers to the city, such as our king—they even came to worship there during the hours of darkness.

As for the bawdy house, a popular expression of the day, *más puta que la Méndez*—more of a whore than La Méndez herself—referred to a real woman called Méndez, whose name was used by don Francisco de Quevedo in his famous ballads about a celebrated figure from the criminal classes called Escarramán, as well as by other men of letters. She had worked as a prostitute in the bawdy house, which offered to the travelers and merchants staying in nearby Calle de Tintores and in other city inns—as well as to locals—gaming, music, and women of the kind described by the great Lope de Vega thus:

How foolish, how mad of a silly young man
To chase, helter-skelter (how he pants and drools),
After one of those women who've already been
Bait to a thousand other young fools.

And which the no less great don Francisco finished off in his own inimitable style:

Stupid the man who trusts in whores
And stupid the man who wants them;

Stupid the money handed over
To pay for whorish flotsam.
Stupid the desire, stupid the delight
The whorish moment imparts,
And stupid the man who doesn't believe—
Madam—you're the queen of tarts!

The bawdy house was run by one Garciposadas, from a family notorious in Seville for two of its brothers: one was a poet at court—a friend of Góngora's, as it happens—who had been burned that very year for sodomizing a mulatto, Pepillo Infante, also a poet and a servant of the Admiral of Castile, and the other had been burnt three years before in Málaga as a Judaizer; and since misfortunes always come in threes, these antecedents had earned Garciposadas the nickname of El Tostao, or Garciposadas the Scorched. This worthy fellow performed the duties of pimp or father of the bawdy house with great aplomb: he kept the authorities suitably lubricated to ensure that his business ran smoothly; and so as not to contravene the regulations laid down by the city's *corregidor,* or governor, he always ensured that weapons of any kind were deposited in the hallway and he forbade entry to any customers under the age of fourteen. The said Garciposadas was also on good terms with the constables and catchpoles, who quite blatantly protected him and his business, a situation that can be aptly summed up in these words:

I am both innocent and devious,
Naïve and promiscuous;
Rile me, yet my wrath is soothed
With a small reward, however lewd.

The reward in question was, of course, a nice fat purse. The place was always packed with petty criminals—rogues who swore upon the soul of Escamilla; scoundrels and rascals from La Heria; dealers in lives and purveyors of stab wounds. It was a picturesque pot, spiced with ruined aristocrats, idle New World nabobs, bourgeois gentlemen with plenty of cash, clerics in disguise, gamblers, pimps, common informers, swindlers, and individuals of every kind, some who had noses so keen they could smell a stranger a harquebus shot away and who were often perfectly safe from a justice of which don Francisco de Quevedo himself wrote:

Sevillean justice can prove scarce,
For the length of sentence handed out
Depends on the size of your purse.

Thus each night, under the protection of the authorities, El Compás was a constant flow of people, a secular feast, where only the finest wines were served, and those who went in as sober friends came out as wine-soaked sots. There they danced the lascivious *zarabanda*, guitar strings

were plucked and so were clients, and everyone did as he
pleased. The bawdy house was home to thirty sirens whose
singing emptied men's purses. Each of these sirens had her
own room, and every Saturday morning—for the people of
quality visited El Compás on Saturday night—a constable
would visit to make sure that none of the girls was infected
with the French disease and would not, therefore, give
their clients cause to curse and swear, and leave them wondering why God didn't give to the Turk and the Lutheran
what He had given to them. They say the archbishop was
in despair, for as one can read in a memoir of the time,
"What one finds most in Seville are men and women living in sin, false witnesses, rogues, murderers, and oppor-
tunists. There are more than three hundred gaming dens
and three thousand prostitutes."

But to return to our story—which does not involve a
very long journey—the fact is that, as ill luck would have
it, just as Guadalmedina was about to bid farewell to us underneath the archway of El Golpe, almost at the entrance
to the bawdy house, a patrol of catchpoles led by a constable with his staff of office passed by. You will recall that
the incident of the hanged soldier days before had caused
hostilities to break out between the law and the soldiers
from the galleys, and both parties were looking for ways to
have their revenge, which is why, during the day, there
wasn't a law officer to be seen on the streets and why, at

night, the soldiers took care to stay outside the city, in Triana.

"Well, well, well," said the constable when he saw us.

Guadalmedina, Quevedo, the captain, and I exchanged bewildered glances. It was equally ill luck that, of all the riffraff coming and going in the shadow of the bawdy house, that particular brooch and all his pins should have alighted on us as a pin cushion in which to stick themselves.

"Out taking the cool, are we, gentlemen?" added the constable scornfully.

His scornful bravado was backed up by his four men, who were armed with swords, shields, and black looks that the dim light made blacker still. Then I understood. By the light of the lantern of the Virgin of Atocha, the clothes worn by Captain Alatriste and Guadalmedina, and even by me, made us look like soldiers. Guadalmedina's buff coat was forbidden in time of peace—ironically enough, he had probably worn it that night in his role as the king's escort—and Captain Alatriste, of course, was the very image of the military man. Quevedo, as quick-thinking as ever, saw the problem coming and tried to put things right.

"Forgive me, sir," he said very courteously to the constable, "but I can assure you that we are all honorable men."

A few curious onlookers gathered around to see what

was happening: a couple of whores, a rogue or two, and a drunk who was already several sheets to the wind. Even Garciposadas himself peered out from beneath the arch. This small crowd emboldened the constable.

"And who asked you to tell us something we can find out for ourselves?"

I heard Guadalmedina tut-tutting impatiently.

"Don't back down now," said an encouraging voice from among the shadows and the throng of inquisitive onlookers. There was laughter too. More people were gathering underneath the arch. Some took the side of the law and others, the majority, urged us to catch as many catchpoles as we could.

"I arrest you in the name of the king."

This did not augur well at all. Guadalmedina and Quevedo looked at each other, and I saw the count wrap his cloak around his body and over his shoulder, revealing his sword arm and his sword but taking care to cover his face.

"It is not the custom of the well-born to suffer such outrages," he said.

"I don't care two figs whether it is or not," retorted the constable in surly tones.

With this refined remark, the scene was set. As for my master, he remained very still and quiet, studying the constable and his companions, the catchpoles. He cut an imposing figure in the half-light, with his aquiline profile and his bushy mustache beneath the broad brim of his hat. Or rather, so it seemed to me, who knew him well. I touched the hilt of my dagger. I would have given anything for a sword, because there were five of them and we were only four. I immediately and regretfully corrected myself. With my few inches of steel, we were really only three and a half.

"Hand over your swords," said the constable, "and be so good as to come with us."

"These are important people," Quevedo said, in one last attempt to save the situation.

"Right, and I'm the Duque de Alba."

It was clear that the constable was determined to have his way, and to make two and two add up to five if necessary. This was his parish, and he was being watched by his parishioners. The four catchpoles unsheathed their swords and spread out to form a wide semicircle around us.

"If we get out of this alive and no one identifies us," Guadalmedina whispered coolly, his voice muffled behind his cloak, "that will be that, but if not, gentlemen, the nearest church in which to seek sanctuary is the San Francisco."

The constable and his men were getting ever closer. In their black clothes, the catchpoles merged with the shadows. Underneath the arch, the onlookers encouraged them with mocking applause. "Go on, teach 'em a lesson,

Sánchez," someone said to the constable in a bantering tone. Unhurriedly, confidently, and boldly, the said Sánchez stuck his staff of office in his belt and grasped his sword in his right hand and a huge pistol in his left.

"I'll count up to three," he said, coming closer. "One . . ."

Don Francisco de Quevedo pushed me gently behind him, interposing himself between the catchpoles and me. Guadalmedina was watching Captain Alatriste, who was still standing impassively in the same place, judging distances and turning his body very slowly so as not to lose sight of the face of the catchpole nearest to him but still keeping an eye on the others. I noticed that Guadalmedina was checking to see who my master was looking at, and then, turning away, he fixed on another, as if satisfied that my master would deal with the first man.

"Two . . ."

Quevedo was removing his short cape. "There's nothing for it et cetera, et cetera," he muttered as he undid the fastening on his cape and wrapped the cloth around his left arm. Guadalmedina, for his part, had arranged his cloak so as to protect his torso from the knife thrusts that were about to rain down upon him. I stepped away from Quevedo and went to stand next to the captain. His right hand was moving toward the guard of his sword and the left was resting on the hilt of his dagger. I could hear his slow, steady breathing. I realized suddenly that I had not seen him kill a man for several months, not since Breda.

"Three," said the constable, raising his pistol and glancing back at the onlookers. "In the name of the king, and of the law . . ."

He had not even finished speaking when Guadalmedina fired one of his pistols at point-blank range, which sent the constable reeling backward, his face still turned away. A woman underneath the archway screamed, and an expectant murmur ran through the shadows, for the spectacle of fellow Spaniards quarreling and knifing one another has long been a popular Spanish sport. And then, as one, Quevedo, Alatriste, and Guadalmedina reached for their blades; seven bare lengths of steel glinted in the street; and then everything happened with diabolical speed: *cling, clang*, sparks flying, catchpoles shouting, "Stop in the name of the king!" and more cries and murmurs from the spectators. I, too, had unsheathed my dagger, though I did nothing with it, for in less time than it takes to say an Ave Maria, Guadalmedina had skewered the upper arm of one catchpole, Quevedo had slashed the face of another, leaving him leaning against the wall, hands pressed to the wound, and bleeding like a stuck pig, and Alatriste, sword in one hand and dagger in the other, wielding both as if they were bolts of lightning, had put two spans of Toledan steel through the chest of a third, who cried out, "Holy

Mother of God," before detaching himself from the blade and falling to the ground, vomiting gobbets of blood as dark as black ink. It all happened so fast that the fourth catchpole didn't think twice and took to his heels when my master suddenly rounded on him as his next victim. At that point, I sheathed my dagger and went over to pick up one of the swords lying on the ground, the constable's sword, and as I did so, two or three of the onlookers, who had misread the situation at the start, stepping forward to come to the aid of the catchpoles, stopped short when they saw how quickly everything had been resolved, and stood very still and circumspect, watching the captain, Guadal-medina, and Quevedo, who turned on them with their naked blades, ready to continue their harvest. I took up a position beside my companions and placed myself on guard; and the hand that held the sword was trembling not with anxiety but with excitement: I would have given any-thing to have contributed a sword thrust of my own to the fight. However, the would-be combatants from the small crowd were fast losing their desire to join in. They hung back prudently, muttering this and that, let's just wait and see, eh, while the other onlookers jeered at them and we walked slowly backward away from the scene, leaving the street bathed in blood: one catchpole dead, the consta-ble with his pistol shot more dead than alive and with not even enough breath to call for a confessor, the one with the cut to his arm stanching the wound the best he could, and the man with the slashed face kneeling by the wall, moaning behind a mask of blood.

"They'll tell you where to find us on the king's galleys!" cried Guadalmedina in a suitably defiant tone, while we dodged around the nearest corner. This was a clever ploy on his part, for it would place the blame for that night's fighting on the soldiers whom the constable had, to his cost, believed us to be.

> *The constable and his catchpoles*
> *Were eager for the kill,*
> *But I taught those turds a lesson*
> *And one was sent to Hell.*

As we strolled along Calle de Harinas, toward the gate of El Arenal, don Francisco de Quevedo was making up a few more scatological lines of poetry, all the while on the lookout for a tavern where he could toast both his poetry and us with some good wine. Guadalmedina was laughing, delighted with the whole business. An excellent move and very well played, damn it! Captain Alatriste, meanwhile, had cleaned the blade of his sword with a kerchief he kept in his pouch, and when he had replaced his sword in its sheath, he walked on in silence, occupied in thoughts impossible to penetrate. And I walked along beside him, carrying the constable's sword and feeling as proud as don Quixote.

4. THE QUEEN'S
MAID OF HONOR

Diego Alatriste was waiting, leaning against a wall, amongst pots of geraniums and basil, in the shade of a porchway in Calle del Mesón del Moro. Without his cloak, but with his hat on, his sword and dagger in his belt, and his doublet open over a clean, neatly darned shirt, he was intently watching the house of the Genoese merchant Garaffa. The house was almost at the gates of the old Jewish quarter in Seville, near the convent of the Discalced Carmelites and the old Doña Elvira playhouse, and it was very quiet at that hour, with few passersby and only the occasional woman sweeping the entrance to her house or watering her plants. In earlier days, when he was serving as a soldier on the king's galleys, Alatriste had often visited that quarter, never imagining that, later on, when he returned from Italy in the year sixteen hundred sixteen, he would spend a long time there, most of it in the company of ruffians and other people quick to draw their swords, in the famous Cathedral courtyard, the Patio de los Naranjos, which was a meeting place for the boldest and most cunning of Seville's criminal class. After the repression of the Moriscos in Valencia, as you may perhaps remember, the captain had asked to leave his regiment in order to enlist as a soldier in Naples—"where," he reasoned, "if I have to slit the throats of infidels, they will at least be able to defend themselves"—and he remained embarked until the naval battle of sixteen hundred fifteen, when, after a devastating raid on the Turkish coast with five galleys and more than a thousand comrades, he and his fellow soldiers returned to Italy with plenty of plunder and he led a life of pleasure in Naples. This ended as such things tend to end in youth, with a woman and another man, with a mark on the face for the woman and a sword thrust for the man, and Diego Alatriste fleeing Naples thanks to the help of his old friend Captain don Alonso de Contreras, who stowed him away on a galley bound for Sanlúcar and Seville. And that was how, before he moved on to Madrid, this former soldier came to earn his living as a paid swordsman in Seville, that Babylon and breeding ground for all vices, taking refuge by day among ruffians and scoundrels in the famous Cathedral courtyard and by night sallying forth to carry out the duties of his profession, one in which any man with courage and a good sword, and with sufficient luck and skill, could easily earn his daily bread. Such legendary ruffians as Gonzalo Xeniz, Gayoso, Ahumada, and the great Pedro Vázquez de Escamilla—who recognized only one kind of king, the king in the deck of cards—they were all long gone, undone by a knife thrust or by the disease of the noose, for in work such as theirs, finding oneself strung up by the neck was a highly contagious complaint. However, in the Patio de los Naranjos and in the royal prison, where he also took up temporary residence with some regularity, Alatriste had met many a worthy successor to such historic rogues, experts in how to stab, cut, and slash, although he, too, soon made a name for himself in that illustrious brotherhood, skilled as he was in the sword thrust perfected by the celebrated ruffian Gayona, as well as in many others proper to his art.

He was recalling all this now with a pang of nostalgia, less perhaps for the past than for his lost youth, and he was doing so not a stone's throw from the very playhouse where, as a young man, he had grown to love the plays of Lope, Tirso de Molina, and others—there he saw for the first time *The Dog in the Manger* and *The Shy Man at the Palace*—on nights that opened with poetry and staged fights and closed with taverns, wine, complaisant whores, jolly companions, and knives. This dangerous, fascinating Seville still existed, and any change was to be sought not in the city but in himself. Time does not pass in vain, he thought, as he stood leaning in the shady porchway. And a man grows old inside, just as his heart does.

"Death and damnation, Captain Alatriste, but it's a small world!"

The captain spun around in surprise to see who it was who had spoken his name. It was strange to see Sebastián Copons so far from a Flemish trench and uttering more than eight words together. It took the captain a few seconds to return to the very recent past: the sea voyage, his recent farewell to Copons in Cádiz, the latter's intention to spend a few days' leave there and then to travel up to Seville on his way north.

"It's good to see you, Sebastián."

This was both true and not true. It was not, in fact, good to see him at that precise moment, and while they clasped each other's arms with the sober affection of two old comrades, he glanced over Copons's shoulder at the far end of the street. Fortunately, Copons could be relied on. He could get rid of Copons without causing offense, knowing that he would understand. That, after all, was the good thing about a real friend: he trusted you to deal the cards fairly and never insisted on checking the deck.

"Are you stopping in Seville?" he asked.

"For a while."

Copons, small, thin, and wiry, was dressed, as ever, in

soldier's garb, in jerkin, baldric, sword, and boots. Beneath his hat, on his left temple, was the scar left by the gash that Alatriste himself had bandaged a year ago, during the battle at the Ruyter mill.

"How about a drink to celebrate, Diego?"

"Later."

Copons looked at him, surprised and intrigued, before half turning to follow the direction of his gaze.

"You're busy."

"Something like that."

Copons again inspected the street, searching for clues as to what was keeping his comrade there. Then, instinctively, he touched the hilt of his sword.

"Do you need me?" he asked phlegmatically.

"Not right now," replied Alatriste with a warm smile that wrinkled his weathered face. "But there might be something for you before you leave Seville. Would you be interested?"

"Are you in on it?"

"Yes, and it's well paid too."

"I'd do it even if it weren't."

At this point, Alatriste spotted the accountant Olmedilla at the end of the street. He was dressed, as always, entirely in black, tightly buttoned up to his ruff, wearing a narrow-brimmed hat and the air of an anonymous government official come straight from the Real Audiencia.

"I have to go, but meet me later at Becerra's."

Placing one hand on his friend's shoulder, he said nothing more, but with apparent unconcern, crossed the street to join the accountant by the house on the corner: a two-story brick building with a discreet gateway leading to an inner courtyard. They went in without knocking and without speaking to each other, exchanging only a brief, knowing glance. Alatriste had his hand on the hilt of his sword and Olmedilla remained as sour-faced as ever. An elderly servant came out, wiping his hands on his apron and looking anxious and inquisitive.

"We are here in the name of the Holy Office of the Inquisition," said Olmedilla with terrible coldness.

The servant's expression changed, for in Garaffa's house and indeed in the whole of Seville, these were not words to be taken lightly. And so when Alatriste, one hand still on the hilt of his sword, indicated a room, the servant entered it as meekly as a lamb, allowing himself, without a murmur of protest, to be bound and gagged and locked in. When Alatriste came back out into the courtyard, he found Olmedilla waiting behind an enormous potted fern and twiddling his thumbs impatiently. There was another silent exchange of glances, and the two men went across the courtyard to a closed door. Then Alatriste unsheathed his sword, flung open the door, and strode into a spacious study furnished with a desk, a cupboard, a copper brazier, and a few leather chairs. The light from a high, barred window, half covered by latticework shutters, cast innumerable tiny luminous squares onto the head and shoulders of a stout, middle-aged man in silk robe and slippers, who started to his feet. This time Olmedilla did not invoke the Holy Office or anything else, he merely followed Alatriste into the room, and after a quick look around, his eye alighted with professional satisfaction on the open cupboard stuffed with papers. Just the way a cat, thought the captain, would have licked its lips at the sight of a sardine placed half an inch from its whiskers. As for the owner of the house, Jerónimo Garaffa, all the blood seemed to have drained from his face; he stood very quietly, mouth agape, both hands resting on the table on which a sealing-wax candle was burning. When he stood up, he spilled half an inkwell over the paper on which he had been writing when the intruders burst in. His dyed hair was covered by a snood and his waxed mustache by a net. He continued to hold the pen between his fingers as if he had forgotten it was there, transfixed in horror by the sword Captain Alatriste was pressing to his throat.

"So you have no idea what we're talking about."

The accountant Olmedilla, as comfortably esconced behind the desk as if he were in his own office, briefly raised his eyes from the papers to see Jerónimo Garaffa, still with his snood on, anxiously shaking his head. He was sitting on a chair, his hands tied to the chair back. It was not particularly warm in the room, but large beads of sweat were already running from his hair into his side-whiskers, and his face smelled of gum arabic, collyria, and barber's lotions.

"I swear to you, sir . . ."

Olmedilla interrupted this protest with an abrupt wave of his hand and resumed his scrutiny of the documents before him. Above the mustache net, which gave his face the grotesque appearance of a Carnival mask, Garaffa's eyes turned to rest on Diego Alatriste, who was listening in silence, leaning against the wall, sword sheathed, arms folded. He must have found Alatriste's icy eyes more troubling even than Olmedilla's abrupt manner, for he turned back to the accountant like someone forced to choose the lesser of two evils. After a long, oppressive silence, the accountant abandoned the documents he was studying, sat back in his chair, hands clasped, and, again twiddling his thumbs, stared at Garaffa. It seemed to Alatriste that he looked even more the part of the gray government-office mouse, except that now his expression was that of a mouse with very bad indigestion who keeps swallowing bile.

"Let's get this quite straight now," said Olmedilla very coldly and deliberately. "You know what I'm talking about and we know that you know. Everything else is a pure waste of time."

Garaffa's mouth was so dry that it took him three attempts before he could articulate a word.

"I swear by Christ Our Lord," he said in a hoarse voice, his foreign accent made more marked by fear, "that I know nothing about this Flemish ship."

"Christ has nothing to do with it!"

"This is an outrage. I demand that the law . . ."

Garaffa's final attempt to give some substance to his protest ended in a sob. The mere sight of Diego Alatriste's face told him that the law to which he was referring—and which he was doubtless accustomed to buying with a few lovely pieces of eight—only existed somewhere very far from that room and that there was no help to be had.

"Where will the *Virgen de Regla* anchor?" asked Olmedilla very quietly.

"I don't know. Holy Mother of God, I swear I don't know what you're talking about."

The accountant scratched his nose indifferently. He gave Alatriste a significant look, and the captain thought to himself that Olmedilla really was the very image of Hapsburg officialdom, always so meticulous and implacable with the unfortunate. He could as easily have been a judge, a scribe, a constable, a lawyer, or any of the other insect life that lived and prospered under the protection of the monarchy. Guadalmedina and Quevedo had told him that Olmedilla was honest, and Alatriste believed them. As to his other qualities and attitudes, he was, Alatriste concluded, no different from the rabble of ruthless, avaricious magpies that populated the courts and offices of lawyers and procurators, and where—not even in one's dreams— would one find more arrogant Lucifers, more thievish Cacuses, or more honor-greedy Tantaluses; no blasphemy uttered by an infidel could ever equal their decrees, which, unfailingly, favored the powerful and damned the humble. They were, in short, loathsome bloodsuckers who lacked all charity and decorum, but who brimmed with intemperance, acquisitiveness, and the fanatical zeal of the hypocrite, so much so that the very people who should be protecting the poor and the destitute were precisely the ones voraciously tearing them apart with their greedy talons. However, the man in their grasp today did not quite fit that image. He was neither poor nor destitute, but he was certainly wretched.

"I see," concluded Olmedilla.

He was tidying the papers on the desk, his eyes still trained on Alatriste, as if signaling that he had nothing more to say. A few seconds passed, during which Olmedilla and the captain continued to observe each other in silence. Then the latter uncrossed his arms, abandoned his position by the wall, and went over to Garaffa. When he reached

Garaffa's side, the expression of terror on the merchant's face was indescribable. Alatriste stood in front of him, leaning slightly forward in order to fix his gaze more intensely. That man and what he represented did not stir his reserves of pity in the least. Beneath the snood, the dyed hair was leaving trails of dark sweat on Garaffa's forehead and neck. Now, despite all the creams and pomades, he gave off a sour smell—of perspiration and fear.

"Jerónimo," whispered Alatriste.

When he heard his name pronounced barely three inches from his face, Garaffa flinched as if he had been slapped. The captain did not draw back but remained for a few moments motionless and silent, regarding him from close up. His mustache was almost touching the prisoner's nose.

"I've seen a lot of men tortured," he said at last, very slowly. "With their arms and legs dislocated by the pulley, I've seen them betray their own children. I've seen renegades flayed alive, screaming and begging to be killed. In Valencia, I saw poor Moorish converts having the soles of their feet burned to make them reveal where they'd hidden their gold, while, in the background, they could hear the cries of their twelve-year-old daughters as they were raped by soldiers."

He fell silent, as if he could go on listing such incidents indefinitely and as if there were, therefore, no point in continuing. Garaffa's face was as pale as if the hand of death had just passed over it. He had suddenly stopped sweating, as though, beneath his skin, yellow with terror, not one drop of blood flowed.

"Everyone talks sooner or later," concluded the captain, "or nearly everyone. Sometimes, if the torturer proves clumsy, the person dies first, but that wouldn't be the case with you."

He remained for a while longer staring at him, almost nose to nose, then went over to the desk. Standing there with his back to the prisoner, he rolled up the shirtsleeve on his left arm. While he was doing so, his eye caught that of Olmedilla, who was watching intently, slightly perplexed. Then he picked up the sealing-wax candle and went back over to Garaffa. When he showed it to him, lifting it up a little, the light from the flame picked out the gray-green of his eyes, once more fixed on Garaffa, like two slivers of ice.

"Watch," he said.

He showed him his brown forearm and the long, slender scar visible amongst the hairs, running from wrist to elbow. And then, right under the nose of the horrified Genoese, Captain Alatriste held the flame to his own bare skin. The flame crackled and there arose a smell of burnt flesh, while the captain clenched his jaw and fist, and the tendons and muscles of his forearm grew as hard as vine shoots carved in stone. The captain's eyes remained green and impassive, but Garaffa's bulged in horror. This lasted for one long, seemingly interminable moment. Then, very calmly, Alatriste put the candlestick down on the desk, returned to the prisoner, and showed him his arm. A hideous burn, the size of a silver piece of eight, was reddening the scorched skin along the edges of the old wound.

"Jerónimo," he said.

He again brought his face very close to Garaffa's, and spoke to him in that same soft, almost confiding tone:

"If I can do this to myself, imagine what I would be capable of doing to you."

A yellowish liquid, emanating from the prisoner, began to form a puddle around the legs of the chair. Garaffa started to moan and shake and did so for some time. When he finally recovered the power of speech, he let out a prodigious, torrential stream of words, while Olmedilla diligently dipped his pen in the inkwell and made what notes he deemed necessary. Alatriste went into the kitchen in search of some lard or grease or oil to apply to the burn. When he returned, bandaging his forearm with a clean piece of cloth, Olmedilla gave him a look that, in a man of a different humor, would have been one of enormous respect. As for Garaffa, oblivious to everything but his own feelings of terror, he continued to gabble on and on, giving names, places, dates, details of Portuguese banks and gold bars.

At this same hour, I was walking under the long vaulted passageway that leads from the Patio de Banderas into Callejón de la Aljama, in what had once been the Jewish quarter. And, albeit for very different reasons from those of Jerónimo Garaffa, I, too, felt as if I had not one drop of blood in my veins. I stopped at the designated place and, fearing that my legs might give way beneath me, placed one hand on the wall to support myself. My instinct for self-preservation, however, had developed over the previous few years and so, despite everything, I remained clearheaded enough to study the situation carefully—the two exits and those troubling little doors set in the walls. I touched the handle of my dagger, which I wore, as always, tucked into my belt at my back, and then I touched the pouch containing the note that had brought me there. It was worthy of a scene in a play by Tirso de Molina or by Lope de Vega:

If you still care for me, now is the moment to prove it. I would like to meet you at eleven o'clock in the passageway leading into the Jewish quarter.

I had received this note at nine o'clock, from a boy who came to the inn in Calle de Tintores, where I was awaiting the captain's return, seated on the little ledge by the door, watching the people go by. There was no signature, but the name of the sender was as clear to me as the deep wounds in my heart and in my memory. You can imagine the conflicting feelings that troubled me following the receipt of that note, and the delicious anxiety that guided my steps. I will not describe in detail all the anxieties of the lover, which would shame me and bore you, the reader. I will say only that I was then sixteen years old and had never loved a girl, or a woman—nor did I ever love anyone afterward—as I loved Angélica de Alquézar.

It really was most odd. I knew that the note could only be another episode in the dangerous game that Angélica had been playing with me ever since we first met outside the Tavern of the Turk in Madrid. A game that had almost cost me my honor and my life and which, many times more over the years, would cause me to walk along the very brink of the abyss, along the deadly edge of the most delicious blade a woman was capable of creating for the man who, throughout her life, and even at the very moment of her early death, would be both lover and enemy. That moment, however, was still far off, and there I was, on that mild winter morning in Seville, striding along with all the vigor and audacity of my youth, to keep an appointment with the girl—perhaps not so much of a girl now, I thought—who, once, almost three years before, at the Fuente del Acero, had responded to my heartfelt "I would die for you" with a sweet, enigmatic smile and the words "Perhaps you will."

The Arco de la Aljama was deserted. Leaving behind me the Cathedral tower, which was silhouetted against the sky above the tops of the orange trees, I walked farther along, until I turned the corner and emerged on the other side, where the water in a fountain was singing softly to itself and where the thick, twining branches of creepers hung down from the battlements of the Alcázares, the Royal Palace. There was no one there either. Perhaps it was all a joke, I thought, retracing my steps and plunging back into the shadows of the passageway. That was when I heard a noise behind me, and as I turned, I put my hand on my dagger. One of the doors stood open, and a burly blond soldier in the German guard was observing me in silence. He gestured to me and I approached very cautiously, fearing some trick, but the German appeared to be friendly. He was examining me with professional curiosity, and when I reached his side, he gestured again, this time indicating that I should surrender my dagger. Beneath the enormous fair side-whiskers and mustache he wore a good-natured smile. Then he said something like *Komensi herein,* which I—having seen more than enough Germans, alive and dead, in Flanders—knew to mean "Come along" or "Come in" or something of the sort. I had no choice, and so I handed him my dagger and went in through the door.

. . .

"Good morning, soldier."

Anyone familiar with the portrait of Angélica de Alquézar painted by Diego Velázquez can easily imagine her just a few years younger. The royal secretary's niece, our queen's maid of honor, was fifteen years old, and her beauty was much more now than a mere promise. She had matured a great deal since the last time I saw her: the laced bodice of her dress with its silver and coral edgings, matching the full brocade skirt held out stiffly around her hips by a farthingale, suggested curves that had not been there before. Ringlets, of a purer gold than any Araucanian could have found in his mines, still framed those blue eyes, complemented by her smooth, white skin, which I imagined—and would one day find to be so—would have the same texture as silk.

"It's been a long time," she said.

She was so beautiful it was painful to look at her. The room, with its Moorish columns, gave onto a small garden in the palace, and the sun behind her created a white halo about her hair. Her smile was the same: mysterious and provocative, with a hint of irony and mischief on her perfect lips.

"Yes, a long time," I said at last.

The German had withdrawn to the garden, where I

glimpsed the wimpled head of a duenna. Angélica sat down on a carved wooden chair and indicated that I should sit on the footstool in front of her. I did as she asked, not fully aware of what I was doing. She was studying me very intently, her hands folded on her lap; from beneath the skirt of her dress emerged one slender satin slipper, and suddenly I was very conscious of my rough sleeveless doublet and darned shirt, my coarse trousers and military gaiters. "Oh, dear God," I murmured. I imagined the court peacocks and fops of good blood and even better purses, dressed in all their finery, paying amorous compliments to Angélica at galas and gatherings. A jealous shiver pierced my soul.

"I hope," she said very softly, "that you bear me no malice."

I remembered—and it took little effort—the humiliation, the prisons of the Inquisition in Toledo, the auto-da-fé in the Plaza Mayor, and the role that Luis de Alquézar's niece had played in my misfortune. This thought had the virtue of restoring to me the coldness I so needed.

"What do you want from me?" I asked.

She took just a second longer than necessary to reply. She was examining me closely, with the same smile on her lips. She seemed pleased by what she saw.

"I don't want anything," she said. "I was simply curious to see you again. I recognized you in the square."

She fell silent for a moment. She looked at my hands and then, again, at my face.

"You've grown, sir."

"So have you."

She bit her lip slightly and nodded very slowly. The ringlets gently brushed the pale skin of her cheeks, and I adored her.

"You've been fighting in Flanders."

This was neither a statement nor a question. She appeared to be thinking out loud.

"I believe I love you," she said suddenly.

I sprang to my feet. Angélica was no longer smiling. She was watching me from her chair, gazing up at me with eyes as blue as the sky, as the sea, as life itself. I swear she was lovely enough to drive a man insane.

"Great God," I murmured.

I was trembling like the leaves on a tree. She remained motionless and silent for a long time. Finally, she gave a slight shrug.

"I want you to know," she said, "that you have some very unfortunate friends. Such as that Captain Batiste or Triste or whatever his name is. Friends who are the enemies of my friends. And I want you to know that this could perhaps cost you your life."

"It already nearly did," I retorted.

"And it will again soon."

Her smile had returned; it was the same smile as before, thoughtful and enigmatic.

"This evening," she went on, "the Duque and Duquesa de Medina Sidonia are giving a party for the king and queen. On the way back, my carriage will stop for a while in the Alameda. With its beautiful fountains and gardens, it's a delightful place to walk in."

I frowned. This was all far too good and far too easy.

"Isn't that a little late for a walk?"

"We're in Seville. The nights here are warm."

The irony of her words did not escape me. I glanced across at the courtyard, at the duenna still pacing up and down. Angélica understood my glance.

"She's not the same one who was with me at the Fuente del Acero. This one turns dumb and blind whenever I want her to. And I thought you might like to be at the Alameda tonight at ten, Íñigo Balboa."

I stood there, perplexed, analyzing everything she had said.

"It's a trap," I concluded, "another ambush."

"Possibly." She held my gaze, her face inscrutable. "It's up to you whether you're brave enough to fall into it or not."

"The captain . . ." I began, but stopped at once. Angélica stared at me with terrible perspicuity. It was as if she had read my thoughts.

"This captain fellow is your friend. You will doubtless have to tell him this little secret, and no friend would allow you to walk alone into an ambush."

She paused to allow the idea to penetrate.

"They say," she added at last, "that he, too, is a brave man."

"Who says so?"

She did not reply, merely smiling more broadly. And I understood then what she had just said to me. This certainty came with such astonishing clarity that I shuddered at the calculated way in which she was throwing this challenge in my face. The black shape of Gualterio Malatesta, like a dark ghost, interposed itself between us. It was all so obvious and so terrible: the old quarrel involved not only Alatriste now. I was of an age to answer for the consequences of my own actions; I knew too much, and as far as our enemies were concerned, I was as troublesome an adversary as the captain. Since I was the pretext for the rendezvous, and since I had, perversely, been warned of the certain danger involved, I couldn't possibly go where Angélica was asking me to go, and yet neither could I not go. The words "You've been fighting in Flanders," spoken only a moment before, now took on a cruelly ironic tone. Ultimately, though, the message was intended for the captain. And I should not, in that case, keep it from him. However, if I told him, he either would forbid me to go to the

Alameda or would forbid me to go alone. The letter of challenge was, inevitably, being issued to us both. It came down to a choice between my shame and certain danger. My conscience thrashed around like a fish caught in a net. Suddenly, Gualterio Malatesta's words surfaced in my memory with a sinister new meaning. Honor, he had said, is a dangerous thing to sustain.

"I wish to know," said Angélica, "if you are still prepared to die for me."

I stared at her in bewilderment, incapable of saying a word. It was as if her gaze were free to walk around inside my mind.

"If you don't come," she added, "I will know that, despite your time spent in Flanders, you are a coward. If you do come, whatever happens, I want you to remember what I said before."

The silk brocade of her dress rustled as she stood up. She was standing close to me now. Very close.

"And that I may well always love you."

She looked across at the garden, where the duenna was walking up and down. Then she came still closer.

"Always remember that—to the very end. Whenever that should come."

"You're lying," I said.

The blood seemed suddenly to have drained from my heart and my veins. Angélica continued studying me intently for what seemed an eternity. And then she did something unexpected, by which I mean that she raised one small, white, perfect hand and placed her fingers on my lips as softly as a kiss.

"Go," she said.

She turned and went out into the garden. I was so shaken that I took a few steps after her, as if intending to follow her up to the royal apartments and into the queen's private chambers. The German with the bushy side-whiskers stopped me and smilingly showed me the door, at the same time returning my dagger to me.

I went and sat on the steps of the Casa Lonja, next to the Cathedral, and stayed there for a long time, sunk in gloomy thoughts. I was filled by conflicting feelings, and my love for Angélica, revived by that disquieting interview, was locked in battle with the certain knowledge of the sinister trap closing around us. At first, I considered saying nothing and making some excuse to slip away that night and go alone to the rendezvous and thus confront my destiny, with, as my only companions, my dagger and the constable's sword, a good blade made by the swordsmith Juanes—I kept it wrapped in old rags, hidden in our room at the inn. But even if I did that, the venture was doomed. The shadowy figure of Malatesta took shape in my imagination like a dark omen. I would have no chance against him. And that, of course, was in the unlikely event that the Italian would come to the rendezvous alone.

I felt like weeping with rage and impotence. I was a Basque and an hidalgo, the son of the soldier Lope Balboa, who had died in Flanders for the king and for the true religion. My honor and the life of the man I respected most in the world hung in the balance, as did my life, but at that point in my existence—brought up, as I had been, from the age of twelve in the harsh worlds of criminality and of war—I had already too often staked my life on the throw of a die and possessed the fatalism of one who takes a breath knowing how very easy it is to stop breathing altogether. I had seen too many men die, some uttering curses or weeping, some praying or silent, some despairing, and others resigned, and dying did not seem to me anything very extraordinary or terrible. Besides, I believed that there was another life beyond, where God, my own good father, and all my old comrades would be waiting for me with open arms. And regardless of whether there was a life to come or not, I had learned that men like Captain Alatriste know that they can die at any moment, and death, in the end, always proves them right.

Such were my thoughts as I sat on the steps outside the Casa Lonja when, in the distance, I spotted the captain and the accountant Olmedilla. They were walking past the

palace wall, toward the Casa de Contratación. My first impulse was to run to meet them, but I stopped myself in
time and, instead, merely observed the slender, silent figure of my master, the broad brim of his hat shading his
face, his sword bobbing at his side, and, next to him, the fu-
nereal presence of the accountant.

I watched them disappear around a corner, then
remained sitting motionless where I was, my arms around
my knees. After all, I concluded, it was a simple enough
matter. That night I merely had to decide between getting
killed alone or getting killed alongside Captain Alatriste.

It was Olmedilla who proposed calling in at a tavern, and
Diego Alatriste agreed, although the suggestion took him
by surprise. This was the first time Olmedilla had ever
proved talkative or sociable. They went into the Seisdedos
tavern, behind the building known as Las Atarazanas—
the arsenal—and sat down at a table outside the door, underneath the porch and the awning that gave shelter from
the sun. Alatriste removed his hat and placed it on a stool.
A girl brought them a jug of Cazalla de la Sierra wine and
a dish of purple olives, and Olmedilla drank with the captain. True, he barely tasted the wine, taking only a sip from
his mug, but before doing so, he took a long look at the man
beside him. His brow unfurrowed slightly.

"Well played," he said.

The captain studied the accountant's gaunt features, his sparse beard, his sallow, parchment-like skin, which seemed to have been contaminated by the candles used to light gloomy government offices. He said nothing, however, but simply raised the wine to his lips and, unlike Olmedilla, drained the mug to the lees. His companion continued to study him with interest.

"They weren't exaggerating when they told me about you," he said at last.

"That business with the Genoese fellow was easy," replied Alatriste grimly, and said no more, but the ensuing silence said, "I've done other far more unsavory things." That, at least, is how Olmedilla appeared to interpret it, because he nodded slowly, with the grave look of someone who understands and is too polite to ask further questions. As for Garaffa and his servant, they were, at that moment, sitting bound and gagged in a carriage driving them out of Seville to some destination unknown to the captain—he neither knew nor cared to know—with an escort of sinister-looking constables, whom Olmedilla had clearly alerted beforehand, for they appeared in Calle del Mesón del Moro as if by magic (the neighbors' natural curiosity having been dampened by the fateful words "Holy Office of the Inquisition"), then vanished very discreetly with their prisoners in the direction of the Puerta de Carmona.

Olmedilla unbuttoned his doublet and took out a folded piece of paper bearing a seal. After holding it in his hand for a moment, as if overcoming a few final scruples, he placed it on the table before the captain.

"It's an order of payment," he said. "To the bearer it's worth fifty old gold doubloons, double-headed. You can convert it into cash at the house of don Joseph Arenzana, in Plaza de San Salvador. No questions asked."

Alatriste looked at the piece of paper but did not touch it. A double-headed doubloon was the most coveted coin of the day. They had been minted from fine gold over a century before, in the reign of the Catholic kings, and no one doubted their value when you slammed them down on the table. He knew men who would knife their own mother for a single one of those doubloons.

"There'll be six times that amount," added Olmedilla, "when it's all over."

"That's good to know."

The accountant gazed thoughtfully into his mug of wine. A fly was swimming about in it, making desperate attempts to clamber out.

"The fleet arrives in three days' time," he said, watching the dying fly.

"How many men will I need?"

Olmedilla pointed with an ink-stained finger at the order of payment. "That's up to you. According to the Genoese fellow, the *Niklaasbergen* is carrying twenty or so sailors, a captain, and a pilot, all of them, apart from the pilot, Flemish or Dutch. In Sanlúcar, a few Spaniards might come on board with the cargo. And we only have one night."

Alatriste made a rapid calculation. "Twelve or fifteen, then. With that amount of gold I can get all the men I need for the job."

Olmedilla made a chary gesture with his hand, making it clear that Alatriste's "job" was no business of his. He said, "You should have them ready the night before. The plan is to go down the river and reach Sanlúcar by evening." He sank his chin in his ruff, as if thinking hard to make sure he had forgotten nothing. "I'll be coming too."

"All the way?"

"We'll see."

The captain made no attempt to conceal his surprise. "It won't be a paper-and-ink affair."

"That doesn't matter. Once the ship is in our hands, I have a duty to check the cargo and organize its transfer."

Alatriste had to suppress a smile. He couldn't imagine the accountant mixing with the kind of people he was considering as recruits, but he could understand that one could never be too careful in such matters. So vast a quantity of gold was a temptation, and the odd ingot could easily get lost along the way.

"Needless to say," added Olmedilla, "any theft will be punished by hanging."

"Does that apply to you as well?"

"Perhaps, yes."

Alatriste smoothed his mustache with one finger, then said drily, "I shouldn't think they pay you enough for such alarming eventualities."

"They pay me sufficient for me to do my duty."

The fly had ceased struggling, but Olmedilla continued to stare at it. The captain poured more wine into his own mug. While he was drinking, he noticed that his companion had looked up again and was studying, with some interest, first the two scars on his forehead and then his left arm where his shirtsleeve concealed the burn beneath the bandage. The burn, by the way, stung like the very devil. Finally, Olmedilla frowned, as if he had been pondering a question he was afraid to ask out loud. "I was just wondering," he said, "what you would have done if Garaffa had been less easily intimidated."

Alatriste glanced up and down the street; the dazzle of sun on the opposite wall made him half close his eyes, so that he appeared even more inscrutable. Then he looked at the drowned fly in Olmedilla's wine, took another sip from his own mug, and said nothing.

5. THE FIGHT

At the entrance to the Alameda, the pillars of Hercules stood in the moonlight like two halberds. The tops of elm trees stretched out behind them as far as the eye could see, making the night seem still darker beneath the arbor of their branches. At that hour, there were no carriages filled with elegant ladies and no Sevillian gentlemen on horseback, capering and caracoling amongst the bushes, fountains, and pools. All I could hear was the sound of water and, sometimes, in the distance, a dog barking anxiously somewhere over near the chapel of La Cruz del Rodeo.

I stopped beside one of the thick stone pillars and listened, holding my breath. My throat was as dry as if it had been dusted with sand, and my pulses were pounding so hard in my wrists and my temples that if, at that moment, someone had cut open my heart, they would have found not a drop of blood in it. As I fearfully scanned the Alameda, I pushed back my short cape to uncover the hilt of the sword I was wearing tucked in my leather belt. In such a deserted place, the weight of the sword, along with that of my dagger, was a great comfort to me. Then I checked the lacing on the buff coat protecting my torso. The coat belonged to Captain Alatriste, and I had "borrowed" it from him while he was downstairs with don Francisco de Quevedo and Sebastián Copons, eating and drinking and talking about Flanders. I had pretended to be feeling unwell and retired early in order to carry out the plan I had been mulling over all day. To this end, I gave my face and hair a thorough wash and then put on a clean shirt, in case, at the end of the night, a scrap of that shirt should end up buried in my flesh. The captain's buff coat was rather too large for me, and so I had padded it out by wearing my old doublet underneath, stuffed with tow. I completed this outfit with a pair of much-patched chamois leather breeches that had survived the siege of Breda—and which would protect my thighs from any possible knife thrusts—a pair of buskins with esparto soles, some gaiters, and a cap. Not exactly the attire to go courting in, I thought, when I saw my reflection in the copper bottom of a saucepan, but better a live ruffian than a dead fop.

I crept out, with my buff coat and my sword concealed beneath my cape. Only don Francisco spotted me briefly from afar, but he merely smiled and went on talking to the captain and to Copons, who, fortunately, both had their backs to the door. Once in the street, I adjusted my clothing as best I could as I walked toward the Plaza de San Francisco, and from there, avoiding the busier thoroughfares, I kept as close as I could to Calle de las Sierpes and Calle del Puerco until I emerged into the deserted Alameda.

It was not, as it turned out, entirely deserted. A mule whinnied from beneath the elms. Frightened, I took a closer look, and when my eyes had grown accustomed to the gloom of that small wood, I could just make out the shape of a carriage standing next to one of the stone fountains. I moved forward very cautiously, my hand resting on the hilt of my sword, until I could see the interior of the carriage, dimly lit by a covered lantern. And step by step, ever more slowly, I reached the running board.

"Good evening, soldier."

That voice stole mine away and made the hand resting on my sword hilt tremble. Perhaps it wasn't a trap after all. Perhaps it was true that she loved me and was there, just as she had promised, waiting for me. I saw a male figure up aloft on the driver's seat, and another at the rear: two silent servants watching over the queen's maid of honor.

"I'm pleased to know you're not a coward," whispered Angélica.

I took off my cap. In the dim lantern glow I could make out only vague shapes in the shadows, but it was enough to light the upholstered interior, the golden glint of her hair, and the satin of her dress when she shifted in her seat. I threw caution to the wind. The door was open, and I stepped up onto the running board. A delicious perfume wrapped about me like a caress. This, I thought, is the very perfume of her skin, and it's worth risking one's life for the mere bliss of being able to breathe it in.

"Have you come alone?"

"Yes."

There was a long silence. When she spoke again, she sounded surprised. "You're very stupid," she said, "and very noble."

I did not respond. I was too happy to spoil the moment with words. In the half-dark I could see her eyes shining. She was looking at me without saying a word. I touched the satin of her skirt and finally managed to murmur, "You said you loved me."

There was an even longer silence, interrupted by the impatient whinnying of the mules. I heard the driver up above quiet them with a flick of the reins. The servant at the back was still only a dark, motionless smudge.

"Did I?"

She paused, as if struggling to remember what it was we had talked about that morning at the Palace. "Perhaps I do," she concluded.

"I love you," I declared.

"Is that why you're here?"

"Yes."

She bent her face toward mine. I swear I felt her hair brush my cheek.

"In that case," she whispered, "you deserve a reward."

She placed one hand on my face with infinite tenderness, and suddenly I felt her lips pressed to mine. For a moment they remained there, soft and cool. Then she withdrew into the carriage.

"That is just an advance payment on my debt to you," she said. "If you survive, you can claim the rest."

She gave an order to the coachman, and he cracked his whip. The carriage moved off. I stood there, dumbstruck, clutching my cap in one hand and with the fingers of my other hand incredulously touching the mouth that Angélica de Alquézar had just kissed. The universe was spinning crazily, and it took me a while to recover my sanity.

Then I looked about me and saw the shadows.

They were emerging out of the darkness, from amongst the trees. Seven dark shapes, men with faces obscured by cloaks and hats. They approached as slowly as if they had all the time in the world, and I felt the skin beneath my buff coat prickle.

"Damnation!" said a voice. "It's the boy, and he's come alone!"

This time there was no *ti-ri-tu, ta-ta*, but I immediately recognized the harsh, hoarse, cracked tone. It came from the shadow nearest to me, which seemed very tall and very black. They were standing around me, not moving, as if uncertain what to do with me.

"Such a very big net," added the voice, "to catch one sardine."

The scorn with which this was spoken had the virtue of heating my blood and restoring my composure. The panic that had begun to fill me vanished. Those faceless men might not know what to do with the sardine, but the sardine had spent all day deliberating and preparing himself for precisely this situation. Every outcome, even the very worst, had been weighed and pondered and considered a hundred times in my imagination, and I was ready. My only regret was that I had no time to perform a proper Act of Contrition, but there was nothing to be done about it. And so I undid my cape, took a deep breath, made the sign of the cross, and unsheathed my sword. What a shame, I thought, that Captain Alatriste cannot see me now. He would have been pleased to know that the son of his friend Lope Balboa also knew how to die.

"Well, well . . ." said Malatesta.

Sheer surprise meant that his comment remained unfinished as I adopted a proper fencing stance and made a lunge that went straight through his cloak, missing his body by an inch. He stepped back to avoid me, and I still had time to deliver a back-edged cut before he had even put hand to sword. That sword, however, now left its sheath with a sinister whisper, and I saw the blade glitter as the Italian moved away to take off his cape and assume the en garde position. Feeling that my one opportunity was slipping away, I steadied myself and closed on him again, and despite my fear, I remained in control, abruptly raised my arm to make a feint to his head, changed sides, and with the same back-edged cut, lunged forward as I had before, with such verve that, if my enemy had not been wearing a hat, his soul would have been sent straight down to Hell.

Gualterio Malatesta stumbled backward, blaspheming loudly in Italian. And then, convinced that any initial advantage I might have had ended there, I swung around, describing a circle with the point of my sword, to confront the others who, taken by surprise at first, had finally unsheathed their weapons and surrounded me, with no consideration for my solitary state. The sentence was clear, as clear as the light of day that I would never see again. The rapid thought crossed my mind that for a boy from Oñate, this wasn't such a bad way to end, and taking my dagger in my left hand, I prepared to defend myself. One against seven.

"Leave him to me," Malatesta said to his companions.

He had recovered from his initial shock and came toward me confidently, sword at the ready, and I knew that I had only a few more seconds of life left. And so instead of waiting for him in the en garde stance, as prescribed in the true art of swordplay, I half crouched down, then sprang up like a hare and aimed straight at his chest. My blade, however, pierced only air. Inexplicably, Malatesta was behind me, and I could feel his knife pressing into one shoulder, in the gap between buff coat and shirt from which protruded the tow from the doublet I was wearing underneath.

"You're going to die like a man, boy," said Malatesta.

There was both anger and admiration in his voice, but I had passed that point of no return where words are of no interest, and I didn't give a fig for his admiration, his anger, or his scorn. And so, without a word, I turned, as I had so often seen Captain Alatriste do: knees bent, dagger in one hand and sword in the other, reserving my breath for the final attack. I had once heard the captain say that the thing that helps a man to die well is knowing that he has done all he can to avoid death.

Then, from the encircling gloom came a pistol shot, and my enemies were briefly lit up by the glare. One of them had not yet hit the ground when the Alameda was lit by another flash, and in that burst of light I saw Captain

Alatriste, Copons, and don Francisco de Quevedo rushing toward us, swords in hand, as if they had sprung from the bowels of the earth.

Thank God they came when they did. The night became a storm of knives, clanging steel, sparks, and shouts. There were two bodies on the ground and eight men fighting— a confusion of shadows who could only occasionally be recognized by their voices—all furiously fencing, shoving, and stumbling. I took my sword in my hand and went straight over to the man nearest to me and, in the melee, with an ease that surprised me, I stuck a good quarter of my blade into his back. I drove it in and pulled it out, and, with a howl, the wounded man spun around—which is how I knew it was not Malatesta—and made a ferocious lunge at me, which I managed to parry with my dagger, although he broke its guard, bruising the fingers of my left hand. I hurled myself at him, drawing back my arm, sword point foremost; I felt his knife graze my buff coat, but I did not jump back; instead, I trapped the blade between my elbow and my side and meanwhile ran him through again, plunging my sword right in this time, so that we both fell to the ground. I raised my dagger to finish him off right there and then, but he was no longer moving and from his throat came the hoarse, stertorous rattle of someone drowning in his own blood. I placed my knee on his chest so as to re-move my sword and then returned to the fray.

Things were more evenhanded now. Copons, whom I could identify by his short stature, was locked in combat with an opponent who, between blows, kept uttering the most terrible oaths, until, suddenly, his curses were re-placed by groans. Don Francisco was limping back and forth between two adversaries—both far less skilled than he—and fighting with his usual panache. Meanwhile, Cap-tain Alatriste, who had sought Malatesta out in the midst of the skirmish, was doing battle with him a little way off, next to one of the stone fountains. They and their swords stood out against the shimmer of moonlight on water, as they lunged and drew back, performing feints and body feints and terrifying thrusts. I noticed that the Italian had abandoned both his loquacity and his wretched whistling. It was not a night to waste one's breath on fripperies.

A shadow came between me and them. My arm was aching now from so much movement, and I was beginning to feel tired. Lunges and slices began to rain down on me, and I retreated, covering myself as best I could, which I did pretty successfully. I was afraid I might fall into one of the ponds, which I knew were somewhere behind me, al-though, of course, a soaking is always preferable to a stab-bing. I was rescued from this dilemma by Copons, who, having rid himself of his adversary, now confronted mine, forcing him to deal with attacks from two fronts. Copons fought like a machine, closing on the other man and forcing him to pay more attention to him than to me. I decided to slip around to his side and knife the man as soon as Copons got in his next blow, and was just about to do so when, from the direction of the Hospital del Amor de Dios, beyond the stone pillars, came lights and voices crying, "Halt!" and "Stop in the name of the king's justice!"

"The bluebottles are here!" muttered Quevedo in between sword thrusts.

The first one to take to his heels was the man under attack by Copons and me, and before you could say knife, don Francisco found himself alone as well. Of our opponents, three lay on the ground, and a fourth was crawling away into the bushes, moaning. We went over to join the captain, and when we reached the fountain, found him, sword in hand, staring into the shadows into which Gualterio Malatesta had disappeared.

"Let's go," said Quevedo.

The lights and voices of the constables were getting ever closer. They were still calling out in the name of the king and of justice, but they were in no hurry to arrive, fearful of the situation they might find themselves in.

"What about Íñigo?" asked the captain, still gazing after his vanished enemy.

"Íñigo's fine."

That was when Alatriste turned to look at me. In the faint glow of moonlight, I thought I could see his eyes fixed on me.

"Never do that again," he said.

I swore that I never would. Then we picked up our hats and cloaks and ran off into the shadows under the elm trees.

Many years have passed since then. Now, whenever I go back to Seville, I visit the Alameda—which has barely changed since I first saw it—and there, time and again, I let my mind fill up with memories. There are certain places that mark the geography of a man's life, and that was one of them, as was the Portillo de las Ánimas, as were the dungeons of Toledo, the plains of Breda, and the fields of Rocroi. The Alameda de Hércules, however, occupies a special place. During my time in Flanders, I had, without noticing it, matured, but I only knew this on that night in Seville, when I found myself alone, face to face with the Italian and his henchmen and wielding a sword. Angélica de Alquézar and Gualterio Malatesta had unwittingly done me the great favor of making me realize that. And thus I learned that it is easy to fight when your comrades are near or when the woman you love is watching you, giving you vigor and courage. The hard thing is to fight alone in the dark, with no other witnesses but your honor and your conscience. With no reward and no hope.

By God, it's been a long road. All the people in this story—the captain, Quevedo, Gualterio Malatesta, Angélica de Alquézar—died a long time ago, and only in these pages can I make them live again and recapture them exactly as they were. Their ghosts, some loved, some loathed, remain intact in my memory, along with that whole harsh, violent, fascinating time that, for me, will always be the Spain of my youth, and the Spain of Captain Alatriste. Now my hair is gray, and my memories are as bittersweet as all clear-sighted memories are, and I share the same weariness with which they all seemed to be burdened. With the passing years I have learned that one pays for clear-sightedness with despair, and that the life we Spaniards lead has always been a slow road to nowhere. While traveling my section of that road I have lost many things and gained a few more. Now, on this apparently interminable journey—it even occurs to me sometimes that perhaps I, Íñigo Balboa, will never die— I can at least enjoy the resignation of memories and silence. And now, at last, I understand why all the heroes I admired then were so very weary.

I hardly slept that night. Lying on my mattress, I could hear the captain's steady breathing while I watched the moon slip behind one corner of the open window. My head was as hot as if I were suffering from the ague and my sheets were drenched in sweat. From the nearby bawdy house came the occasional sound of a woman laughing or the chords of a guitar.

Feverish and unable to sleep, I left my bed, went over to the window in my bare feet, and leaned on the sill. In the moonlight, the rooftops looked unreal and the clothes hung out to dry on the flat roofs resembled white shrouds. I was, of course, thinking about Angélica.

I didn't hear Captain Alatriste until he was by my side. He was wearing only his nightshirt and was, like me, barefoot. He, too, stood gazing into the darkness, saying nothing, and out of the corner of my eye I could see his aquiline nose, his pale eyes absorbed in the strange light from outside, and the bushy mustache that only emphasized his formidable soldier's profile.

"She is loyal to her own," he said at last.

That "she" in his mouth made me tremble. Then I nodded, still without saying a word. I was at an age when I would have argued with anything else he might have had to say on the subject, but not with that unexpected comment. It was something I could understand.

"It's only natural," he added.

I didn't know whether he was referring to Angélica or to my own warring emotions. Suddenly I felt a feeling of unease rising up inside me, a strange sadness.

"I love her," I murmured.

No sooner had I spoken these words than I felt intensely ashamed, but the captain did not make fun of me, nor did he offer me any trite words of advice. He simply stood there, not moving, contemplating the night.

"We all love once," he said. "Or, indeed, several times."

"Several times?"

My question seemed to catch him off guard. He paused for a moment, as if he thought it his duty to say something more but didn't quite know what. He cleared his throat. I noticed him shifting uncomfortably.

"One day it stops," he said at last. "That's all."

"I'll always love her."

The captain hesitated before responding. "Of course," he said.

He remained silent for a moment, then said again very softly, "Of course."

I felt him raising one hand to place it on my shoulder, just as he had in Flanders on the day that Sebastián Copons slit the throat of that wounded Dutchman after the battle of the Ruyter mill. This time, however, he did not complete his gesture.

"Your father . . ."

Again, he left these words hanging inconclusively in the air. Perhaps, I thought, he wanted to tell me that his friend Lope Balboa would have been proud to see me that night, sword and dagger in hand, alone against seven men, and only sixteen years old. Or to hear his son saying that he was in love with a woman.

"You did very well in the Alameda just now."

I blushed with pride. In Captain Alatriste's mouth these words were worth a Genoese banker's ransom. It was the equivalent of a king commanding a subject to don his hat in his presence.

"I knew it was a trap," I said. The last thing I wanted was for him to think that I had fallen into the trap like some novice.

The captain nodded reassuringly. "I know you did. And I know that it wasn't intended for you."

"Angélica de Alquézar," I said as steadily as I could, "is entirely my affair."

Now he remained silent for a long time. I was staring obstinately out of the window and the captain was watching me.

"Of course," he said again at last.

The scenes of that day kept crowding into my mind. I touched my mouth, where she had placed her lips. "If you survive," she had said, "you can claim the rest." Then I turned pale at the thought of those seven shadows emerging out of the darkness beneath the trees. My shoulder still hurt from the knife thrust stopped by the captain's buff coat and my tow-stuffed doublet.

"One day," I muttered, almost thinking out loud, "I'll kill Gualterio Malatesta."

I heard the captain chuckle. There was no mockery in that laughter, no scorn for my young man's arrogance. It was a gentle laugh, warm and affectionate.

"Possibly," he said, "but first, I must have a go at killing him myself."

The next day, we planted our imaginary flag and started recruiting. We did so as discreetly as possible, with no ensigns, no drumroll, and no sergeants. And Seville was the ideal place to provide the kind of men we required. If you bear in mind that man's first father was a thief, his first mother a liar, and their first son a murderer—for there's nothing new under the sun—this was all confirmed in that rich and turbulent city, where the Ten Commandments weren't so much broken as hacked to pieces with a knife. Seville, with its taverns, bawdy houses, and gaming dens, with the Patio de Los Naranjos and even the royal prison— which quite rightly bore the title of the Spanish Empire's capital of crime—abounded in purveyors of stranglings and dealers in sword thrusts; and this was only natural in a city populated by gentlemen of fortune, hidalgos of thievery, caballeros who appeared to live on air and with not a thought for the morrow, and monks of the Holy Order of Intrigue, where judges and constables could be silenced with a gag of silver. It was, in short, a university for the biggest rogues God ever created, full of churches offering sanctuary, and a place where men would kill on credit for a *maravedí*, for a woman, or for a word.

> *Remember Gonzalo Xeniz,*
> *Gayoso and Ahumada,*
> *Those butchers of bodies*
> *And scarrers of faces . . .*

The problem was that in a city like Seville and, indeed, in the whole of Spain, where all was bravado and effrontery, many of these self-proclaimed killers were nothing but talk, young ruffians full of valiant oaths, who, in their cups, claimed to have dispatched between twenty and thirty men, boasting of murders they hadn't committed and of wars in which they hadn't served, of how they were as happy to kill with their bare hands as with a knife or a sword, strutting and swaggering, in buff coats and hats as large as parasols, and sporting black looks, goatees, and mustaches that resembled the guard on a dagger; however, come the moment of truth, twenty of them together wouldn't have been capable of seeing off one drunk constable, and if tortured on the rack, they would have confessed everything at the first turn of the screw. If you were not to be dazzled by such an apparent abundance of fine swordsmen, you had to know who you were dealing with, as Captain Alatriste certainly did. Thus, trusting to the captain's keen eye, we began our levy in the taverns of La Heria and Triana, in search of old acquaintances who were men of few words but had a ready hand with the sword, who were not stage villains but genuine ruffians, men who would kill without giving their victims time to confess, so that no one afterward could go telling tales to the law. The kind of man who, when questioned under pain of death, and when the torturer turned the screw, would offer as guarantors only his own throat and spine, and remain entirely dumb, except to say naught or "My name's Nobody" or to call on the Church itself for aid, but otherwise offer no information, not even if someone promised to dub him a Knight of Calatrava.

Alonso Fierro, fencing master
Skilled with sword and dagger,
Slit many a throat in old Seville,
One doubloon per funeral.

Calling on the Church wasn't, in fact, such a bad idea, for Seville boasted the most famous rogues' refuge in the world—the Cathedral's Patio de los Naranjos, whose renown and usefulness is captured in these lines:

I ran away from Córdoba
And reached Seville a tired man.
There I became a gardener
In the Corral de los Naranjos.

This was one of the courtyards in the Cathedral, or Iglesia Mayor, which had been built on the site of a former Moorish mosque, just as the Giralda tower had been modeled on a minaret. It was a pleasant, spacious area with a fountain in the middle and was shaded by the orange trees from which it took its name; the main door of this famous courtyard opened onto the Cathedral square and the surrounding steps, which, during the day, like the steps of San Felipe in Madrid, were the favored place for idlers and rogues to meet and talk. Because of the courtyard's role as sanctuary, it became the chosen place of asylum for desperados and scoundrels and criminals on the run from justice, and there they lived freely and well, visited both day and night by their whores and companions; and those men whom the law was most eager to apprehend only ventured forth into the city in large gangs, so that even the constables themselves dared not confront them. The place has been described by the sharpest quills of Spanish letters, from the great don Miguel de Cervantes to don Francisco de Quevedo, so I need not provide much detail. No picaresque novel, no soldier's tale or rogue's story is complete without a mention of Seville and the Patio de los Naranjos. Simply try to imagine the atmosphere of that legendary place, close by the Casa Lonja and the shops selling silk, a place where fugitives from justice and the whole criminal world were as thick as thieves and as snug as bugs in a rug.

I accompanied the captain on his recruiting campaign, and we visited the Patio during the day, when the light was still good and it was easy to recognize faces. On the steps up to the main entrance beat the pulse of that multifarious and sometimes cruel city of Seville. At that hour, the steps were seething with idlers, sellers of cheap trinkets, strollers, rogues, streetwalkers with their faces half veiled, girl pickpockets disguised as innocent maids accompanied by ancient chaperones and little pages, with light-fingered thieves, beggars, and blades for hire. In the midst of them all, a blind man was selling ballad sheets and singing about the death of Escamilla:

Brave, bold Escamilla,
Glory and pride of all Sevilla . . .

Half a dozen ruffians were gathered beneath the arch of the main doorway and nodded approvingly as they listened to the turbulent story of that legendary swordsman and hired assassin, the very cream of the local villainry. We passed them as we went into the courtyard, and I couldn't help noticing that the whole group turned to watch Captain Alatriste. Inside, thirty or so fellows, identical in appearance to those at the entrance, were lounging in the shade of the orange trees next to the pleasant fountain. In this market of death, contracts to kill were regularly drawn up and agreed upon. This was the refuge of those who had sliced open someone's face or relieved many a soul of its corruptible matter. They had more steel about their persons than a Toledo swordsmith, and they all sported Córdoba leather jerkins, turned-down boots, broad-brimmed hats, large mustaches, and a swaggering, bowlegged gait. Otherwise, the Patio resembled a Gypsy encampment, with pots being heated over fires, blankets spread on the ground, bundles of clothing, a few mats on which men were dozing, and a couple of gaming tables, one for cards and the other for dice, where a jug of wine was doing the rounds amongst gamblers intent on wagering their very souls, even though the latter had been in hock to the Devil ever since their owners were weaned. A few ruffians were in close conversation with their women, some of whom were young and others less so, but who all conformed to the same whorish pattern, hard-faced and hardworking, accounting to their pimps for the money they had earned on the street corners of Seville.

Alatriste stopped by the fountain and looked quickly around. I was right behind him, fascinated by everything I saw. One bold doxy, her cloak folded and draped across her chest as if she were ready for a knife fight, casually and brazenly accosted him, and when they heard her do this, two cutthroats playing dice at one of the tables got up very slowly, giving us a mean, appraising look. They were dressed in typical ruffian style: open-necked shirts with wide Walloon collars, colored hose, and baldrics about a span wide, and equipped with all kinds of swords and daggers. The younger of the two men was carrying on his belt a pistol instead of a dagger and a light cork shield.

"What can we do for you, sir?" asked one.

The captain turned to them calmly, his thumbs in his belt, his hat down over his eyes.

"Nothing, gentlemen," he said. "I'm looking for a friend."

"Perhaps we know him," said the other man.

"Perhaps," replied the captain, again looking around him.

The two fellows exchanged a glance. A third man who had been watching came over, curious to know what was going on. I shot a sideways look at the captain and saw that he was entirely unruffled. After all, this was his world too, and he knew it like the back of his hand.

"You probably want—" began one.

Alatriste ignored him and walked on. I went behind, keeping my eye on the two cutthroats, who were discussing in low voices whether the captain's behavior constituted an affront and, if so, whether or not they should knife him in the back. They were clearly unable to reach an agreement, for nothing happened. The captain was now studying a group sitting in the shade by the wall, three men and two women apparently engaged in animated conversation as they swigged from a capacious leather wineskin. Then I saw that he was smiling.

He went over to the group, and I followed. When they saw us approaching, the conversation gradually petered out, and the various members of the group eyed us warily. One of the men had very dark skin and hair and huge side-whiskers that reached right down to his jaw. He had a couple of marks on his face, which had clearly not been there since birth, and large, blunt-nailed hands. He was dressed almost entirely in leather and had a short, broad Toledo sword—the blade of which bore its maker's unusual mark: the engraving of a puppy—and his coarse canvas breeches were adorned with strange green and yellow bows. He sat staring at my master as the latter came toward him, and his words died on his lips.

"Well, I'll be hanged," he said at last, openmouthed, "if it isn't Captain Alatriste."

"The only thing that surprises me, Señor don Juan Jaqueta, is that they haven't hanged you already."

The man uttered a couple of oaths and a loud guffaw and then stood up, brushing off his breeches.

"So where have you sprung from?" he asked, shaking the captain's proffered hand.

"Here and there."

"Are you in hiding too?"

"No, just visiting."

"By my faith, I'm pleased to see you!"

Jaqueta cheerily demanded the wineskin from his companions, and this was duly passed around, and even I drank my share. After exchanging memories of mutual friends and of the odd shared experience—which is how I learned that Jaqueta had also been in Naples as a soldier, and one of the best too, and that, years before, Alatriste had himself taken refuge in that very place—Jaqueta, my master, and I moved away from the group. The captain came straight to the point and told Jaqueta that he had some work for him, his kind of work, and with a promise of gold paid in advance.

"Here?"

"In Sanlúcar."

Jaqueta made a despairing gesture.

"If it was something easy and at night," he explained, "that would be fine. But I can't stray very far at the moment. A week ago, I knifed a merchant, the brother-in-law of a Cathedral canon, and the law are after me."

"That can be sorted out."

Jaqueta gave my master a keen look.

"Blind me, have you got a letter from the archbishop or something?"

"Better than that," said the captain, patting his doublet. "I have a document authorizing me to recruit whatever friends I can and to place them beyond the reach of the law."

"Are you serious?"

"I certainly am."

"Things are obviously going well for you." Jaqueta spoke more respectfully now. "I imagine the job will involve some, shall we say, hand work."

"You imagine correctly."

"Just you and me?"

"Plus a few others."

Jaqueta was scratching his side-whiskers. He glanced over at his companions and lowered his voice.

"And there's pelf aplenty to be had, is there?"

"There is."

"And part payment in advance?"

"Three double-headed doubloons."

Jaqueta let out an admiring whistle. "Well, I could certainly do with them, because the wages for our kind of work have gone right down, Captain. Only yesterday, someone came to see me about doing away with his good lady's lover and all he was offering was twenty *ducados*. What do you think to that?"

"Shameful."

"Too true," agreed Jaqueta, his fist on his hip, every inch the ruffian now. "So I told him that all he could get for that price was a cut to the face that would require ten stitches, or, at most, twelve. We argued, got nowhere, and I very nearly knifed him there and then, and I'd have done it for free too."

Alatriste was once more looking around him. "I need men I can trust, good swordsmen, not playhouse villains. And I want no talebearers either."

Jaqueta nodded authoritatively. "How many?"

"A good dozen."

"It's a big job, then."

"You don't think I'd be looking for such a rabble of rogues just to knife an old lady, do you?"

"No, of course not. Is it dangerous work?"

"Fairly."

Jaqueta frowned thoughtfully. "Most of the men here are pure dross," he said, "no good for anything but cutting the ears off cripples or giving their whores a good belting when they bring back four *reales* less than they should after a day's work." He discreetly indicated one man in his group. "He might be all right. His name's Sangonera and he's been a soldier too. He's a nasty piece of work, but good with his hands and fast on his feet. And I know a mulatto who's in hiding at San Salvador church at the moment. His name's Campuzano. He's as strong as an ox and knows how to hold his tongue. Why, only six months ago, they tried to pin a murder on him, which him and another lad had, in fact, done, but he survived four bouts of strappado like a pure-bred hidalgo, because he knows that you pay for any slip of the tongue with your throat."

"Sensible man," commented Alatriste.

"After all," went on Jaqueta philosophically, "it takes no more effort to say a 'no' than a 'yes,' does it?"

"Very true."

Alatriste looked at the man called Sangonera, who was sitting with the rest of the group by the wall. He was thinking.

"Sangonera it is, then," he said at last, "if you can vouch for him and if I still like him when we've spoken. I'll take a look at that mulatto too, but I still need more people."

Jaqueta wore an expression of deep concentration.

"There are some other good comrades in Seville at the moment, like Ginesillo el Lindo or Guzmán Ramírez, who are both men with blood in their veins. I'm sure you remember Ginesillo, because he once killed a catchpole who called him a shirt lifter, oh, it must be ten or fifteen years ago now, around the time you were still living here in Seville."

"Yes, I remember Ginesillo," said Alatriste.

"Well, you'll remember, too, that they tortured him by holding his head under water. Three times they did it, and he didn't so much as blink, far less peach on anyone."

"I'm surprised they didn't burn him at the stake, as they usually do to such as him."

Jaqueta burst out laughing. "He's not only turned mute, he's gotten very dangerous indeed, and there's not a catchpole with any mettle who'll lay a hand on him. I don't know where he lives, but he's sure to be at the royal prison tonight for Nicasio Ganzúa's wake."

"Who's Ganzúa? I don't know him."

Jaqueta quickly told Alatriste all about Ganzúa, one of the most celebrated ruffians in Seville, the terror of catch-poles and the pride of Seville's taverns, gaming dens, and bawdy houses. He had been walking along a narrow street one day when the Conde de Niebla's carriage spattered him with mud. The count was with his servants and a few young friends of his; there was an exchange of words, swords were drawn, Ganzúa dispatched one of the servants and one of the friends, and, by a miracle, the count him-self escaped with only a stab wound to the thigh. A regi-ment of constables and catchpoles came after him, and at the hearing, even though Ganzúa didn't say a word, some-one mentioned a few other little matters pending, includ-ing a couple of murders and a notorious jewel robbery carried out in Calle Platería. In short, Ganzúa was now to be garroted the next day in Plaza de San Francisco.

"A shame, really, because he would have been perfect for what we have in mind," said Jaqueta regretfully, "but there's no getting him out of tomorrow's execution. Tonight, though, his comrades—as they always do on these occasions—will join him for a final meal and help him on his way. Ginesillo and Ramírez are good friends of his, so you'll probably find them there."

"I'll go to the prison, then," said Alatriste.

"Well, greet Ganzúa from me. This is one of those occasions when your friends really should be by your side, and I'd be there like a shot if I wasn't in such difficulties myself." Jaqueta examined me closely. "Who's the boy?"

"A friend."

"A bit green, isn't he?" Jaqueta continued to study me inquisitively and noticed the dagger in my belt. "Is he involved in this?"

"On and off."

"That's a nice weapon he's carrying."

"You might not think it, but he knows how to use it too."

"Well, we ruffians have to start young, don't we?"

The conversation moved on, and everything was agreed for the next day, with Alatriste promising to alert the law officers so that Jaqueta could safely leave the Corral. We said our goodbyes and spent the rest of the day on our recruiting campaign, which took us first to La Heria and Triana, and then to San Salvador, where the mulatto Campuzano—a giant Negro with a sword like a scimitar—also proved to be to the captain's liking. By evening, my master had signed up half a dozen men to his company: Jaqueta, Sangonera, the mulatto, an extremely hirsute Murcian called Pencho Bullas—highly thought of by the other rogues—and two former soldiers from the galleys known as Enríquez el Zurdo (Enrique the Lefthander) and

Andresito el de los Cincuenta, the latter having earned his nickname from the time when he had received fifty lashes and taken them like a man; a week later, the sergeant who had ordered the flogging was found lying near the Puerta de la Carne with his throat neatly cut, and no one could ever prove—although they could easily imagine—who had done the job.

We still needed more pairs of hands, and in order to complete our singular and well-armed company, Diego Alatriste decided to go to the royal prison that night and attend the ruffian Ganzúa's final meal. But I will tell you all about that in more detail, for Seville's prison, I can assure you, deserves a chapter to itself.

6. THE ROYAL PRISON

That night, we attended Nicasio Ganzúa's last meal, but
first I spent some time on a personal matter that was
greatly troubling me. And although I learned nothing new
from the exercise, it served at least to distract me from the
unease I was feeling about Angélica de Alquézar's role in
what had happened in the Alameda. My steps thus led me
once more to the palace, where I patrolled the entire length
of its walls, as well as to the Arco de la Judería and the
palace gate, where I stood watching for a while amongst
other onlookers. This time, the soldiers guarding the palace
were not the ones in red-and-yellow uniforms but Burgundy archers dressed in their striking red-checkered garb
and carrying short pikes, and I was relieved not to see the
fat sergeant, which meant that there would be no repeat of
our earlier confrontation. The square opposite the palace

was teeming with people, for the king and queen were going to the Cathedral to pray a solemn rosary, after which they would receive a delegation from the city of Jerez.

There was more to this latter engagement than met the eye, and it might be worth explaining that, at the time, Jerez, like Galicia before it, was hoping to buy representation at the Cortes de la Corona, the Cortes of the King, in order to escape their current subjection to the influence of Seville. In that Hapsburg-Spain-cum-marketplace, there was nothing unusual about buying a seat at the Cortes—the city of Palencia was trying to do the same thing—and the amount offered by the men from Jerez came to the respectable sum of 85,000 *ducados,* all of which would, of course, end up in the king's coffers. The deal, however, foundered when Seville counterattacked by bribing the Council of the Treasury, and the final judgment made was that the request would only be granted on condition that the money came not from contributions made by the citizens but from the private wealth of the twenty-four municipal magistrates who wanted the seat. The prospect of having to dip into their own pockets put a completely different complexion on the matter, and the Jerez corporation withdrew the request. This all helps to explain the role that the Cortes played at the time, as well as the submissive attitude of the Cortes of Castile and of others, for—rights and privileges apart—these other Cortes were listened to only when their votes were needed for new taxes or for subsidies to replenish the royal treasury, or to pay for wars or for the general expenses of a monarchy that the Conde-Duque de Olivares deemed to be a powerful and unifying force. Unlike in France and England, where the kings had destroyed the power of the feudal lords and agreed on terms with the merchants and traders—for neither that red-haired bitch Elizabeth nor that vile Frenchie Richelieu were ever ones for half-measures—in Spain, the noble and the powerful formed two groups: those who obeyed royal authority meekly and almost abjectly (these were, by and large, ruined Castilians who had no other protection than that of the king) and those on the periphery, cushioned by local charters and ancient privileges, who protested loudly whenever called upon to defray costs or to equip armies. The Church, of course, did exactly as it chose. Most political activity, therefore, consisted in a constant to-and-fro of haggling, usually over money; and all the subsequent crises that we endured under Philip IV— the Medina Sidonia plot in Andalusia, the Duque de Híjar's conspiracy in Aragon, the secession of Portugal, and the Catalonia War—were created by two things: the royal treasury's greed and a reluctance on the part of the nobility, the clerics, and the great local merchants to pay anything at all. The sole object of the king's visit to Seville in sixteen twenty-four and of this present visit was to crush local opposition to a vote in favor of new taxes. The sole obsession of that unhappy Spain was money, which is why the route to the Indies was so crucial. To demonstrate how little this had to do with justice or decency, suffice it to say that two or three years earlier, the Cortes had rejected outright a luxury tax that was to be levied on sinecures, gratuities, pensions, and rents—that is to say, on the rich. The Venetian ambassador, Contarini, was, alas, quite right when he wrote at the time, "The most effective war one can wage on the Spanish is to leave them to be devoured and destroyed by their own bad governance."

But let us return to my own troubles. As I was saying, I spent the whole afternoon near the palace, and in the end, my determination was rewarded, albeit only in part, for the gates finally opened, the Burgundy archers formed a guard of honor, and the king and queen in person— accompanied by the nobility and the authorities of Seville—walked the short distance to the Cathedral. The young and very beautiful Queen Isabel nodded graciously to the crowd. Sometimes she smiled with that peculiarly French charm that did not always quite fit with the rigid etiquette of the Spanish court. She was carrying a gold rosary and a small prayerbook decorated with mother-of-pearl, and was dressed according to the Spanish fashion in a gold-embroidered costume of blue satin with sleeves slashed to reveal an underlayer of silver cloth, and draped over head and shoulders she wore an exquisite white lace mantilla sewn with pearls. Arm-in-arm with her walked the equally youthful king, Philip IV, as fair, pale, stern-faced, and inscrutable as ever. He was wearing a costume made of silver-gray velvet, with a neat Walloon collar, a gold Agnus Dei medallion studded with diamonds, a golden sword, and a hat topped with white feathers. The queen's pleasant demeanor and friendly smile were in marked contrast to her august husband's solemn presence, for he still conformed to the grave Burgundian model of behavior brought from Flanders by the Emperor Charles and which meant that—apart from when he was actually walking, of course—he never moved foot, hand, or head but always kept his gaze directed upward as if the only person to whom he had to justify himself was God. No one, either in public or in private, had ever seen him lose his perfect composure and no one ever would. On that afternoon, I could never have dreamed that life would later present me with the opportunity to serve and escort the king at a very difficult time for both him and for Spain, and I can state categorically that he always maintained that same imperturbable—and ultimately legendary—sangfroid. Not that he was a disagreeable king; he was extremely fond of poetry, plays, and other literary diversions, of the arts, and of gentlemanly pursuits. Neither did he lack personal courage, although he never set foot on a battlefield except from afar and years later, during the war with Catalonia; however, when it came to his great passion, hunting, he often ran real risks and even killed wild boar on his own. He was a consummate horseman, and once, as I have recounted before, he won the admiration of the people by dispatching a bull in the Plaza Mayor in Madrid with a single shot from a harquebus. His failings were two: a certain weakness of character that led him to leave the business of the monarchy entirely in the hands of the count-duke, and his unbounded liking for women, which once—as I will describe on another occasion—very nearly cost him his life. Otherwise, he never had the grandeur or the energy of his great-grandfather the emperor or the tenacious intelligence of his grandfather Philip II; but although he devoted far too much time to his own amusements, indifferent to the clamor of a hungry population, to the anger of ill-governed territories and kingdoms, to the fragmentation of the empire he had inherited, and to Spain's military and maritime ruin, it is fair to say that his kindly nature never provoked any feelings of personal hostility, and right up until his death, he was loved by the people, who attributed most of these misfortunes to his favorites, his ministers, and his advisors, in a Spain that was, at the time, far too large, beleaguered by far too many enemies, and so subject to base

human nature that not even the risen Christ would have
been capable of preserving it intact.

In the cortège I spotted the Conde-Duque de Olivares,
cutting as imposing a figure as ever, both physically and in
the way his every gesture and look exuded absolute power;
also present was the elegant young son of the Duque de
Medina Sidonia, the Conde de Niebla, who was accompanying Their Majesties, along with the flower of Seville's
nobility. The count was then only twenty years old or so,
and a long way from the time when, as ninth Duque de
Medina Sidonia, hounded by the enmity and envy of Olivares and weary of the crown's rapacious demands on his
prosperous estates—whose value had increased because of
Sanlúcar de Barrameda's role in the route to and from the
Indies—he was drawn into a plot with Portugal to turn Andalusia into an independent kingdom, a conspiracy that
brought him dishonor, ruin, and disgrace. Behind him
came a large retinue of ladies and gentlemen, including
the queen's ladies-in-waiting. And as I searched among
them, my heart turned over, because Angélica de Alquézar
was there too, exquisitely dressed in yellow velvet trimmed
with gold braid, and daintily holding up her skirt, which
was held out stiffly by an ample farthingale. Beneath her
fine lace mantilla, the same golden ringlets that had
brushed my face only hours before gleamed in the afternoon sun. I tried frantically to push my way through the

crowd to reach her but was prevented from doing so by the broad back of a Burgundian guard. Thus Angélica passed by only a few steps away without seeing me. I tried to catch her blue eyes, but she moved off without reading in mine the mixture of reproach and scorn and love and madness troubling my mind.

But let us change scenes again, for I promised to tell you about our visit to the royal prison and about Nicasio Ganzúa's final supper. Ganzúa was a prince among outlaws, a notorious ruffian from the quarter known as La Heria, a fine example of the criminal classes of Seville, and much admired by his fellow ruffians. The next day, to the discordant sound of drums and preceded by a cross, he was to be marched from the prison to have a rope placed around his neck, a rope that would rob him of his final breath. For this reason, the most illustrious members of that brotherhood of the blade were gathering—with all the requisite gravity, stoicism, and solemnity—to join him for a final supper. This unusual way of bidding farewell to a comrade was known, in criminal jargon, as *echar tajada*. And it was a perfectly normal occurrence, for everyone knew that a life of crime or "hard graft"—the common term at the time for earning one's living by the sword or by other illicit means—usually ended in the galleys, plowing the seas, hands firmly grasping the neck of an oar, beneath the lash of the galleymaster, or else in a fatal dose of that much more dependable and highly contagious disease: the malady of the rope, all too common a malaise amongst rogues.

Nothing 'scapes the maw of time,
Scoundrels barely reach their prime
Before the hangman stops their crime.

A dozen or so inebriated male voices were softly singing these words when, at the first watch, a constable—whose hand had been greased and spirits lifted with Alatriste's bribe of a silver piece of eight—led us to the infirmary, which is where they put any prisoners about to be executed. Far better pens than mine have described the picaresque life lived within the prison's three gates, barred windows, and dark corridors, and the curious reader wishing to know more should turn to don Miguel de Cervantes, Mateo Alemán, or Cristóbal de Chaves. I will merely relate what I saw on that first visit, when the doors had been closed, and the prisoners who enjoyed the favor of the mayor or of the prison guards and were allowed to come and go as they pleased were all back snug in their cells—apart, that is, from the even more privileged few who, by reason of social position or wealth, could sleep wherever they chose. Wives, whores, and relatives had also left the building, and the

four taverns and inns that served the prison parish—
wine courtesy of the prison governor and water courtesy
of the innkeeper—were closed until the following day, as
were the gaming tables in the courtyard and the stalls selling food and vegetables. In short, this miniature Spain had
gone to sleep, along with the bugs in the walls and the fleas
in the blankets, even in the very best cells, which prisoners
with the wherewithal could rent for six *reales* a month
from the undergovernor, who had bought his post for four
hundred *ducados* from the governor, who, as corrupt as they
come, grew rich on bribes and contraband of every sort. As
in the rest of Spain, everything could be bought and sold,
and you could more safely rely on money than you could on
justice. All of which only confirmed the truth of that old
Spanish proverb, that says, *Why go hungry, when it's dark
and there are another man's fig trees to pick?*

On our way to the supper, we had an unexpected encounter. We had just walked down one long, railinged corridor and past the women's prison—on the left as one
entered—when we came to a room that was temporary
home to those about to be sent to the galleys. A few inmates
were standing there behind the bars, chatting. They peered
out at us. A large torch on the wall lit up that part of the
corridor, and by its light one of the men inside recognized
my master.

"Either I'm blind drunk," he said, "or that's Captain
Alatriste."

We paused. The man who had spoken was very tall and burly, and he had thick, black eyebrows that met in the middle. He was wearing a filthy shirt and breeches made of rough cloth.

"Ye gods, Cagafuego," said the captain, "what are you doing in Seville?"

In his delight and surprise, the giant opened his huge mouth and beamed from ear to ear, revealing, in place of an upper set of teeth, only a black hole.

"As you can see, they're packing me off to the galleys. I've got six years of pounding the waves to look forward to."

"The last time I saw you, you were safe in San Ginés church."

"Oh, that was a long time ago," said Bartolo Cagafuego with a stoical shrug. "You know what life's like."

"And what crime are you paying for this time?"

"Oh, for my crimes and for other people's. They say that me and my comrades here"—his comrades smiled fiercely from the back of the cell—"robbed a few bars in Cava Baja and a few travelers at the Venta de Bubillos, near the Puerto de la Fuenfría."

"So?"

"So, nothing. I didn't have the cash to bribe the scribe with, and once they'd strung me and plucked me like a guitar, they sent me here, where I'm busy preparing my back for the rigors of life on the galleys."

"When did you arrive?"

"Six days ago. After a jolly little jaunt of seventy-five leagues on foot, all of us shackled together, surrounded by guards, and in the freezing cold. It was pissing with rain when we reached Adamuz, where we tried to make a run for it, but the catchpoles caught up with us and brought us here. They're taking us down to El Puerto de Santa María on Monday."

"I'm sorry to hear that."

"Oh, don't be sorry, Captain. I don't expect much from life, and, besides, it's all part of the job really. And it could have been worse. Some of my comrades were sent to the mercury mines in Almadén, and that's the real finibusterre, that is. Not many men make it out of there alive, I can tell you."

"Is there some way I can help?"

Cagafuego lowered his voice. "If you have a bit of spare cash on you, I'd be very grateful. Me and my friends here haven't got a bean."

Alatriste took out his purse and placed four silver escudos in Cagafuego's great paw. "How's Blasa Pizorra?"

"Dead, poor woman." Cagafuego discreetly pocketed the coins, eyeing his companions warily. "She was taken into the Hospital de Atocha. Her hair had fallen out and she had swellings all over her body. It was awful to see her like that, poor thing!"

"Did she leave you anything?"

"Only a sense of relief really. Given her profession, she had the pox, of course, but by some miracle, I didn't get it."

"My condolences anyway."

"Thank you."

Alatriste gave a half-smile. "You never know," he said, "perhaps you'll get lucky. The Turks might capture the galley, and you might decide to convert and end up in Constantinople in charge of a harem."

"Don't say such things," said Cagafuego, apparently genuinely offended. "Let's get this straight, neither the king nor Jesus Christ is to blame for me being where I am now."

"You're quite right, Cagafuego. I wish you luck."

"Same to you, Captain Alatriste."

And he stayed there, leaning against the bars, watching as we walked down the corridor. As I mentioned before, we could hear singing and the strumming of a guitar coming from the infirmary, and the prisoners in nearby cells were now providing an accompaniment, banging knives on bars, clapping, and playing improvised flutes. The room set aside for the meal contained a couple of benches and a small altar with a crucifix and a candle, and in the center was a table adorned with tallow candles and surrounded by several stools, which were occupied at that moment, as were the benches, by a select sample of the local ruffianry. They had begun arriving at nightfall and continued to do so, grave-faced and solemn, wearing capes thrown back over their shoulders, old buff coats, tow-stuffed doublets—which had been holed more often than La Méndez herself—hats with the brims turned up at the front, huge curled mustaches, scars, patches, verdigris hearts bearing the names of their ladyloves and other such things tattooed on hands and arms, Turkish beards, medallions of Virgins and saints, rosaries of black beads worn around the neck, and all manner of swords and daggers, as well as yellow-handled slaughterer's knives tucked in the leg of gaiters and boots. This dangerous rabble of rogues were making short work of the pitchers of wine arranged on the table along with queen olives, capers, Flemish cheese, and slices of fried bacon; they addressed each other as "sir," "comrade," "friend," and spoke with the accents of the criminal classes, mixing up their *h*'s and their *j*'s and their *g*'s and saying, for example, *gerida* instead of *herida*, *jumo* instead of *humo*, *harro* instead of *jarro*. They toasted the souls of Escamilla and of Escarramán and drank to the soul of Nicasio Ganzúa, the last still very much there and safely ensconced in its owner's body. They drank, as well, to the honor of Nicasio himself—"To your honor, comrade," cried the ruffians—and every man there would very gravely raise his mug to his lips to make the toast. Not even at a wake in Vizcaya or at a Flemish wedding would you see such a thing. And as I watched them drinking and heard them, over and over, mentioning Ganzúa's honor, I marveled that it should be so great.

> *Go for hearts or diamonds*
> *If you seek a winning knave;*
> *Avoid black-hearted spades,*
> *For they will dig your grave.*

The songs continued, as did the drinking and the talk, and more comrades kept arriving. Sallow-skinned and menacing, with broad hands and face, and a huge mustache whose ferocious waxed ends reached almost to his eyes, Ganzúa was a strapping man in his late thirties and still as sharp as a razor. He had dressed for the occasion in his Sunday best: a purple, slightly darned doublet, slashed sleeves, green canvas breeches, shoes for promenading in, and a four-inch-wide belt with a silver buckle. It was a pleasure to see him looking so smart and so solemn, accompanied, encouraged, and cheered by his confreres, every one of them wearing a fine hat and looking for all the world like a Spanish grandee, gaily downing the wine, of which several pints had already been drunk and which showed no signs of running out because—not trusting the wine sold by the prison governor—they had brought a large supply of pitchers and bottles from a tavern in Calle

Cordoneros. As for Ganzúa, he appeared not to be taking his early-morning appointment too much to heart, and he played his part with courage, decorum, and a proper sense of gravity.

"Death, my friends, is of no importance," he would declare now and then with great aplomb.

Captain Alatriste, who understood this world well, went over and very courteously introduced himself to Ganzúa and company, passing on greetings from Juan Jaqueta, whose situation in the Patio de los Naranjos, he explained, meant that he could not have the pleasure of coming with him that night to bid farewell to his friend. Ganzúa responded equally courteously, inviting us to take a seat, which Alatriste did, having first greeted a few acquaintances who were all busily eating and drinking. Ginesillo el Lindo—a fair-haired, elegantly dressed ruffian, with an affable look and a dangerous smile, and long, silky, shoulder-length hair *a la milanesa*—greeted him warmly, delighted to see him well and in Seville. Ginesillo was, as everyone knew, effeminate—by which I mean that he had little taste for the act of Venus—but he was as brave as any man, and as deadly as a scorpion with a doctorate in the art of fencing. Others of his ilk proved less fortunate, and were arrested on the slightest pretext and treated by everyone, even by other prison inmates, with terrible cruelty, which only ended when they were burnt at the stake. In this frequently hypocritical and contemptible Spain, a man could, with impunity, lie with his own sister or daughters or even his grandmother, but, as with blasphemy and heresy, committing the abominable sin of sodomy meant only one thing: the pyre. By contrast, killing, stealing, corruption, and bribery were considered mere bagatelles.

I took my place on a stool, sipped some wine, ate a few capers, and listened to the conversation and the solemn arguments that each man offered Nicasio Ganzúa by way of consolation or encouragement. Doctors kill more people than the executioner, one said. Another colleague pointed out that behind every bad lawsuit there's a sly scribe. Another said that death, though a nuisance, was the inevitable fate of all men, even dukes and popes. Someone else cursed the whole race of lawyers, who had no equal, he affirmed, even amongst Turks and Lutherans. May God be our judge, said another, and leave justice to the fools. Yet another regretted that the sentence imposed on Ganzúa would deprive the world of such an illustrious member of the criminal classes.

"My only regret," said another prisoner who was also at the wake, "is that my own sentence hasn't been signed yet, although I'm expecting it any moment. It's a damned shame it didn't arrive today, really, because I would gladly have joined you on the scaffold tomorrow."

Everyone thought this the sentiment of a true comrade

and, praising its aptness, pointed out to Ganzúa how much his friends admired him and how honored they were to be able to keep him company at this time, just as they would be the following morning in Plaza de San Francisco—those of them, that is, who could walk the streets without fear of constables. They would all do the same for one another one day, and whatever a fellow ruffian might suffer, he would always have his friends.

"You have to face death with courage, just as you've always faced life," said a man with a much-scarred face and a fringe as greasy as the collar of his shirt. He was El Bravo de los Galeones—a sharp-witted rogue from Chipiona.

"On my grandmother's grave, that's true," replied Ganzúa serenely. "No one did me a wrong they didn't pay for later, and if ever a man did, then come the Resurrection, when I step out into the new world, I'll really let him have it."

All nodded sagely: this was how real men talked, and they all knew that at his execution the following day, he would neither blanch nor turn religious; he was, after all, a brave man and a scion of Seville, and everyone knew that La Heria did not breed cowards, and that others before him had drunk from that same cup and never quailed. A man with a Portuguese accent offered the consoling thought that at least the sentence had been imposed by the king's justice, and therefore almost by the king himself, and so it was not just anyone who was taking Ganzúa's life. It would be a mark of dishonor for such a famous rogue to be dispatched by a mere nobody. This last remark was roundly applauded by the other men there, and Ganzúa himself smoothed his mustaches, pleased with such a measured assessment of the situation. The idea had come from a ruffian in a knee-length buff coat; he had little fat on him and little hair, and what hair he had grew gray and curly and abundant around the noble, bronzed dome of his head. It was said that he'd been a theologian at the University of Coimbra until some misfortune had set him on the path of crime. Everyone considered him to be a man of the law and of letters, as well as a swordsman; he was known as Saramago el Portugués; he had a stately air about him, and was said to kill only out of necessity, hoarding all his money like a Jew in order to print, at his own expense, an endless epic poem on which he'd been working for the last twenty years, and in which he described how the Iberian Peninsula broke away from Europe and drifted off like a raft on the ocean, crewed entirely by the blind. Or something like that.

"It's my Maripizca I feel sorry for," said Ganzúa, between mugs of wine.

Maripizca la Aliviosa was Ganzúa's doxy, and he believed that his execution would leave her all alone in the world. She had come to see him that very evening, crying

and weeping: ah, light of my eyes and love of my life, et
cetera, fainting away every five steps or so into the arms of
twenty or so of the condemned man's comrades. During
the tender conversation that followed, Ganzúa had apparently commended his soul to her by asking her to pay for
a few masses to be said—because a ruffian would never
confess, not even on his way to the scaffold, on the grounds
that it was dishonorable to go bleating to God about something he had refused to reveal under torture—and to come
to some agreement with the executioner, by offering him
either money or her own body, so that, the next day, everything would be done in an honorable and dignified fashion, ensuring that he did not cut a foolish figure when the
rope was tightened around his neck in Plaza de San Francisco, in full view of all his acquaintances. La Aliviosa finally bade a graceful farewell, praising her man's courage
and expressing the hope that she would see him again in
the next world, "looking just as healthy and handsome and
brave." La Aliviosa, said Ganzúa to his guests, was a good,
hardworking woman, very clean about her person and a
good earner too, and who only needed the occasional beating to keep her in order. However, there was scarcely any
need to praise her further, because she was well known to
all the men present, and indeed to all of Seville and half
of Spain. And as for the razor scar on her face, well, it
hardly spoiled her appearance at all, and besides, he had

done it while blind drunk on good Sanlúcar *oloroso*. All couples had their little misunderstandings, didn't they? Indeed, a timely cut to the face was a healthy sign of affection, the proof of this being that whenever he felt obliged to give her a good hiding, his eyes always filled with tears. La Aliviosa had shown herself to be a dutiful, faithful companion by taking care of him in prison with money earned by works that would be discounted from her sins, if, indeed, it was a sin to make sure that the man of her heart lacked for nothing. And that was all there was to be said on the matter. At this point, he grew a little emotional, although in a very manly way; he sniffed and took another sip of wine, and various voices chimed in to reassure him. Don't worry, she'll come to no harm, my word on it, said one. Mine too, said another. That's what friends are for, put in a third. Comforted to know that he was leaving her in such good hands, Ganzúa continued drinking while Ginesillo el Lindo warbled a *seguidilla* or two in tribute to Maripizca.

"As for the grass snake who mentioned my name," said Ganzúa, "you will, of course, take care of him too."

These words were greeted with another chorus of protests. It went without saying that the snake who had placed Señor Ganzúa in this woeful situation would, at the earliest opportunity, be relieved of both breath and money; his friends owed the prisoner this and more. For the worst sin any ruffian could commit was to peach on a comrade;

and even if that comrade had done said ruffian some offense or harm, it was felt to be entirely unacceptable to betray that person to the law, the chosen option being to remain silent and to exact one's own revenge.

"If you can, and if it's not too much trouble, get rid of Catchpole Mojarrilla too, will you? He handled me very roughly at the arrest, and showed me no respect at all."

Ganzúa could count on it, his friends assured him. They swore on God and all his angels that Mojarrilla could be safely considered to have received the last rites already.

"It might be a good idea," added Ganzúa after a moment's thought, "to send the silversmith my greetings as well."

The silversmith was added to the list. And while they were on the subject, they agreed that if, on the following morning, the executioner proved not to have been sufficiently rewarded by La Aliviosa and failed to do a decent job, by not tightening the garrote as cleanly and efficiently as required, he, too, would get his just deserts. It was one thing to execute someone—after all, everyone had his job to do—but quite another, worthy of traitors and prettyboys, not to show due respect for a man of honor, et cetera, et cetera. There were many other remarks in the same vein, and Ganzúa was left feeling both satisfied and comforted. He looked at Alatriste, grateful that he should have come to keep him company in this way.

"I don't believe I have the pleasure of your acquaintance," he said.

"Some of the other gentlemen here know me already," replied the captain in the same tone. "And I am pleased to be able to accompany you on behalf of those friends who cannot be here."

"Say no more." Ganzúa was looking at me amiably from behind his vast mustaches. "Is the boy with you?"

The captain said that I was, and I in turn nodded in a courteous way that provoked murmurs of approval from the other men present, for no one appreciates modesty and good manners in the young more than the criminal classes.

"He's a fine-looking lad," said Ganzúa. "I hope it will be a very long time before he finds himself in my situation."

"Amen to that," agreed Alatriste.

Saramago el Portugués also praised my presence there. It was, he remarked—with a Lusitanian slur to his *s*'s—an edifying spectacle for a young lad to see how men of courage and honor take their leave of this world, especially in these troubled times when shamelessness and ill manners are so rife. Aside from having the good fortune to have been born in Portugal—which was not, alas, a possibility open to everyone—nothing was more instructive than to witness a good death, to speak with wise men, to know other lands, and to read widely and well. He concluded poetically, "Thus the boy will be able to say with Virgil *'Arma virumque cano'* and with Lucan *'Plus quam civilia campos.'"*

This was followed by much talk and more wine. Ganzúa then proposed a last game of cards with his friends, and Guzmán Ramírez, a silent, grave-faced ruffian, took a grimy pack from his doublet and placed it on the table. The cards were dealt out to the eight players, while the others watched and all of us drank. Wagers were made and, whether by luck or because his comrades were letting him win, Ganzúa had some good hands.

"I'll wager six *ducados*, my life on it."

"It's your turn to cut the cards."

"I'll deal."

"What a hand!"

"I'll buy it from you, if you like."

And they were happily occupied in this fashion when steps were heard in the corridor and in came the court scribe, the prison governor with his constables, and the prison chaplain, all black as crows, to read the final sentence. And apart from Ginesillo el Lindo, who stopped playing the guitar, no one took the slightest notice; not even the condemned man himself showed a flicker of interest; instead, they all continued downing their wine, each player holding his three cards and keeping one eye on the card that had just been turned up, which happened to be the two of hearts. The scribe cleared his throat and declared that, according to the king's justice, and the prisoner's appeal having been refused on such and such a date and for such and such a reason, the aforementioned Nicasio Ganzúa would be executed in the morning. Ganzúa listened impassively, concentrating on his cards, and only when the sentence had been read did he open his mouth to look at his partner and raise his eyebrows.

"I'll see you," he said.

The game continued as before. Saramago el Portugués put down a jack of clubs, another comrade played a king, and another an ace of diamonds.

"The jack of hearts," announced a comrade known as El Rojo Carmona, placing that card on the table.

"The two of hearts," said another, putting his card down as well.

Luck was with Ganzúa that night, because he had a card that beat a two of any suit, and with one hand placed defiantly on his hip, he flung down the four of hearts. And only then, while he was picking up the coins and adding them to his pile, did he look up at the scribe.

"Could you just repeat what you said? I wasn't listening."

The scribe grew angry, saying that such statements could be read only once, and that it was Ganzúa's own fault if, as he put it, he blew out the candle without first making sure he'd understood the deal.

"To a man like me," replied Ganzúa with great aplomb,

"who has never bowed his head except to take communion, and then only when I was a boy, and who has since fought five hundred duels and been in five hundred scraps and fearlessly fought in a thousand more, the details are about as important to me as a fleabite. All I want to know is do I face execution tomorrow or not?"

"You do. At eight o'clock prompt."

"And who signed the death sentence?"

"Judge Fonseca."

Ganzúa gave his companions a meaningful look, and they responded with winks and silent nods. It would seem that the informer, the catchpole, and the silversmith would not be making their journey alone.

"The judge," said Ganzúa philosophically to the scribe, "is perfectly at liberty to hand down a sentence and take away my life, but if he ever had the decency to face me, sword in hand, then we'd see who would take whose life."

There were more solemn nods from the circle of ruffians. What he had said was as true as the Gospel. The scribe shrugged. The friar, an Augustine with a gentle air and filthy fingernails, came over to Ganzúa.

"Do you wish to confess?"

Ganzúa looked at him while he shuffled the cards.

"You wouldn't want me to blurt out now what I refused to reveal under torture."

"I was referring to your soul."

Ganzúa touched the rosary and the medallions that he

wore around his neck. "I'll take care of my soul," he said after a long pause. "And tomorrow, in the next world, I'll have a few words with the appropriate person."

His fellow players nodded approvingly. Some had known Gonzalo Barba, a famous rogue who began his confession to a young and inexperienced priest by admitting straight out to eight murders. Seeing the look of alarm on the young priest's face, he said, "Honestly, I start with the small stuff, and already you're shocked. If you react like that to the first eight, then I'm not the right man for you, Father, and you're not the right man for me." And when the priest insisted, he added, "Look at it this way, Father, you were ordained the day before yesterday and here you are trying to confess a man with hundreds of murders under his belt."

They returned to their cards while the friar and the others headed for the door. Just as they were about to leave, however, Ganzúa remembered something and called them back.

"Just one thing, Señor Scribe. Last month, when they tied the rope around my friend Lucas Ortega's neck, one of the steps on the scaffold was loose, and Lucas nearly fell when he was climbing them. It doesn't bother me particularly, but be so kind as to repair it for whoever comes after, because not all men have my courage."

"I'll make a note of it," the scribe assured him.

"I'll say no more, then."

The men of law and the friar left, and those who re-mained carried on playing cards and drinking while Ginesillo el Lindo resumed his strumming.

Though he killed his father and his mother
And did his elder brother in,
And put two sisters on the game,
They hung him high on the gallows tree
Of old Seville because he stole
The lives of strangers, one, two, three.

The game continued in the grubby light of the tallow candles. The ruffians drank and played, solemnly keeping watch over their comrade with many "Ye gods" and "I'faiths" and "By my troths."

"It hasn't been a bad life," Ganzúa suddenly said very thoughtfully. "Hard, but not bad."

Through the window came the sound of the bells of the church of San Salvador. Out of respect, Ginesillo el Lindo stopped his singing and his strumming. Everyone, including Ganzúa, doffed his hat and interrupted the game to make the sign of the cross. It was the Hour of All Souls—midnight.

The next day dawned with a sky worthy to be painted by Diego Velázquez, and in the Plaza de San Francisco, Nicasio Ganzúa climbed the steps of the scaffold with great aplomb. I went to watch with Alatriste and a few companions from the previous night. We were just in time to get a place, because the square was crammed from end to end with people who crowded around the platform and filled the surrounding balconies, and it was said that from a shuttered window of the Audiencia, even the king and queen were watching. Country folk and important figures alike had come to see, and the best places, which had been hired out for the occasion, gleamed and glittered with the finest stuffs: ladies' mantillas and skirts, gentlemen's velvets and feathered felt hats and gold chains. The crowd below was full of the usual selection of idlers, thieves, and ne'er-do-wells, and those skilled in the art of picking pockets were making their fortunes by slipping two sly fingers into other men's purses and drawing out a fistful of coins. Don Francisco de Quevedo pushed his way through the crowd to join us and was observing the spectacle with keen interest, because, he said, the execution would prove really useful for one particular passage in *The Swindler*, the book on which he was currently working.

"One doesn't always draw one's inspiration from Seneca or Tacitus," he explained, adjusting his eyeglasses the better to see with.

Someone must have told Ganzúa that the king and queen were there, because when they brought him from the prison dressed in his smock, mounted on a mule, his hands bound in front of him, he raised both hands to his face to smooth his mustaches and even gestured up at the balconies. His hair was combed, he looked clean and elegant and utterly calm, and the only sign of last night's carousing was a slight redness of the eyes. Along the way, whenever he spotted a familiar face amongst the crowd, he would again wave graciously, as if he were part of a religious procession heading for the Prado de Santa Justa. In short, he bore himself with such grace that it almost made one feel like being executed oneself.

The executioner was waiting beside the garrote. When Ganzúa climbed slowly up the scaffold steps—the rickety step was still rickety, and this earned the scribe, who was standing nearby, a stern look—everyone commented on his excellent manners and his courage. With his raised hands he greeted his comrades and La Aliviosa, who was standing right at the front, comforted by some dozen ruffians, and who, despite her copious tears, nonetheless felt proud of how handsome her man looked as he made his way to death. Then he allowed the Augustine friar of the previous night to preach to him a little, and nodded solemnly whenever the friar said something pithy or pleasing. The executioner was becoming visibly grumpy and impatient, and Ganzúa said to him, "Don't hurry me, I'll be with you in a moment. After all, the world's not about to end and there are no Moors to fight." He then recited the Creed from beginning to end in a strong, steady voice, kissed the cross with great feeling, and asked the executioner to ensure that he placed the hood properly on his head and, afterward, wiped any drool from his mustache, so that he would not look undignified. And when the executioner said the customary words—"Forgive me, brother, I am only doing my duty"—Ganzúa retorted that he was forgiven from there to Lima, but to make sure he did a good job, because they would see each other in the next life, where Ganzúa would have nothing to lose if he took his revenge. Then he sat down and did not flinch or grimace when they placed the rope around his neck, looking, instead, almost bored. He smoothed his mustaches one last time, and at the second turn of the garrote, his face grew perfectly calm and serene, as if he was sunk in thought.

7. ALL'S FISH THAT COMES TO THE NET

The treasure fleet was about to arrive, and Seville, along with all the rest of Spain and Europe, was preparing to make the most of the torrent of gold and silver it was carrying in its holds. The vast squadron now filling the horizon with sails had arrived at the mouth of the Guadalquivir, escorted from the Azores by the Atlantic Armada, and the first galleons, laden almost to the gunwales with merchandise and other riches, were beginning to drop anchor opposite Sanlúcar or in the Bay of Cádiz. In gratitude to God for having kept the fleet safe from storms, pirates, and the English, the churches were organizing masses and Te Deums. Shipowners and those employed in unloading the ships were already counting their profits; merchants were clearing their shops to make room for the new merchandise or arranging for it to be transported elsewhere;

bankers were writing to their correspondents to draw up letters of exchange; the king's creditors were drafting invoices that they hoped would soon be paid; and customs clerks were rubbing their hands at the thought of lining their own pockets. All Seville was smartening itself up for the great event; business picked up; crucibles and dies were made ready for minting coins; the two towers, the Torre de Oro and the Torre de la Plata, were prepared as storehouses; and El Arenal was a hive of activity, crowded with carts, piles of provisions, curious onlookers, and black and Moorish slaves laboring by the quayside. The doorways of houses and shops were scrubbed and swept; inns, taverns, and bawdy houses were spruced up; and everyone, from the proudest aristocrat to the humblest beggar and the oldest jade, rejoiced at the prospect of the fortune in which they all hoped to have a share.

"You're lucky," said the Conde de Guadalmedina, looking up at the sky. "You'll have good weather in Sanlúcar."

That same afternoon, before we set off on our mission—we were to meet the accountant Olmedilla on the pontoon bridge at six o'clock prompt—Guadalmedina and don Francisco de Quevedo came to say goodbye to Captain Alatriste. We had met in El Arenal at a small inn, by the wall of the old arsenal, constructed out of planks and canvas rifled from the nearby careening-wharf. Tables and stools stood outside beneath a makeshift porch. At that hour, the inn, frequented only by a few sailors, was quiet and private, and a good place for a drink and a chat. It enjoyed a pleasant view, too, over the lively port, where longshoremen, carpenters, and shipwrights were working on the boats moored on either shore. Triana—all whites and reds and ochers—gleamed resplendent on the far side of the Guadalquivir, with the caravels of the sardine fleet and the little ferryboats coming and going between the two shores, their lateen sails unfurled to catch the late-afternoon breeze.

"Here's to plenty of booty," said Guadalmedina.

We all raised our mugs and drank. The wine might not have been special, but the occasion was. Don Francisco de Quevedo, who would, in a way, have liked to join us on that expedition downriver, was irritated by the fact that, for obvious reasons, he could not. He was still very much a man of action, and it would not have bothered him in the least to add the boarding of the *Niklaasbergen* to his other experiences.

"I wish I could have just a glimpse of your recruits," he said, polishing his spectacles with a handkerchief that he produced from the sleeve of his doublet.

"Oh, so do I," agreed Guadalmedina. "I'm sure they form a highly picturesque band, but we cannot involve ourselves further. From now on, the responsibility is entirely yours, Alatriste."

The poet put on his spectacles and twirled his mustache, and a sly look appeared on his face. "This is so typical of Olivares. If things go well, there will be no need to bestow any public honors, but if things go badly, heads will roll." He took two long swigs of wine and sat staring thoughtfully into his mug.

"Sometimes, Captain," he said gravely, "I regret ever having gotten you into this."

"No one's forcing me to do it," said Alatriste, expressionless. He was staring across at the Triana shore.

The captain's stoical tone made the count smile.

"They say," he said in an insinuating murmur, "that our King Philip knows all about the plan. He's delighted to have this chance to play a trick on the old Duque de Medina Sidonia and to imagine the look on his face when he finds out. And, of course, gold is gold, and His Catholic Majesty needs it just as much as any other man."

"Possibly more," Quevedo said with a sigh.

Guadalmedina leaned across the table and lowered his voice: "Last night, in circumstances I need not go into here, His Majesty asked who was in charge of the attack." He left these words hanging in the air for a moment to allow their meaning to penetrate. "He asked this of a particular friend of yours, Alatriste, and that friend told him all about you."

"And praised him to the skies, I suppose," said Quevedo.

The count shot him a look, offended by that "I suppose."

"As I said, he was a friend of the captain's."

"And what did the great Philip say?"

"Being young and adventurous, he showed consider-
able interest. He even spoke of turning up tonight at the
embarkation point—incognito, of course—just to satisfy
his curiosity. Naturally, Olivares was horrified at the idea."

An awkward silence fell.

"That's all we need," commented Quevedo, "to have
the king on our backs."

Guadalmedina was turning his mug around and around
in his hands.

"But whatever happens," he said after a pause, "a suc-
cess would suit us all very well."

He suddenly remembered something, put his hand inside his doublet and removed a piece of paper folded in
four. It bore the seal of the Audiencia Real and another
from the master of the king's galleys.

"I was forgetting your safe-conduct pass," he said, handing it to the captain. "It authorizes you to go downriver to
Sanlúcar. Needless to say, once there, you must burn the
document. From that moment on, if anyone asks why
you're going to Sanlúcar, you'll have to find your own excuse." The count was smiling and stroking his goatee. "You
can always say you're going fishing for tuna and palm them
off with that old saying: *All's fish that comes to the net.*"

"I wonder how Olmedilla will acquit himself," said
Quevedo.

"There's no need for him actually to board the ship.

He's only required to take charge of the gold once it's been unloaded. His well-being depends on you, Alatriste."

The captain was studying the document. "I'll do what I can."

"Please do. For all our sakes."

The captain tucked the piece of paper into the leather band inside his hat. While he remained as cool and collected as ever, I kept fidgeting about on my stool. There were too many kings and count-dukes involved in this affair for a simple lad like me to be expected to sit still.

"There will, of course, be protests from the ship's owners," said the count. "Medina Sidonia will be furious, but no one involved in the plot itself will breathe a word. With the Flemish, though, it will be different. We're sure to get protests from that quarter, exchanges of letters, and storms in the chanceries. That's why we need to make it look like a private affair—an attack by bandits or pirates." He raised his mug of wine to his lips, smiling mischievously. "Although no one can demand the return of gold that doesn't officially exist."

"Remember," said Quevedo to the captain, "if anything goes wrong, everyone will deny all knowledge of the matter."

"Even don Francisco and myself," added Guadalmedina bluntly.

"Precisely. *Ignoramus atque ignorabimus.*"

The poet and the aristocrat sat looking at Alatriste, but the captain, who was still staring across at the Triana shore, merely gave a brief nod and said nothing.

"If things do go wrong," Guadalmedina went on, "be very careful, because there will be hell to pay. And you will have to cover the cost of any broken pots."

"If, that is, they catch you," said Quevedo.

"In short," concluded the count, "under no circumstances must anyone be captured"—he shot me a quick glance—"no one."

"Which means," explained Quevedo with his usual pithiness, "that there are only two options: you either succeed, or you die with your mouth closed."

And he said this so clearly and frankly that his words barely weighed on me.

After saying goodbye to our friends, the captain and I walked through El Arenal to the pontoon, where the accountant Olmedilla was waiting for us, as punctual and proper as ever. He walked beside us, a thin, austere, silent figure, all in black. Beneath the slanting rays of the setting sun we crossed the river, heading for the sinister walls of the castle of the Inquisition, a sight that stirred my worst memories. We were all equipped for the journey: Olmedilla was wearing a long black cape, and the captain his cloak, hat, sword, and dagger, and I was carrying an enormous bundle containing, more discreetly, a few provisions, two cotton

blankets, a full wineskin, a pair of pistols, my dagger—
its hilt having been repaired in Calle de Vizcaínos—
gunpowder, bullets, Constable Sánchez's sword, my master's
buff coat, and a newer, much lighter one for myself, made
of good, stout buffalo skin, which we had bought for
twenty escudos in a shop in Calle Francos. The meeting
point was the Corral del Negro, near the Cruz del Altozano.
Leaving behind us the bridge and the collection of long-
boats, galleys, and skiffs moored along the shore as far up
as the harbor used by the local shrimpers, we reached the
Corral just as night was falling. Triana was full of cheap
inns, taverns, gaming rooms, and places where soldiers con-
gregated, and so there was nothing unusual about the sight
of men bearing swords. The Corral del Negro was, it tran-
spired, a vile inn with an open-air courtyard that served as
a drinking den, which on rainy days was covered over with
an old awning. People sat out there with their hats down
over their eyes and their cloaks wrapped about them, and
given that it was a cool night and given the nature of the
customers who frequented the inn, it seemed perfectly normal for everyone to have his face covered so that only his
eyes were visible, and to wear a dagger in his belt and a
sword beneath his cloak. The captain, Olmedilla, and I
took a seat in one corner, ordered some wine and some
food, and cast a cool eye around us. Some of our men were
already there. At one table, I recognized Ginesillo el

Lindo—without his guitar this time but with an enormous sword at his belt—and Guzmán Ramírez, both of them with hats pulled down low and cloaks muffling their faces, and a moment later I saw Saramago el Portugués enter alone and take a seat, where, by the light of a candle, he immediately took a book out of his pouch and started reading. Then in came Sebastián Copons, as small, compact, and silent as ever. He sat himself down with a pitcher of wine without so much as a glance at anyone, not even his own shadow. Not one of them betrayed by the merest flicker that they knew one another, and gradually, alone and in pairs, the others arrived too, swaggering and shifty-eyed, swords clanking, finding a place to sit wherever they could, but never saying a word. The largest group to arrive was a threesome: Juan Jaqueta of the long side-whiskers, his friend Sangonera, and the mulatto Campuzano, who had all been allowed to leave their ecclesiastical seclusion thanks to the opportune intervention of the captain, courtesy of Guadalmedina.

Although accustomed to a fairly rough clientele, the innkeeper observed such an influx of ruffians with a suspicion that the captain soon dissipated by placing a few silver coins in his hand, the perfect way to render even the most curious of innkeepers blind, deaf, and dumb, as well as acting as a warning that if he talked too much, he might easily end up with his throat neatly slit. Within half an

hour, the whole crew was there. To my surprise, for Alatriste had made no mention of him, the last to arrive was
Bartolo Cagafuego. With his cap worn low over his bushy
brows and wearing a broad smile that revealed his dark,
toothless mouth, he paced up and down beneath the arcade
near our table, winking at the captain and generally be-
having about as discreetly as a bear at a requiem mass. My
master never passed any comment on the matter, but I suspect that, although Cagafuego was more braggart than
blade, and although the captain could doubtless have
recruited another man made of sterner stuff, he had
arranged for Cagafuego to be set free more for reasons of
sentiment—if such reasons are attributable to the captain.
Anyway, there he was, and he could barely conceal his gratitude. And well might he be grateful, for the captain had
saved him from six long years chained to an oar in the galleys with a galleymaster yelling at him to row ever harder
and faster.

This completed the group, and no one failed to make
the rendezvous. I watched Olmedilla's face to see his reac-
tion to the fruits of the captain's recruitment campaign,
and although the accountant maintained his usual cold,
inexpressive, mute façade, I thought I saw a glimmer of approval. Apart from those already mentioned—and as I
learned shortly afterward when told their real or assumed
names—there was Pencho Bullas, the man from Murcia,

the old soldiers Enríquez el Zurdo and Andresito el de los Cincuenta, the grimy and much-scarred Bravo de los Galeones, a sailor from Triana called Suárez, another called Mascarúa, a very pale, hollow-eyed man looking every inch the down-at-heel hidalgo known as El Caballero de Illescas, and a rubicund, bearded smiling fellow from Jaén, with a shaved head and strong arms, Juan Eslava by name, who was notorious in Seville as a pimp (he lived off the earnings of four or five women and cared for them, almost, as if they were his daughters), a fact that justified his sobriquet, earned fair and square, namely the Lothario of the Alameda.

Imagine, then, the scene, dear reader, with all these brave fellows in the Corral del Negro, their faces muffled by cloaks and who, with every movement, gave off a menacing clank of daggers, pistols, and swords. If you hadn't known they were on your side—at least temporarily—you would have been hard put to find your own pulse, because your heart would have stopped beating out of sheer dread. Once this fearsome retinue was all assembled, Diego Alatriste put a few coins on the table, and, to the great relief of the innkeeper, we set off with Olmedilla to the river, through the pitch-black narrow streets. There was no need to look around. From the sound of footsteps echoing at our backs, we knew that the recruits were slipping one by one out of the inn door and following behind us.

Triana slumbered in the darkness, and anyone still up and about prudently stepped out of our path. The waning crescent of the moon was bright enough to provide us with a little light, enough for us to see a boat, sail furled, silhouetted against the shore. There was one lantern lit at the prow and another on land, and two motionless shapes, master and sailor, were waiting on board. Alatriste stopped at that point, with Olmedilla and me by his side, while the shadows following us gathered around. The captain sent me to fetch one of the lanterns, which I did, placing it at his feet. The tenuous light of the candle lent a gloomier aspect to the gathering. Faces were barely visible, only the tips of mustaches and beards, the dark shapes of cloaks and hats, and the dull metallic gleam of the weapons they all carried at their waists. There was a general murmuring and whispering amongst the comrades as they recognized one another, but the captain abruptly silenced them all.

"We will be going downriver to perform a task which I will explain to you once we reach our destination. You have all been paid something in advance, so there is no going back. And I need hardly say that we are all of us dumb."

"You need hardly tell *us* that," said someone. "More than one of our number has been on the rack and never uttered a word."

"Yes, but it's always good to make these things clear. Any questions?"

"When do we get the rest of the money?" asked one anonymous voice.

"When we've completed our mission, but, in principle, the day after tomorrow."

"Will we be paid in gold again?"

"You certainly will, in double-headed doubloons, just like those you've each received as an advance."

"Will there be much killing involved?"

I glanced at the accountant Olmedilla, a dark figure in his black cloak, and I noticed that he was scraping at the ground with the tip of his shoe, as if embarrassed, or else far away, thinking of something else. He was, after all, a man of paper and ink and unaccustomed to certain harsh facts of life.

"I would hardly bother recruiting men of your caliber," replied Alatriste, "merely to dance the chaconne."

There was some laughter and a few appreciative oaths. When this had died away, the captain pointed to the boat.

"Get on board and make yourselves as comfortable as you can. And from now on, consider yourselves part of a militia."

"What does that mean?"

In the dim lantern light, everyone could see how the captain rested his left hand, as if casually, on the hilt of his sword. His eyes pierced the darkness.

"It means," he said slowly, "that if anyone disobeys an order or even so much as pulls a face, I'll kill him."

Olmedilla looked hard at the captain. We could hear the whine of a mosquito. Each man was thinking about what the captain had said and resolving not to arouse his leader's displeasure. Then, in the silence, not far off, near the boats moored by the bank of the river, came the sound of oars. Everyone turned to look: a small boat had emerged from the shadows. Against the gleam of lights on the farther shore, we could make out half a dozen oarsmen and three black shapes standing in the prow. In less time than it takes to describe, Sebastián Copons, ever ready, had leapt into action; as if by magic, two enormous pistols appeared in his hand, and he had them trained on the people in the boat; Captain Alatriste, meanwhile, had whipped out his sword and was already brandishing its bare steel blade.

"All's fish that comes to the net," said a familiar voice in the darkness.

As if this were a password, both the captain and I relaxed, for I, too, had been about to reach for my dagger.

"They're friends," said Alatriste.

This calmed the men, and my master sheathed his sword and Copons put away his pistols. The boat had come to shore just beyond the prow of our vessel, and in the faint light of the lantern we could now make out the three men standing up. Alatriste walked past Copons and went over to them. I followed.

"We've come to say goodbye to a friend," said the same voice.

I, too, had recognized the Conde de Guadalmedina's voice. Like his companions, he kept his face almost concealed with cloak and hat. Behind them, amongst the oarsmen, I caught the glow of the slow-burning matches on two harquebuses. The count's companions were clearly men of a cautious nature.

"We don't have much time," said the captain bluntly.

"We wouldn't want to get in your way," replied Guadalmedina, who was still with his companions in the boat. "You carry on."

Alatriste looked at the other two men. One was heavily built, a cloak wrapped about his powerful chest and shoulders. The other man was slimmer, wearing a featherless hat and a brownish-gray cloak that covered him from eyes to feet. The captain lingered for a moment longer, studying them. He himself was lit by the lantern on the prow of the boat, with his hawklike profile and mustache red in the light, his eyes vigilant beneath the dark brim of his hat, and his hand touching the bright hilt of his sword. In the gloom, he cut a somber, menacing figure, and I imagine that he must have made the same impression on the men in the boat. Finally, he turned to Copons, who had hung back a little, and to the other members of the group, who were waiting farther off, concealed by the darkness.

"Get on board," he said.

One by one, with Copons at their head, the ruffians filed past Alatriste, and the lantern on the prow lit each one as they boarded the boat with a great scrape and clang of ironware. Most of them covered their faces as they passed the light, but others, indifferent or defiant, left them uncovered. Some even stopped to cast a curious glance at the three cloaked figures, who watched this strange procession without uttering a word. The accountant Olmedilla paused for a moment at the captain's side, anxiously observing the men in the boat, as if uncertain whether or not he should speak to them. He finally decided against doing so, put one leg over the gunwale of our boat, and, encumbered by his cape, would have fallen into the water had not a pair of strong hands hauled him on board. The last to get on was Bartolo Cagafuego, who was carrying the other lantern, which he handed to me before clambering on board, making so much clatter that one would have thought he had half of all the steel produced in Vizcaya either buckled to his belt or in his pockets. My master had still not moved, watching the men in the other boat.

"There you have it," he said in the same brusque tone.

"Not a bad troop of men," commented the taller and stronger of the three.

Alatriste looked at him, trying to penetrate the gloom. He had heard that voice before. The third man, slimmer and slighter, who was standing between the other man and Guadalmedina, and who had watched the embarkation in silence, was now scrutinizing the captain's face.

"Well," he said at last, "they certainly frighten me."

He spoke in a neutral, well-educated voice, a voice accustomed to being obeyed. When he heard it, Alatriste stood as still as a statue. For a few seconds, I could hear his breathing, calm and very slow. Then he put his hand on my shoulder. "Get on board," he ordered.

I obeyed, carrying with me our luggage and the lantern. I jumped over the gunwale and took a seat in the prow, among the other men, who were wrapped in their cloaks and who smelled of sweat, iron, and leather. Copons made room for me, and I used the bundle as a seat. From there I could see that Alatriste, on the shore, was still looking at the men in the smaller boat. He raised one hand as if to doff his hat, although without completing the gesture—merely touching the brim—then threw his cloak over his shoulder and climbed into the boat.

"Good fishing," said Guadalmedina.

No one responded. The master of the boat had cast off, and the sailor, once he had rowed us away from the shore, hoisted the sail. And so, with the help of the current and the gentle breeze blowing from the land, our boat slipped silently downriver, cutting through the black water with its tremulous reflection of Seville's and Triana's few lights.

There were countless stars in the sky, and the trees and the bushes paraded past to right and left, like dense, dark shadows, as we followed the course of the Guadalquivir.

Seville was left far behind us, beyond the bends in the river, and the damp night air drenched the wood of the boat and our cloaks. Olmedilla was lying close by me, shivering. I lay contemplating the night, my blanket up to my chin and my head resting on our bundle of provisions, occasionally glancing across at the motionless silhouette of Alatriste, sitting in the stern with the master of the boat. Above my head, the pale smudge of the sail trembled in the breeze, by turns concealing and revealing the tiny luminous points of light studding the sky.

Almost everyone was silent, a collection of black shapes huddled together in the narrow space of the boat. Apart from the lapping of the water, I could hear the steady breathing of those asleep, as well as loud snores, or else the occasional whispered comment from those who remained awake. Someone was humming a tune in a high falsetto voice. Beside me, his hat over his face and well wrapped up in his cloak, Sebastián Copons was sleeping soundly.

My dagger was sticking in my ribs, and so, in the end, I took it off. For a while, staring up at the stars with wide eyes, I tried to think of Angélica de Alquézar, but her image kept fading, obscured by the uncertainty of what awaited us downriver. I had heard the count's instructions to the captain, as well as the latter's conversations with

Olmedilla, and I knew the broad lines of the planned attack on the Flemish ship. The idea was to board her while
she was anchored at Barra de Sanlúcar, cut her moorings,
and take advantage of the current and the favorable night
tide to carry her to the coast, where we would run her
aground and then transport the booty to the beach; there
we would be met by an official escort who had been
forewarned of our arrival, a picket from the Spanish guard,
who should, at that very moment, be arriving in Sanlúcar
by land, and who would discreetly await the right moment
to intervene. As for the crew of the *Niklaasbergen*, they
were sailors, not soldiers, and would, besides, be taken by
surprise. As for their fate, our orders were clear-cut: the
assault was to look like a bold incursion by pirates. And if
there is one certainty in life, the dead do not talk.

It grew colder toward dawn, with the first light illuminating the tops of the poplars that edged the eastern shore.
The cold woke some of the men, and they moved closer to
one another in search of warmth. Those not sleeping chat-
ted quietly to pass the time, handing around a wineskin.
Some men nearby were whispering, assuming I was asleep.
They were Juan Jaqueta, his friend Sangonera, and another
man. They were talking about Captain Alatriste.

"He hasn't changed," Jaqueta was saying. "He's still the
same cool, silent son-of-a-mongrel-bitch."

"Can he be trusted?" asked one.

"Like a papal bull. He was in Seville for a while, living from his sword like the best of them. We spent some time in the Patio de los Naranjos together. He got into trouble in Naples. Killed someone apparently."

"They say he's an old soldier and has fought in Flanders."

"He has," said Jaqueta, lowering his voice a little. "Along with that Aragonese fellow asleep over there and the boy. But he fought in the other war too, at Nieuwpoort and Ostend."

"Is he good with a sword?"

"I'll say. He's clever too and cunning." Jaqueta stopped speaking to take a swig from the wineskin; I heard the gurgle of the wine as he poured it into his mouth. "When he looks at you with those ice-cold eyes of his, you'd better get out of his way and fast. I've seen him skewer and slash and generally do more damage than a bullet through a buff coat."

There was a pause and more swigs of wine. I imagined they were looking at Alatriste, still sitting motionless in the bow, next to the master, who kept his hand on the tiller.

"Is he really a captain?" asked Sangonera.

"I don't think so," replied his friend. "But everyone calls him Captain Alatriste."

"He's certainly a man of few words."

"Yes, he's the sort who does his talking with his sword.

And he's even better at fighting than he is at holding his tongue. I knew someone who was with him on the galleys in Naples ten or fifteen years ago, on a raid in the channel of Constantinople. Apparently, the Turks boarded the ship he was on, having first killed most of the crew, and Alatriste and a dozen or so others were forced to retreat, defending the gangway inch by inch, finally holing themselves up on the half-deck, fighting like savages, fending off the Turks with their knives, until they were all either dead or wounded. The Turks were taking them and the ship back up the channel, when, as good fortune would have it, two galleys from Malta came to their aid and rescued them from life on a Turkish galley."

"Sounds like a plucky bastard," said one.

"You bet, comrade."

"And he's known the rack too, I'll bargain," added another man.

"That I don't know, but for the moment, at least, things don't seem to be going too badly for him. If he can spring us from prison and slap a *noli me tangere* on us, he's obviously got influence."

"Who were those three men in the other boat?"

"No idea. But they smelled like nobs to me. Perhaps they're the people supplying the lucre."

"And what about the man in black? I mean the clumsy clod who almost fell in the water?"

"No idea, but if he's a fellow ruffian, my name's Luther."

There were more gurgling sounds of wine being drunk, followed by a couple of satisfied belches.

"Not a bad job so far, though," said someone after a while. "Plenty of gold and good company too."

Jaqueta chuckled. "Yeah, but you heard what the boss said. First, we have to earn it. And they're not going to give us the money just for strolling up and down of a Sunday."

"Oh, I can live with that," said one. "For one thousand two hundred *reales,* I'd steal the morning star."

"Me too," agreed another man.

"Besides, he certainly deals a fair hand—I'll be happy to have a few more gold'uns like the ones I've got in my pocket now."

I heard them whispering. Those who knew how to add up were busy making calculations.

"Is it a fixed amount?" asked Sangonera. "Or do they share out the total among those who survive?"

Jaqueta gave the same low chuckle.

"We won't find out until afterward. It's a way of making sure that in the heat and noise of the fighting, we don't stab one another in the back."

The horizon was growing red behind the trees, allowing glimpses of scrub and of the pleasant orchards that sometimes grew down as far as the banks of the river. In the end, I got up and made my way past the sleeping bodies to the stern, to join the captain. The master of the boat, who wore a serge smock and a faded cap on his head, declined when I offered him some wine from the wineskin I'd brought for the captain. He was leaning one elbow on the tiller, intent on estimating the distance from the banks, on the breeze filling the sail, and on any loose logs on the shore that might be dragged downstream. He had a very tanned face, and up until then I hadn't heard him say a word, nor would I thereafter. Alatriste took a draft of wine and ate the proffered piece of bread and cured meat. I stayed by his side, watching the cloudless sky and the light growing brighter on the horizon. On the river, everything was still very gray and hazy, and the men lying in the bottom of the boat remained immersed in darkness.

"How's Olmedilla doing?" asked the captain, looking across at where the accountant lay.

"He's finally managed to fall asleep after spending all night shivering."

My master gave a faint smile. "He's not used to this kind of thing," he said.

I smiled too. We were used to it. He and I. "Is he coming aboard the *urca* with us?" I asked.

Alatriste shrugged. "Who knows?" he said.

"We'll have to look out for him," I murmured, somewhat concerned.

"Every man will have to look out for himself. When the moment comes, you just worry about yourself."

We fell silent, passing the wineskin from one to the other. My master chewed on his bread for a while.

"You've grown up a lot," he said between mouthfuls.

He was still watching me thoughtfully. I felt a sweet wave of satisfaction warm my blood.

"I want to be a soldier," I blurted out.

"I thought after Breda, you'd have had enough."

"No, that's what I want to be. Like my father."

He stopped chewing and studied me for a while longer, then, in the end, he gave a lift of his chin, indicating the men lying in the boat. "It's hardly a great future," he said.

We remained for a while without talking, rocked by the swaying of the boat. Now the landscape behind the trees was growing red and the shadows less gray.

"Besides," Alatriste said suddenly, "it'll be a couple of years before they'd let you join a company. And we've been neglecting your education. So, the day after tomorrow—"

"I read well," I said, interrupting him. "I have a reasonably neat hand, I know the Latin declensions and how to add, subtract, multiply, and divide."

"That's not enough. Master Pérez is a good man and he can complete your education once we're back in Madrid."

He fell silent again in order to cast another glance at the sleeping men. The easterly light emphasized the scars on his face.

"In this world," he said at last, "the pen can sometimes take you where the sword cannot."

"Well, it's not fair," I retorted.

"Possibly not."

He had taken a while to respond, and I thought there was a good deal of bitterness in that "possibly not." For my part, I merely shrugged beneath my blanket. At sixteen, I was sure that I would go wherever I needed to go and arrive wherever I needed to arrive. And as far as I was concerned, Master Pérez had nothing to do with it.

"It isn't yet the day after tomorrow, Captain."

I said this with something like relief, defiantly, staring obstinately at the river ahead. I didn't need to turn around to know that Alatriste was studying me closely, and when I did turn my face, I saw that his sea-green eyes were tinged with red from the rising sun.

"You're right," he said, handing me the wineskin. "We still have a long way to go."

8. BARRA DE SANLÚCAR

The sun was directly above us as we passed the inn at Tarifa, where the Guadalquivir turns westward and you begin to see the marshlands of Doña Ana on the right-hand bank. The fertile fields of Aljarafe and the leafy shores of Coria and Puebla slowly gave way to sand dunes, pinewoods, and dense scrub, out of which emerged the occasional fallow deer or wild boar. It grew hotter and more humid, and in the boat, the men folded up their cloaks, unclasped capes, and unbuttoned buff coats and doublets. They were crammed together like herrings in a barrel, and the bright light of day revealed scarred, ill-shaved faces, as well as ferocious beards and mustaches that did little to belie the piles of weapons, leather belts, and baldrics, the swords, half-swords, daggers, and pistols that each of them kept nearby. Their grubby clothes and skin—made grimy by the elements, and by lack of sleep and the journey—gave off a raw, rough smell that I knew so well from Flanders. It was the smell of men at war. The smell of war itself.

I sat slightly apart with Sebastián Copons and the accountant Olmedilla, for although the latter kept as aloof as ever, I nevertheless felt under a moral obligation, among such a rabble, to keep an eye on him. We shared the wine and the provisions, and although neither Copons, the old soldier from Huesca, nor the functionary from the royal treasury were men of many—or indeed even few—words, I kept close by them out of a sense of loyalty: Copons because of our shared experience in Flanders, and Olmedilla because of the particular circumstances we found ourselves in. As for Captain Alatriste, he spent the twelve leagues of the journey in his own fashion, seated in the stern with the master of the boat, occasionally dropping asleep but only for a matter of minutes at a time and otherwise barely taking his eyes off the other men. When he did sleep, he lowered his hat over his face, in order, it seemed, not to be seen to be sleeping. When awake, he studied each man carefully in turn, as if he had the ability to delve into their virtues and their vices and to know them better. He watched how they ate, yawned, slept, how they reacted—phlegmatically or with ill humor—as they were each dealt a hand from Guzmán Ramírez's deck of cards, gambling away money they did not yet have. He noticed who drank a lot and who little, who was talkative, who boastful, and who silent; he noticed Enríquez el Zurdo's oaths, the mulatto Campuzano's thunderous laugh, and the stillness of Saramago el Portugués, who spent the whole voyage lying on his cape, serenely reading a book. Some were silent or discreet, like El Caballero de Illescas, the sailor Suárez, or the Vizcayan Mascarúa, and some seemed awkward and out of place, like Bartolo Cagafuego, who knew no one and kept making abortive attempts to strike up conversations. There was no shortage of witty and amusing talkers, such as Pencho Bullas or the ever-cheerful ruffian Juan Eslava, who was regaling his fellows with details of how he had personally benefited from the wonders of powdered rhinoceros horn. Then there were the pricklier characters like Ginesillo el Lindo, with his immaculate appearance, equivocal smile, and dangerous gaze, or Andresito el de los Cincuenta, who had a way of spitting out of the side of his mouth, or mean bastards like El Bravo de los Galeones, with his face crisscrossed with scars that were clearly not just the work of a particularly careless barber. And so while our boat sailed downriver, one man would be telling tales of his adventures with women or at the gaming table, another would be roundly cursing as he threw the dice to pass the time, and yet another would be retailing anecdotes, whether true or false, from some hypothetical soldier's life that embraced the Battle of Roncesvalles and even took in a couple of campaigns fought under the leadership of the Lusitanian, Viriathus. And all of this was spiced with a large dose of oaths, curses, braggartry, and hyperbole.

"I swear by Christ that I'm a Christian as pure of blood and as noble as the king himself," I heard one man say.

"Well, I, by God, am purer than that," retorted another. "After all, the king is half Flemish."

To hear them, you would have thought our boat was filled by the very cream of Aragon, Navarre, and the two Castiles, Old and New. This was a coinage common to every purse, and even in such a restricted space and among such a small group as ours, each man played the part of a proud, distinguished native of this region or that, one side joining forces against another, with Extremadurans, Andalusians, Vizcayans, and Valencians taking it in turns to heap reproaches on one another, brandishing the vices and misfortunes of every province, with much heavy banter and joking, and all agreeing on one thing: their shared hatred of the Castilians—and with every man presuming to be a hundred times worthier than he actually was. This gang of roughs thrown together by chance was like a Spain in miniature, for the gravity and honor and national pride depicted in the plays of Lope, Tirso, and others had vanished with the old century and now existed only in the theater. All that remained was arrogance and cruelty, and when you considered the high regard in which we held ourselves, our violent customs, and our scorn for other provinces and nations, one could understand why the Spanish were, quite rightly, hated throughout Europe and half the known world.

Our own expedition naturally enjoyed its share of all these vices, and virtue would have been about as natural a sight as the Devil plucking a harp and wearing a halo and a pair of white wings. However nasty, cruel, and boastful our fellow travelers were, they nonetheless had certain things in common: they were bound by their greed for the promised gold; their baldrics, belts, and sheaths were kept oiled and polished with professional care; and their burnished weapons glinted in the sunlight when they took them out to sharpen or clean them. Accustomed as he was to these people and this life, Captain Alatriste was doubtless coolly comparing these men with others he had known in other places, and would thus be able to guess or foresee how each man would react when night fell. He could, in other words, tell who would be worthy of his trust and who not.

It was still light when we rounded the final long bend of the river, on whose banks rose the white mountains of the salt marshes. Between the sandy shore and the pinewoods

we could see the port of Bonanza, its bay already crowded
with moored galleys and ships, and farther off, clearly visible in the afternoon sun, stood the tower of the Iglesia
Mayor and the tallest of Sanlúcar de Barrameda's houses.
Then the sailor furled the sail, and the master steered the
boat toward the opposite shore, seeking out the right-hand
margin of the broad current that, a league and a half
downstream, would flow out into the sea.

We disembarked—getting our feet wet in the process—
in the shelter of a large dune that reached its tongue of
sand down into the river. Three men watching from a
clump of pines came to meet us. They were dressed in
dun-colored clothes, like hunters, but as they approached,
we saw that their swords and pistols were hardly the kind
one would use to go hunting for rabbits. Olmedilla greeted
the apparent leader, a man with a ginger mustache and a
military bearing that his rustic outfit did little to disguise.
While they withdrew to converse in private, our troop
of men clustered together in the shade of the pines. We
lay for a while on the needle-carpeted sand, watching
Olmedilla, who was still talking and occasionally nodding
impassively. Now and then, the two men would look across
at a raised area of land farther off, about five hundred
paces along the riverbank, and about which the man with
the ginger mustache seemed to be giving detailed expla-
nations. Olmedilla finally bade farewell to the supposed

hunters, who, after casting an inquisitive glance in our direction, set off into the pines; the accountant then rejoined us, moving across the sandy landscape like some strange black smudge.

"Everything is in place," he said.

Then he took my master aside and they spoke together for a while in low voices. And sometimes, while he was talking, Alatriste stopped staring down at his boots to look across at us. Then Olmedilla fell silent, and I saw the captain ask two questions to which Olmedilla replied twice in the affirmative. Then they crouched down, and Alatriste took out his dagger and started tracing lines with it in the sand; and whenever he glanced up to ask Olmedilla something, the latter nodded again. All of this took some time, and afterward the captain stood quite still, thinking. Then he rejoined us and explained how we were to attack the *Niklaasbergen*. He did this succinctly, with no superfluous comments.

"We'll split into two groups, one per boat. The first group will attack the quarterdeck, trying to make as much noise as possible, but there must be no firing of guns. We will leave our pistols here."

There was some murmuring, and a few of the men exchanged disgruntled looks. A timely pistol shot meant you could kill a man straight off, more quickly than with a sword and from a safe distance too.

The captain went on: "We're going to be fighting in the dark and at very close quarters, and I don't want us killing one another by mistake. Besides, if someone's pistol should go off accidentally, they'll fire on us with their harquebuses from the galleon before we've even climbed on board."

He paused, quietly observing the men.

"Who amongst you has served the king?"

Almost everyone raised his hand.

Grave-faced and with his thumbs hooked in his belt, Alatriste studied them one by one. His voice was as ice-cold as his eyes. "I mean those of you who really have fought as soldiers."

Many hesitated, embarrassed and looking shiftily around. A couple of men put their hands down, but others kept them up, until, under Alatriste's sustained gaze, more men lowered their hands as well. Only Copons, Juan Jaqueta, Sangonera, Enríquez el Zurdo, and Andresito el de los Cincuenta kept their hands up. Alatriste also picked out Eslava, Saramago el Portugués, Ginesillo el Lindo, and the sailor Suárez.

"These nine men will form the group that will attack from the bow. In order to take the crew by surprise and from behind, you will only board the ship when those at the stern are already fighting on the quarterdeck. The idea is that you board very quietly via the anchor and make your way along the deck, and then we all meet up at the stern."

"Is there someone in charge of each group?" asked Pencho Bullas.

"There is: Sebastián Copons at the bow, and me at the stern with you, Cagafuego, Campuzano, Guzmán Ramírez, Mascarúa, El Caballero de Illescas, and El Bravo de los Galeones."

I looked from one to the other, confused at first. The difference in the quality of the men in the two groups was glaringly obvious. Then I realized that Alatriste was placing the best men under Copons's command, and keeping the least disciplined or least trustworthy men for himself, with the exception perhaps of the mulatto Campuzano and possibly Bartolo Cagafuego, who despite being more braggart than brave, would fight well under the captain's gaze, if only out of a sense of obligation. This meant that the group attacking the bow was the one that would decide the battle, while those at the stern—mere cannon fodder—would bear the brunt of the fighting. And if things went wrong or those boarding at the bow were greatly delayed, the group at the stern would also suffer the greatest losses.

"The plan," went on Alatriste, "is to cut the anchor chain so that the ship drifts toward the coast and runs aground on one of the sandbanks opposite San Jacinto Point. For that purpose, the group at the bow will carry with them two axes. We will all remain on board until the ship touches bottom on the bar. Then we will come ashore—the water there is only at chest height—and leave the matter in the hands of others who will be waiting."

The men again exchanged looks. From the pinewoods came the monotonous whir of cicadas. Apart from the buzz of flies swarming about our heads, that was the only sound to be heard while each man thought his own thoughts.

"Will there be much resistance?" asked Juan Jaqueta, pensively chewing the ends of his mustache.

"I don't know, but we certainly expect there to be some."

"How many heretics are there on board?"

"They're not heretics, they're Flemish Catholics, but it comes to the same thing. We estimate between twenty and thirty, although many will jump overboard. And there is one important point: As long as there are crew members alive, not one of us will utter a word of Spanish." Alatriste looked at Saramago el Portugués, who was listening intently with the grave demeanor of a scrawny hidalgo, and with, as usual, a book stuffed in the pocket of his doublet. "It would not go amiss if this gentleman here were to shout something in his own language, and for those of you who know English or Flemish words to let fly with those as well." The captain allowed himself the flicker of a smile. "The idea is . . . that we are pirates."

This remark eased the tension. There was laughter, and the men shared amused looks. Amongst such a band of men, this idea was not so very far from the truth.

"And what about those who don't jump overboard?" asked Mascarúa.

"No crew member will reach the sandbank alive. The more people we frighten at the beginning, the fewer we will have to kill."

"And what about the wounded, or those who cry mercy?"

"Tonight there is no mercy."

Some whistled through their teeth. There was mocking applause and subdued laughter.

"And what about our own wounded?" asked Ginesillo el Lindo.

"They will leave the ship with us and be attended to on land. There we will all be paid and, after that, it will be a matter of every owl to his olive tree."

"And if there are deaths?" El Bravo de los Galeones had a smile on his scarred face. "Do we still earn the same amount each, or divide what's left between us?"

"We'll see."

The ruffian glanced at his comrades and his smile grew wider. "Perhaps it would be a good idea if we could see right now," he said insinuatingly.

Alatriste very slowly removed his hat and smoothed his

hair. Then he put his hat on again. The way he looked at the other man left no room for doubt. "Good? For whom exactly?"

He said these words softly, almost in a drawl, in a tone of solicitous inquiry that would not have fooled even a babe in arms. It did not fool El Bravo de los Galeones either, for he got the message, averted his eyes, and said no more. Olmedilla had sidled up to the captain and whispered something in his ear. My master nodded.

"This gentleman has just reminded me of another important point. No one, absolutely no one," said Alatriste, fixing his icy gaze on each man in the group in turn, "will, for any reason, go down into the ship's hold. There will be no personal booty, none at all."

Sangonera raised his hand and asked curiously, "And what if a crew member holes himself up in there?"

"Should that happen, then I will decide who goes down to fetch him."

El Bravo de los Galeones was thoughtfully stroking his hair, which he wore caught back in a greasy pigtail. Then he asked the question that was in everyone's mind:

"And what is there in this 'tabernacle' that we can't see?"

"That's none of your business. It's not even my business. And I hope not to have to remind anyone of that fact."

El Bravo gave a jeering laugh. "Not if my life depended on it."

Alatriste stared at him hard. "It does."

"Now you're going too far, by God." El Bravo was standing, legs apart, shifting his weight from one to the other. "By my faith, we're not a load of sheep to put up with being threatened like that. Me and my comrades here—"

"I don't give a damn what you can and can't put up with," Alatriste broke in. "That's the way it is. You were all warned, and there's no going back."

"And what if we want to go back?"

"You talk boldly enough in the plural, I see." The captain ran two fingers over his mustache, then pointed to the pinewoods. "As for the singular you, I will be happy to discuss the matter alone, just the two of us, in that wood."

The ruffian made a silent appeal to his comrades. Some regarded him with what seemed like a glimmer of solidarity, and others did not. For his part, Bartolo Cagafuego had stood up, brows beetling, and was approaching menacingly in support of the captain. I, too, reached for my dagger. Most of the men looked away, half smiling or watching as Alatriste's hand brushed the hilt of his sword. No one appeared bothered by the prospect of a good fight, with the captain in charge of the fencing lessons. Those who knew his past record had already informed the others, and El Bravo de los Galeones, with his low arrogance and ridiculous swagger—hardly necessary amongst such a crew—was not much liked.

"We'll talk about it some other time," he said at last.

He had thought it over, and preferred not to lose face. Some of his fellow ruffians nudged one another, disappointed that there would be no fight in the woods that afternoon.

"Yes, let's do that," replied Alatriste gently, "whenever you like."

No one said anything more, no one took him up on his offer or even looked as if he would. Peace was restored, Cagafuego's brows unbeetled, and everyone went about his own business. Then I noticed Sebastián Copons withdrawing his hand from the butt of his pistol.

The flies buzzed around our faces as we peered cautiously over the top of the dune. Before us lay Barra de Sanlúcar, brightly lit by the evening sun. Between the inlet at Bonanza and Chipiona Point about a league farther on, where the Guadalquivir flowed into the sea, the mouth of the river was a forest of masts with flags flying and the sails of ships—*urcas*, frigates, caravels, small vessels and large, both oceangoing and coastal—either anchored amongst the sandbanks or else in constant movement back and forth, this same panorama stretching eastward along the coast toward Rota and the Bay of Cádiz. Some were waiting for the rising tide in order to travel up to Seville, others were unloading merchandise onto smaller boats or rigging their ships so as to sail on to Cádiz once the royal officials had checked their cargo. On the farther shore, we could see, in the distance, prosperous Sanlúcar, with its houses reaching right down to the water's edge, and on top of the hill, the old, walled enclave, the castle turrets, the ducal palace, the Cathedral, and the customhouse, which, on days such as this, brought wealth to so many. The harbor sands were speckled with beached fishing boats, and the lower city, gilded by the sun, teemed with people and with the small sailing boats that came and went between the ships.

"There's the *Virgen de Regla*," said Olmedilla.

He lowered his voice when he spoke, as if they might be able to hear us on the other side of the river, and he wiped the sweat from his face with an already sodden handkerchief. He seemed even paler than usual. He was not a man for long walks or for traipsing over sand dunes and through scrub, and the effort and the heat were beginning to take their toll. His ink-stained forefinger was pointing out a large galleon, anchored between Bonanza and Sanlúcar, and sheltering behind a sandbank just beginning to be revealed by the low tide. Its prow was facing into the southerly breeze rippling the surface of the water.

"And that," he said, pointing to another ship moored closer to us, "is the *Niklaasbergen*."

I followed Alatriste's gaze. With the brim of his hat shading his eyes from the sun, the captain was scrutinizing the Dutch galleon. It was anchored separately, near our shore, toward San Jacinto Point and the watchtower that had been erected there to prevent incursions by Berber, Dutch, and English pirates. The *Niklaasbergen* was a tar-black, three-masted *urca*, or merchant ship, its sails furled. It was a short, ugly, rather clumsy-looking vessel, with a high prow above which hung a lantern painted in white, red, and yellow, a perfectly ordinary cargo ship that would not attract attention. It, too, had its prow facing south, and its gunports had been left open to air the lower decks. There appeared to be little movement on board.

"It was anchored next to the *Virgen de Regla* until daybreak," explained Olmedilla. "Then it went and dropped anchor over there."

The captain was studying each detail of the landscape, like a bird of prey that will only be able to pounce on its victim in the dark.

"Is all the gold on board?" he asked.

"No, one part is missing. They chose not to remain moored next to the other ship because they were afraid it might look suspicious. The rest will be brought at nightfall by boat."

"How much time do we have?"

"It doesn't set sail until tomorrow, with the high tide."

Olmedilla indicated the rubble of an old ruined netting shed on the shore. Beyond could be seen a sandy bank that the low tide had left uncovered.

"That's the place," he said. "Even at high tide, you can wade ashore."

Alatriste screwed up his eyes more tightly. He was studying the black rocks barely covered by water, a little farther in to shore.

"I remember those shallows well," he said. "The galleys always did their best to avoid them."

"I don't think they need worry us," replied Olmedilla. "At that hour, the tide, the breeze, and the river current will all be working in our favor."

"I certainly hope so. Because if instead of running into the sand, our keel collides with those rocks, we'll go straight under . . . and the gold with us."

We crawled back, keeping our heads down, to join the rest of the men. They were lying on cloaks and capes, waiting with the stolid patience of their profession; and without anyone having said a word, they had instinctively gathered together into the two groups they would form when it came to boarding the ship.

The sun was disappearing behind the pinewoods. Alatriste went and sat on his cloak, picked up the wineskin, and drank from it. I spread my blanket on the ground, beside Sebastián Copons; Copons was on his back, dozing, with a handkerchief covering his face to keep off the flies and his hands folded over the hilt of his dagger. Olmedilla came over to the captain. He had his fingers interlaced and was twiddling his thumbs.

"I'm going with you," he said softly.

Alatriste, about to take another drink from the wineskin, stopped and regarded him intently. "That's not a good idea," he said after a moment.

With his pale skin, sparse mustache, and beard unkempt after the journey, the accountant cut a frail figure. However, he insisted, tight-lipped, "It's my duty. I'm the king's agent."

The captain thought for a moment, wiping the wine from his mustache with the back of his hand. Then he placed the wineskin on the sand and lay down. "As you wish," he said suddenly. "I never meddle in matters of duty."

He remained thoughtful, though, and silent. Then, with a shrug of his shoulders, he announced, "You'll board at the bow."

"Why can't I go with you?"

"We don't want to put all our eggs in one basket, do we?"

Olmedilla shot me a glance, which I held unblinking. "And the boy?"

Alatriste looked at me, as if indifferent, then unbuckled the belt bearing his sword and dagger, and wrapped the belt around them. He placed this bundle beneath the folded blanket that served as a pillow, and unfastened his doublet.

"Íñigo goes with me."

He lay down to rest with his hat over his face. Olmedilla again interlaced his fingers and resumed his thumb-twiddling. He seemed less impenetrably impassive than usual, as if an idea he could not quite bring himself to express was going around and around in his head.

"And what will happen," he said at last, "if the group boarding at the bow is delayed and fails to reach the quarterdeck in time? I mean . . . what if something should happen to you?"

Beneath the hat hiding his face, Alatriste did not stir.

"In that case," he said, "the *Niklaasbergen* will no longer be my problem."

I fell asleep. I closed my eyes as I often had in Flanders before a march or a battle, and made the most of what time there was to gather my strength. At first, I fell into a superficial doze, opening eyes and ears from time to time to the fading daylight, the bodies lying around me, their breathing and their snores, the murmured conversations and the motionless shape of the captain with his hat over

his face. Then I fell into a deeper sleep and allowed myself
to float on the gentle black water, adrift on a vast sea filled,
as far as the horizon, with innumerable sails. Then
Angélica de Alquézar appeared, as she had so many times.
And this time I plunged into her eyes and felt again the
sweet pressure of her lips on mine. I looked around for
someone to whom I could shout my joy, and there they
were, lying very still amongst the dank mists of a Flemish
canal: the shadows of my father and Captain Alatriste. I
squelched through the mud to join them, ready to unsheathe my sword and fight the vast army of ghosts clambering out of tombs, dead soldiers in rusty breastplates and
helmets, brandishing weapons in their bony hands, and
staring at us from hollow sockets. And I opened my mouth
to cry out in silence—old words that had lost their mean-
ings, because time was plucking them from me, one by one.

I woke with Captain Alatriste's hand on my shoulder. "It's
time," he whispered, almost brushing my ear with his mustache. I opened my eyes to the darkness. No one had lit
fires, and there were no lanterns. The slender, waning
moon shed only enough light now to be able to make out
the vague, black shapes moving around me. I heard swords
being slipped out of sheaths, belts being buckled, hooks
fastened, short muttered sentences. The men were prepar-

ing themselves, exchanging hats for kerchiefs tied around their heads, and wrapping their weapons in cloth so that there would be no telltale clank of metal. As the captain had ordered, all pistols were left on the beach, along with the other baggage. We were to board the *Niklaasbergen* armed only with swords and daggers.

I fumbled open our bundle of clothes and donned my new buff coat, still stiff and thick enough to protect my upper body from knife thrusts. Then I made sure my sandals were firmly tied on and that my dagger was securely attached to my belt with a length of cord wound around the hilt, and, finally, I placed the stolen constable's sword in my leather baldric. All around me, men were speaking softly, taking one last swig from the wineskins, and relieving themselves before going into action. Alatriste and Copons had their heads close together as the latter received his final instructions. When I stepped back, I bumped into Olmedilla, who recognized me and gave me a little pat on the back, which, in a man of such sourness, might be considered an expression of affection. I saw that he, too, was wearing a sword at his waist.

"Let's go," said Alatriste.

We set off, our feet sinking into the sand. I could identify some of the shadows who passed me: the tall, slender figure of Saramago el Portugués, the heavy bulk of Bartolo Cagafuego, the slight silhouette of Sebastián Copons. Someone made some derisory remark, and I heard the muffled laughter of the mulatto Campuzano. The captain's voice boomed out, demanding silence, and after that no one spoke.

As we passed the wood, I heard the braying of a mule and, curious, peered into the dark. There were mules and horses hidden amongst the trees and the indistinct shapes of people standing next to them. These were doubtless the people who, later on, when the galleon had foundered on the bar, would be in charge of unloading all the gold. As if to confirm my suspicions, three black silhouettes emerged from behind the pines, and Olmedilla and the captain paused to hold a whispered conversation with them. I thought I recognized the "hunters" we had seen earlier. Then they vanished, Alatriste gave an order, and we set off again. Now we were climbing the steep slope of a dune, plunging in up to our ankles, the outlines of our bodies standing out more clearly against the pale sand. At the top, the sound of the sea reached us and the breeze caressed our faces. As far as the horizon—as black as the sky itself—stretched a long dark stain filled with the tiny luminous dots of ship's lanterns, so that it seemed as if the stars were reflected in the sea. Far off, on the other shore, we could see the lights of Sanlúcar.

We went down to the beach, the sand dulling the sound of our steps. Behind me, I heard the voice of Saramago el Portugués, reciting softly to himself:

"But staying with the pilots on the sand,
And being eager to determine where I stand,
I pause and calculate the bright sun's height
Then mark our spot, exactly, on the chart."

Someone asked what the devil he was mumbling about, and Saramago responded calmly, in his soft, cultivated Portuguese voice, that he was reciting some lines from Camões, which made a change from those wretches Lope and Cervantes, and that before he went into battle, he always recited whatever came into his heart, and that if anyone was affronted to hear a few lines from *The Lusiads*, he would be more than happy to fight it out with him *and* his mother.

"That's all we need," muttered someone.

There were no further comments. Saramago el Portugués resumed his mumbled recitation, and we continued on. Next to the cane fence surrounding the tidal pool created by the fishermen for their fish stocks, we saw two boats waiting, with a man in each of them. We gathered expectantly on the shore.

"The men in my group, come with me," said Alatriste.

He was hatless, but had now donned his buff coat, and his sword and dagger hung at his belt. The men duly divided into their allotted groups. They exchanged farewells and wishes of good luck, even the odd joke and the inevitable boasts about how many men they intended to relieve of their souls. There were also cases of ill-disguised nerves, stumblings in the dark, and curses. Sebastián Copons walked past us, followed by his men.

"Give me a little time," the captain said to him in a low voice. "But not too much."

Copons gave his usual silent nod and waited while his men got into the boat. The last to embark was the accountant Olmedilla. His black clothes made him seem darker still. He splashed about heroically in the water, tangled up in his own sword, while they helped him in.

"And take care of him, too, if you can," Alatriste said to Copons.

"God's teeth, Diego," replied Copons, who was tying his neckerchief around his head. "That's too many orders for one night."

Alatriste chuckled. "Who would have thought it, eh, Sebastián? Cutting Flemish throats in Sanlúcar."

Copons grunted. "Well, when it comes to cutting throats, one place is as good as any other."

The group assigned to the attack on the bow was also embarking. I went with them, waded into the water, scrambled over the edge of the boat, and sat down on a bench. A moment later, the captain joined us.

"Start rowing," he said.

We tied the oars to the tholes and began rowing away

from the shore, while the sailor took the tiller and guided us toward a nearby light that shimmered on the water ruffled by the breeze. The other boat remained a silent presence close by, the oars entering and leaving the water as quietly as possible.

"Slowly now," said Alatriste, "slowly."

Seated next to Bartolo Cagafuego, my feet resting on the bench in front of me, I bent forward with each stroke, then threw my body back, pulling hard on the oar. Thus the end of each movement left me staring up at the stars shining brightly in the vault of the sky. As I bent forward, I sometimes turned and looked back past the heads of my comrades. The lantern at the galleon's stern was getting closer and closer.

"So," muttered Cagafuego to himself, "I didn't escape the galleys after all."

The other boat began to move away from ours, with the small figure of Copons standing up in the prow. It soon vanished into the dark and all we could hear was the faint sound of its oars. Then, not even that. The breeze was fresher now and the boat rocked on the slight swell, forcing us to pay more attention to the rhythm of our rowing. At the halfway point, the captain told us to change places, so that we would not be too tired by the time it came to boarding the ship. Pencho Bullas took my place and Mascarúa took that occupied by Cagafuego.

"Quiet now, and be careful," said Alatriste.

We were very close to the galleon. I could see in more detail its dark, solid bulk, the masts silhouetted against the night sky. The lantern lit on the quarterdeck indicated exactly where the stern was. There was another lantern illuminating the shrouds, the rigging, and the bottom of the mainmast, and light filtered out from two of the gunports that had been left open. There was no one to be seen.

"Stop rowing!" Alatriste whispered urgently.

The men stopped, and the boat bobbed about on the swell. We were less than twenty yards from the vast stern. The light from the lantern was reflected in the water, almost right under our noses. On the side nearest the stern, a small rowing boat was moored, and a rope ladder dangled down into it.

"Prepare the grappling irons."

From beneath the benches, the men produced four grappling hooks with knotted ropes attached to them.

"Start rowing again, but very quietly and very slowly."

We began to move, with the sailor steering us toward the rowing boat and the ladder. Thus we passed beneath the high, black stern, seeking out the shadows where the light from the lantern did not reach. We were all looking up, holding our breath, afraid that a face might appear at any moment and be followed swiftly by a warning shout and a hail of bullets or a cannonade. Finally, the oars were placed in the bottom of the boat, and we glided forward until we touched the side of the galleon, next to the rowing boat and immediately beneath the ladder. The noise of that collision was, I thought, enough to have woken the entire bay, but no one inside cried out; there was no word of alarm. A shiver of tension ran through the boat while the men unwrapped their weapons and got ready to climb the ladder. I fastened the hooks on my buff coat. For a moment, Captain Alatriste's face came very close to mine. I couldn't see his eyes, but I knew he was looking at me.

"It's every man for himself now," he said quietly.

I nodded, knowing that he could not see me nod. Then I felt his hand squeeze my shoulder, firmly, briefly. I looked up and swallowed hard. The deck was some five or six cubits above our heads.

"Up you go!" whispered the captain.

At last I could see his face lit by the distant light of the lantern, the hawklike nose above his mustache as he began to scale the ladder, looking upward, his sword and dagger clinking at his waist. I followed without thinking and heard the other men, making no attempt to be quiet now, throw the grappling irons over the edge of the ship where they clattered onto the deck and clunked into place as they attached to the gunwale. Now there was only the effort of climbing, the sense of haste, the almost painful tension that gripped muscles and stomach as I grasped the sides of the rope ladder and hauled myself up, step by step, feet slipping on the damp, slimy planks that formed the hull of the ship.

"Oh, shit!" someone said below me.

A cry of alarm rang out above our heads, and when I looked up, I saw a face peering down at us, half lit by the lantern. The expression on the man's face was one of horror, as if unable to believe his eyes, as he watched us climbing toward him. He may have died still not quite believing, because Captain Alatriste, who had reached him by then, stuck his dagger in his throat, right up to the hilt, and the man disappeared from view. Now more voices could be heard above, and the sound of people running about below-decks. A few heads peeped cautiously out from the gunports and immediately drew back, shouting in Flemish. The captain's boots scuffed against my face when he reached the top and jumped onto the deck. At that moment, another face appeared over the edge, a little farther off, on the quarterdeck; we saw a lit fuse, then a flash, and a harquebus shot rang out; something very fast and hard ripped past us, ending in a squelch of pierced flesh and broken bones. Someone beside me, climbing up from the boat, fell backward into the sea with a splash, but without uttering a word.

"Go on! Keep going!" shouted the men behind me, driving one another onward.

Teeth gritted, head hunched right down between my shoulders, I climbed what remained of the ladder as quickly as possible, clambered over the edge, stepped onto the deck, and immediately slipped in a huge puddle of blood. I got to my feet, sticky and stunned, leaning on the motionless body of the slain sailor, and behind me the bearded face of Bartolo Cagafuego appeared over the edge, his eyes bulging with tension, his gap-toothed grimace made even fiercer by the enormous machete gripped between his few remaining teeth. We were standing at the foot of the mizzenmast, next to the ladder that led up to the quarterdeck. More of our group had now reached the deck via the ropes secured by grappling hooks, and it was a miracle that the whole galleon wasn't awake to give us a warm welcome, what with that single harquebus shot and the racket made by sundry noises—the clatter of footsteps and the hiss of swords as they left their sheaths.

I took my sword in my right hand and my dagger in my left, looking wildly about in search of the enemy. And then I saw a whole horde of armed men swarming onto the deck from down below, and I saw that most were as blond and burly as the men I had known in Flanders, and that there were more of them to the stern and in the waist, between the quarterdeck and the forecastle, and I saw as well that there were far too many of them, and that Captain Alatriste was fighting like a madman to reach the quarterdeck. I rushed to help my master, without waiting to see if Cagafuego and the others were following or not. I did so muttering the name of Angélica as a final prayer, and my last lucid thought, as I hurled myself into the fight with a furious howl, was that if Sebastián Copons did not arrive in time, the *Niklaasbergen* adventure would be our last.

9. OLD FRIENDS AND OLD ENEMIES

The hand and the arm grow tired of killing too. Diego Alatriste would gladly have given what remained of his life—which was perhaps very little—to lay down his weapons and lie quietly in a corner, just for a while. At that stage, he was fighting out of a mixture of fatalism and habit, and his feeling of indifference as to the result may, paradoxically, have been what kept him alive in the midst of all the clash and confusion. He was fighting with his usual serenity, without thinking, trusting in his keen eye and swift reactions. For men like him and in situations like that, the most effective way of keeping fate at bay was to leave imagination aside and put one's trust in pure instinct.

Using his foot for leverage, he wrenched his sword from the body of the man he had just skewered. All around him there were shouts, curses, moans, and from time to time the gloom was lit up by a shot from a pistol or from a Flemish harquebus, offering a glimpse of groups of men furiously knifing one another and of puddles of blood that slithered into the scuppers as the ship tilted.

In the grip of a singular clarity, he parried a thrust from a scimitar, dodged another, and responded by plunging his sword vainly into the void, yet he gave this error no thought. The other man drew back and turned his attention to someone else, who was attacking him from behind. Alatriste took advantage of that pause to lean against the bulkhead for a moment and rest. The steps to the quarterdeck stood before him, lit from above by a lantern; they appeared to be free. He had had to fight three men to get there; no one had warned him that there would be such a large company on board. The high poop deck, he thought, would provide a useful stronghold until Copons arrived with his men, but when Alatriste looked around him, he found that most of his party were engaged in fighting for their lives and had barely moved from the spot where they had boarded.

He forgot about the quarterdeck and returned to the fray. He encountered someone's back, possibly that of the man who had escaped him before, and plunged his dagger into his opponent's kidneys, turning the blade so as to cause as much damage as possible, and then yanking it out as the fellow dropped to the floor, screaming like a man condemned. A shot nearby dazzled him, and knowing that none of his men was carrying a pistol, he slashed his way blindly toward the source of that flash. He collided with someone, made a grab for him, but skidded and fell on the blood-washed deck, meanwhile headbutting the other man in the face, again and again, until he could get a grip on his own dagger and slip it in between them. The Fleming screamed as he felt the knife go in and crawled away on all fours. Alatriste spun around, and a body fell on top of him, murmuring in Spanish, "Holy Mother of God, Holy Mother of God." He had no idea who the man was and had no time to find out. He pushed the body away and, sword in his right hand and dagger in his left, scrambled to his feet, with a sense that the darkness around him was growing red. The screams and the shouting were truly horrendous, and it was impossible now to take more than three steps without slipping in the blood.

Cling, clang. Everything seemed to happen so slowly that he was surprised that in between each thrust he made his adversaries did not dish out ten or twelve in return. He felt a blow to his cheek, very hard, and his mouth filled with the familiar, metallic taste of blood. He raised his sword up high in order to slash a nearby face—a whitish blur that vanished with a yelp. In the come-and-go of battle, Alatriste found himself back at the steps leading to the quarterdeck, where there was more light. Then he realized that he was

still clutching under his arm a sword he had taken off someone who knows how long ago. He dropped it and whirled
around, dagger at the ready, sensing that there were enemies
behind him, and at that moment, just as he was about to
deal a counterblow with his sword, he recognized the fierce,
bearded face of Bartolo Cagafuego, who was crazily hitting
out at anyone in his path, his lips flecked with foam. Alatriste
turned in the other direction, seeking someone to fight,
just in time to see a boarding pike being propelled toward
his face. He dodged, parried, thrust, and then drove his
sword in, bruising his fingers when the point of his blade
stopped with a crunch as it hit bone. He stepped back to free
his weapon and, when he did so, stumbled over some coiled
cordage and fell so heavily against the ladder that he thought
for a moment he had broken his spine. Now someone was
trying to batter him with the butt of a harquebus and so he
crouched down to protect his head. He collided with yet another man, whether friend or foe he could not tell; he hesitated, then stuck his knife in and drew it out again. His back
really hurt, and he longed to cry out to gain some relief—
emitting a long, half-suppressed moan was always a good
way to take the edge off pain—but not a sound did he utter.
His head was buzzing, he could still taste blood in his mouth,
and his fingers were numb from gripping sword and dagger.
For a moment, he was filled by a desire to jump overboard.
I'm too old for this, he thought desolately.

He paused long enough to catch his breath, then returned reluctantly to the fray. This is where you die, he said to himself. And at that precise moment, as he stood at the foot of the steps, encircled by the light from the lantern, someone shouted his name. Bewildered, Alatriste turned, sword at the ready. And he swallowed hard, scarcely able to believe his eyes. May they crucify me on Golgotha, he thought, if it isn't Gualterio Malatesta.

Pencho Bullas died at my side. The Murcian was caught up in a knife fight with a Flemish sailor, when, suddenly, the latter shot him in the head, at such close range that his head was ripped off at the jaw, spattering me with blood and brain. However, even before the Fleming had lowered his pistol, I had slit his throat with my sword, very hard and fast, and the man fell on top of Bullas, gurgling something in his own strange tongue. I whirled my sword about my head to fend off anyone attempting to close on me. The steps up to the quarterdeck were too far away for me to reach, and so I did as everyone else was trying to do: tried to keep myself alive long enough for Sebastián Copons to get us out of there. I didn't even have breath enough to utter the names of Angélica or Christ himself; I needed all the breath I had to save my own skin. For a while, I managed to dodge whatever thrusts and blows came my way, returning as many as I could. Sometimes, amid the confusion of the fight, I thought I could see Captain Alatriste in the distance, but my efforts to reach him were in vain. We were separated by too many men killing and being killed.

Our comrades were putting on a brave face like the practiced swordsmen they were, fighting with the professional resolve of someone who has bet all his money on the knave of spades, but there were far more men on board the galleon than we had expected, and they were gradually driving us back toward the gunwale over which we had boarded. At least I can swim, I thought. The deck was full of motionless bodies or moaning figures dragging themselves along, and causing us to stumble at every step. I started to feel afraid, not of death exactly—death is of no importance, Nicasio Ganzúa had said in the prison in Seville—but of shame, mutilation, defeat, and failure.

Someone else attacked. He wasn't tall and blond like most Flemings but sallow-skinned and bearded. He struck out at me, grasping his sword with both hands, but had little luck. I kept my head and stood firm, and the third or fourth time that he drew back his arm, I stuck my sword into his breast swift as lightning, right up to the guard. My face almost touched his when I did so—I could feel his breath on mine—and we crashed to the floor together, with me still grasping the hilt, and I heard the blade of my sword snap as his back hit the deck. Then, for good measure, I stabbed him five or six times in the belly. At first, I was surprised to hear him cry out in Spanish and, for a moment, thought I must have made a mistake and killed one of my own. The light from a lantern near the quarterdeck, however, fell on an unfamiliar face. So there were Spaniards on board too, I thought. Given the fellow's general appearance and the doublet he was wearing, he was clearly a professional swordsman.

I got to my feet, confused. This altered things, and not, by God, for the better. I tried to think what it could mean, but in the white heat of fighting there was no time to mull things over. I looked for some weapon other than my dagger, and found a cutlass; it had a short, broad blade and an enormous guard on the hilt. It felt satisfyingly heavy in my hand. Unlike an ordinary sword, with its more subtle blade and sharp point to inflict penetrating wounds, the cutlass was excellent for slashing one's way through a throng. Which is what I did, *chaf, chaf,* impressed by the slick sound it made as I struck. I finished up next to a small group composed of the mulatto Campuzano, who continued to fight despite a great gash to his forehead, and El Caballero de Illescas, who was battling on exhausted, with little resolve, clearly seeking the first opportunity to hurl himself into the sea.

An enemy sword glittered before me. I raised the cutlass to deflect the blow and had barely completed that move when, with a sudden sense of panic, I realized my error. But it was too late, and at that moment, near the small of my back, something sharp and metallic pierced my buff coat, entering the flesh. I shuddered to feel the steel slide sleekly between my ribs.

A fleeting thought went through Diego Alatriste's mind as he assumed the en garde position. It all made sense: the gold, Luis de Alquézar, the presence of Gualterio Malatesta in Seville and now here, on board the Flemish galleon. The Italian was acting as escort to the cargo, which is why they had encountered such unexpectedly stiff resistance: most of the men he had been fighting were Spanish mercenaries like them, not sailors. In fact, this was a fight to the death between dogs of the same pack.

He had no time to think anything more, because after the initial surprise—Malatesta seemed as taken aback as he—the Italian advanced on him, black and menacing, sword foremost. As if by magic, the captain's weariness vanished. There is no greater tonic to the humors than an ancient hatred, and his burned as brightly as ever. The desire to kill proved stronger than mere survival instinct. Alatriste moved faster than his adversary, for when it came to the first thrust, he was already on guard, deflecting it with one short, sharp flick, sending Malatesta staggering backward as the point of his sword came within an inch of his face. When the captain bore down upon him again, he noticed that the bastard wasn't even whistling his usual wretched little tune—*ti-ri-tu, ta-ta*—or anything else for that matter.

Before the Italian could recover, Alatriste moved in close, wielding his sword and jabbing with his knife, so that Malatesta had no alternative but to continue backing away, looking for an opportunity to get in his first proper strike. They clashed fiercely right beneath the steps leading to the quarterdeck, and then, still fighting, traveled as far as the shrouds on the other side of the ship, in hand-to-hand combat, wielding their daggers, the guards of their swords locked together. Then the Italian lost his balance when he collided with the cascabel on one of the bronze cannon positioned there; Alatriste savored the look of fear in his enemy's eyes, then turned sideways on and gave a left thrust and then a right, point and reverse, but as luck would have it, he performed that last slashing attack with the flat of his sword not the edge. This was enough to provoke a ferocious yelp of glee from Malatesta, who, sly as a snake, drove his dagger forward with such vigor that if a startled Alatriste had not jumped out of the way, he would have surrendered his soul there and then.

"Well, well," murmured Malatesta, out of breath, "what a small world."

He still appeared surprised to find his old foe on board. For his part, the captain said nothing, but merely waited for the next onslaught. They paused, studying each other, swords and daggers in hand, crouched and ready to join battle again. All around them, the fighting continued, and Alatriste's men were still getting the worst of it. Malatesta glanced across at them.

"This time, Captain, you lose. This time, you've bitten off more than you can chew."

The Italian was smiling serenely, as black as the Fates themselves, the murky light from the lantern throwing into sharp relief the scars and pockmarks on his face.

"I hope," he added, "you haven't got the boy involved in this scrimmage."

That was one of Malatesta's weak points, thought Alatriste as he made a downward thrust: he talked too much and thus opened up gaps in his defense. The point of his sword caught the Italian's left arm, forcing him to drop his dagger with an oath. The captain took immediate advantage of this "gap" and gave such a fearsomely fast, low thrust with his dagger that the blade broke when he missed and hit the cannon instead. For a moment, he and Malatesta stood very close, almost embracing, looking at each other. They both swiftly drew back their swords to gain some space and try to get their knife in before the other one did; then the captain, resting his free—badly bruised— hand on the cannon, gave the Italian a sly kick that sent him slamming into the gunwale and the shrouds. At that point, behind them, they heard loud shouts coming from the waist of the ship, and a renewed clatter of swords spread throughout the deck. Alatriste did not turn round, intent as he was on his enemy, but from the expression on the latter's face, suddenly grim and desperate, he could tell that Sebastián Copons must finally have boarded at the prow. To confirm this, the Italian opened his mouth and let out a stream of blasphemies in his mother tongue, something about *il cazzo di Cristo* and *la sporca Madonna*.

Pressing my hands to my wound, I managed to drag myself over to the gunwale, where I could lean against some coiled ropes. I unfastened my clothes so that I could find out what damage had been done to my right side, but I could see nothing in the darkness. It hardly hurt at all, apart from the ribs bruised by the steel blade. I could feel the blood running gently over my fingers, down my waist to my thighs, and onto the already gore-soaked deck. I had to do something, I thought, or else bleed to death like a stuck pig. This idea made me feel faint, and I took deep breaths of air, struggling to remain conscious; fainting was the surest way to bleed to death. All around, the struggle continued, and everyone was far too occupied for me to ask for help, plus, of course, it might be an enemy who came to my aid, and an enemy would blithely slit my throat. And so I decided to keep quiet and manage on my own. Sliding slowly down onto my good side, I poked a finger into the wound to find out how deep it was—only about two inches, I reckoned. My new buff coat had more than repaid the twenty escudos I had given for it. I could still breathe easily, which meant that my lung was presumably unharmed, but the blood continued to flow, and I was growing weaker by the minute. I've got to stop the flow, I said to myself, or else order a mass for my soul right now. Anywhere else, a handful of earth would have been enough to clot the blood, but here there was nothing, not even a clean handkerchief. Somehow or other, I had kept my dagger with me, because it was there gripped between my legs. I cut off a section of my shirttail and pushed it into the wound. This stung most violently—indeed, it hurt so much that I had to bite my lip in order not to cry out.

I was beginning to lose consciousness. I've done all I could, I thought, trying to console myself before falling into the black hole opening up at my feet. I wasn't thinking about Angélica or about anything else. As I grew steadily weaker, I rested my head against the gunwale, and then it seemed to me that everything around me was moving. It must be my head spinning, I decided. But then I noticed that the noise of battle had abated and all the shouting and the ruckus were happening farther off, toward the waist of the ship and toward the prow. A few men ran past, jumping over me, almost kicking me in their haste to escape and plunge into the water. I heard splashes and cries of panic. I looked up, bewildered. Someone had apparently climbed the mainmast and was cutting the gaskets, because the mainsail suddenly unfurled and dropped down, half filled by the breeze. Then my mouth twisted into a foolish, happy grimace intended as a smile, for I knew then that we had won, that the group boarding at the prow had managed to cut the anchor cable, and the galleon was now drifting in the night toward the sandbanks of San Jacinto.

I hope I have what it takes and that I don't give in, thought Diego Alatriste, steadying himself again and grasping his sword. I hope this Sicilian dog has the decency not to ask for mercy, because I'm going to kill him anyway, and I don't want to do it when he's disarmed. With that thought, and spurred on by the urgent need to finish the business there and then and make no last-minute errors, he gathered together what strength he had and unleashed a series of furious thrusts, so fast and brutal that even the best fencer in the world would have been unable to riposte. Malatesta retreated, defending himself with difficulty, but he still had sufficient sangfroid, when the captain was delivering his final thrust, to make a high, oblique slashing movement with his knife that missed the captain's face by a hair's breadth. This pause was enough for Malatesta to cast a rapid glance around him, to see how things stood on the deck, and to realize that the galleon was drifting toward the shore.

"I was wrong, Alatriste. This time you win."

He had barely finished speaking when the captain made a jab at his eye with the point of his sword, and the Italian ground his teeth and let out a scream, raising the back of his free hand to his cut face, now streaming with blood. Even then he showed great aplomb and managed to strike out furiously and blindly, almost piercing Alatriste's buff coat and forcing him to retreat a little.

"Oh, go to hell," muttered Malatesta. "You and the gold."

Then he hurled his sword at the captain, hoping to hit his face, scrambled onto the shrouds, and leapt like a shadow into the darkness. Alatriste ran to the gunwale, lashing the air with his blade, but all he could hear was a dull splash in the black waters. And he stood there, stock-still and exhausted, staring stupidly into the dark sea.

"Sorry I'm late, Diego," said a voice behind him.

Sebastián Copons was at his side, breathing hard, his scarf still tied around his head and his sword in his hand, his face covered in blood as if by a mask. Alatriste nodded, his thoughts still absent.

"Many losses?" asked the captain.

"About half."

"And Íñigo?"

"Not too bad. A small wound to the chest but no damage to the lung."

Alatriste nodded again, and continued staring at the sinister black stain of the sea. Behind him, he heard the triumphant shouts of his men, and the screams of the last defenders of the *Niklaasbergen* having their throats cut as they surrendered.

I felt better once I had stanched the flow of blood and the strength returned to my legs. Sebastián Copons had put a makeshift bandage on my wound, and with the help of Bartolo Cagafuego I went to join the others at the foot of the quarterdeck steps. Various men were clearing the deck by throwing corpses overboard, first plundering them for any objects of value they might find. The bodies dropped into the sea with a macabre splash, and I never found out exactly how many of the ship's crew, Flemish and Spanish, died that night. Fifteen or twenty, possibly more. The others had jumped overboard during the fighting and were swimming or drowning in the wake left by the galleon, which was now heading for the sandbanks, nudged along by a breeze from the northeast.

On the deck, still slippery with blood, lay our own dead. Those of us who had boarded at the stern had borne the brunt. There they lay, motionless, hair disheveled, eyes open or closed, in the precise pose in which the Fates had struck: Sangonera, Mascarúa, El Caballero de Illescas, and the Murcian, Pencho Bullas. Guzmán Ramírez had been lost to the sea, and Andresito el de los Cincuenta was moaning softly as he lay huddled and dying next to a gun carriage, a doublet thrown over him to cover his spilled guts. Less badly wounded were Enríquez el Zurdo, the mulatto Campuzano, and Saramago el Portugués. There was another corpse stretched out on deck, and I stared at it for a while in surprise at the unexpectedness of the sight: the accountant Olmedilla's eyes remained half open, as if, right up until the last moment, he had kept watch to ensure that his duty to those who paid his salary was duly carried out. He was rather paler than usual, his customary ill-tempered sneer fixed forever beneath the mousy mustache, as if he regretted not having had time to set everything down in ink and in a neat hand on the standard official document. The mask of death made him look more than usually insignificant, very still and very alone. They told me he had boarded along with the group at the prow, clambering over ropes with touching ineptitude, lashing out blindly with a sword he barely knew how to use, and that he had died at once, without a murmur of complaint, and all for some gold that was not his own, for a king whom he had glimpsed only occasionally from afar, who did not know his name, and who would not even have spoken to him had he walked past him in a room.

When Alatriste saw me, he came over and gently touched the wound, then placed one hand on my shoulder. By the light of the lantern I could see that his eyes retained the same absorbed expression as during the fighting, indifferent to everything around us.

"Pleased to see you, lad."

But I knew this wasn't true. He might well feel pleased later on, when his pulse had returned to normal and order was restored, but at that moment, his words were mere words. His thoughts were still fixed on Gualterio Malatesta and on the galleon now drifting toward the sandbanks of San Jacinto. He scarcely looked at our dead comrades and gave Olmedilla's body only the most cursory of glances. Nothing seemed to surprise him, or alter the fact that he was still alive and still had things to do. He dispatched Juan Eslava to the leeward side to report on whether we had yet reached the sandbank or the shallows; he ordered Juan Jaqueta to make sure that no enemies remained hidden on board; and repeated the order that no one, for any reason, should go belowdecks. On pain of death, he said somberly, and Jaqueta, after looking at him hard, nodded. Then, accompanied by Sebastián Copons, Alatriste went down into the bowels of the ship. I would not have missed this for the world, and so I took advantage of my position as my master's page and followed behind, despite the pain from my wound, and doing my best to make no sudden movements that might make it bleed still more.

Copons was carrying a lantern and a pistol he'd picked up from the deck, and Alatriste had his sword unsheathed. We scoured every berth and hold, but found no one—we saw a table set, with the food untouched on the dozen or so plates—and finally we reached some steps that led down into the darkness. At the bottom was a door closed with a great iron bar and two padlocks. Copons handed me the lantern and went in search of a boarding ax, and it took only a few blows to break down the door. I held the lantern up to light the interior.

"God's teeth!" murmured Copons.

There were the gold and silver for which we had fought and killed. Stored away like ballast in the hold, the treasure was piled up in various barrels and boxes, all roped securely together. The ingots and bars lining the hold glowed like some extraordinary golden dream. In the distant mines of Peru and Mexico, far from the light of the sun, thousands of Indian slaves, under the lash of the overseer, had ruined their health and lost their lives in order that this precious metal should reach these shores, and all to repay the Empire's debts, to finance the armies and wars in which Spain was enbroiled with half of Europe, to swell the fortunes of bankers, officials, and unscrupulous aristocrats, and, in this case, to line the pockets of the king himself. The gold bars glinted in Captain Alatriste's dark pupils and in Copons's wide eyes. And I watched, fascinated.

"What fools we are, Diego," said Copons.

And there was no doubt about it, we were fools. I saw the captain slowly nod agreement. We were fools not to hoist the sails—had we known how to do it—and to keep sailing, not toward the sandbanks but out toward the open sea, into waters that bathed shores inhabited by free men, with no master, no god, and no king.

"Holy Mother!" said a voice behind us.

We turned around. El Bravo de los Galeones and the sailor Suárez were standing on the steps, staring at the treasure, slack-jawed with amazement. They were carrying their weapons in their hands and, over their shoulders, sacks into which they had been stashing anything of value they came across.

"What are you doing here?" asked Alatriste.

Anyone who knew him would have taken great care how he answered. El Bravo de los Galeones, however, did not.

"Just having a bit of a walkabout," he replied brazenly.

The captain smoothed his mustache, his eyes as hard and fixed as glass beads. "I said no one was to come down here."

"Yeah, well," said El Bravo dismissively. He was smiling greedily, a fierce look on his scarred, marked face. "And now we know why."

He was gazing wildly at the glittering treasure. Then he exchanged a glance with Suárez, who had put his sack down on the steps and was scratching his head incredulously, stunned by what lay before him.

"It seems to me, comrade," said El Bravo de los Galeones, "that we should tell the others about this. That would be a fine trick—"

The word became a mere gurgle in his throat as Alatriste, without warning, stuck his sword through El Bravo's breast, so quickly that by the time the ruffian had a chance to stare down in stupefaction at the wound inflicted, the blade had already been removed. Mouth agape and uttering an agonized sigh, El Bravo fell forward onto the captain, who pushed him away, leaving him to roll down the steps and land at the very foot of a barrel of silver. When he saw this, Suárez let out a horrified "Dear God!" and instinctively raised the scimitar he was carrying; then he seemed to think better of it, for he turned on his heel and started climbing back up the steps as fast as he could, stifling a scream of terror. And he continued to scream that muffled scream until Sebastián Copons, who had unsheathed his dagger, caught up with him, grabbed his foot, and knocked him down; then, straddling his body, he yanked Suárez's head up by the hair and deftly cut his throat. I watched this scene, frozen in horror. Not daring to move a muscle, I saw Alatriste wiping the gore from his sword on the prone body of El Bravo, whose blood was now soiling the gold ingots piled up on the floor. Then he did something strange: he spat, as if he had something dirty in his mouth. He spat into the air as if he were making some comment to himself, or like someone uttering a silent oath, and when his eyes met mine, I shuddered, because he was looking at me as if he didn't know me, and for an instant I was afraid he might kill me as well.

"Watch the stairs," he said to Copons.

From where he was kneeling beside the inert corpse on which he was cleaning his dagger, Copons nodded. Then Alatriste walked past him, without so much as a glance at the sailor's dead body, and went back up on deck. I followed him, glad to leave behind me the awful scene in the hold, and once up aloft, I noticed that Alatriste had paused to take a deep breath, as if desperate for the air that had been lacking down below. Then Juan Eslava shouted to us from the gunwale and, almost simultaneously, we felt the keel of the ship grind into the sand. All movement ceased, and the deck listed slightly to one side. The men were pointing at the lights moving on the shore, coming to meet us. The *Niklaasbergen* had run aground in the shallows of San Jacinto.

We went over to the gunwale. There were boats rowing

toward us in the dark, and a line of lights was approaching slowly from the end of the spit of sand, where the water beneath the galleon looked bright and clear in the lantern light.

Alatriste glanced at the deck.

"Right, let's go," he said to Juan Jaqueta.

The latter hesitated for a moment.

"Where are Suárez and El Bravo?" he asked uneasily. "I'm sorry, Captain, but I couldn't help it." He suddenly paused, studying my master's face in the light near the quarterdeck. "I'm sorry, but to stop them, I'd have had to kill them."

He fell silent.

"Kill them," he repeated in soft, bewildered tones.

This sounded more like a question than a statement. But there was no reply. Alatriste was still looking around him.

"It's time we left the ship," he said, addressing the men on deck. "Help the wounded off."

Jaqueta was still watching him. He seemed to be waiting for an answer.

"What happened?" he asked grimly.

"They're not coming."

He had turned at last to face Jaqueta, very coldly and calmly. Jaqueta opened his mouth, but said nothing. He stood like that for a moment, then turned to the other men, urging them to obey the captain's orders. The boats and the lights were coming nearer, and our men began to climb down the rope ladder to the tongue of sand, uncovered by the low tide, on which the galleon had run aground. Bartolo Cagafuego and the mulatto Campuzano, whose head was swathed in a huge bandage like a turban, were carefully helping Enríquez el Zurdo off the ship; El Zurdo was bleeding profusely from a broken nose and had a couple of nasty cuts to his arms. Ginesillo el Lindo, in turn, went to the aid of Saramago, who was limping painfully from a long gash in his thigh.

"Any closer, and they'd have had my balls," Saramago said mournfully.

The last to leave were Jaqueta—once he had closed the eyes of his comrade Sangonera—and Juan Eslava. No one had to bother with Andresito el de los Cincuenta, because by then he had been dead for some time. Copons appeared at the top of the steps to the hold and went straight over to the side of the ship. At that moment, a man climbed on board, and I recognized the fellow with the ginger mustache who had spoken to Olmedilla earlier. He was still dressed as a hunter and was armed to the teeth; behind him came several more men. Despite their disguise, they were all clearly soldiers. They eyed with professional curiosity the bodies of our dead comrades and the bloodstained deck, and the man with the ginger mustache stood for a while studying Olmedilla's corpse. Then he came over to the captain.

"How did it happen?" he asked, pointing to the accountant.

"As these things do," said Alatriste laconically.

The other man looked at him intently, then said very equably, "Good work."

Alatriste did not respond. Heavily armed men continued to clamber on board. Some were carrying harquebuses with the fuses lit.

"In the name of the king," said the man with the ginger mustache, "I take charge of this ship."

I saw my master nod, and then I followed him over to the gunwale, where Sebastián Copons was already climbing down the rope ladder. Alatriste turned to me with that same distracted air, and put a helping arm around me. I leaned against him, and breathed in from his clothes the smell of leather and steel mixed with the smell of blood from the men he had killed that night. He went down the ladder, all the while supporting me, until we reached the sand. The water came up to our ankles. We got wetter as we waded toward the beach, plunging in up to our waists, and my wound stung fiercely. Shortly afterward, with me still leaning on the captain for support, we reached land, where our men were gathered in the darkness. Around them were the shadows of more armed men, as well as the blurred shapes of many mules and carts ready to carry off what lay in the ship's holds.

"Ye gods," said one man, "we certainly earned our keep tonight."

These words, spoken in a cheery tone of voice, broke the silence and the tension. As always after combat—and I had seen this over and over in Flanders—the men gradually began to talk and open up, with just a comment here and there at first, brief remarks, complaints, and sighs. Then they launched into oaths and boasts and laughter: I did this, someone else did that. Some described in detail how they had boarded the ship or else asked how such and such a comrade had died. I heard no one regret the passing of the accountant Olmedilla: they had never taken to that scrawny individual dressed all in black, and it was as clear as day that he was ill-equipped for such work. As far as everyone there was concerned, his life wasn't worth a candle.

"What happened to El Bravo de los Galeones?" asked someone. "I didn't see him peg it."

"No, he was alive at the end," said another.

"Suárez didn't get off the ship either," added a third.

No one had an explanation, and those who did kept quiet. There were a few muttered comments, but Suárez had no friends amongst that crew, most of whom also loathed El Bravo. No one really felt their absence.

"All the more for us, I suppose," remarked one man.

Someone gave a coarse guffaw, and the subject was dropped. And I wondered—and had few illusions about the answer—if I were lying on deck, stiff and cold as a piece of salt tuna, would I merit the same epitaph? I saw the silent shadow of Juan Jaqueta, and although I couldn't see his face, I knew he was looking at Captain Alatriste.

We walked to a nearby inn, which was all prepared to receive us for the night. The innkeeper—a scurvy knave if ever there was one—had only to see our faces, our bandages, and our ironware to treat us as diligently and obsequiously as if we were grandees of Spain. And so there was wine from Jerez and Sanlúcar for everyone, a fire to dry our clothes by, and abundant food, of which we ate every crumb, for the recent violent fracas had left us all with empty bellies. Mugs of wine and plates of roast kid were quickly dispatched, and we drank to our dead comrades and to the gleaming gold coins piled up on the table before us; they had been delivered before dawn by the man with the ginger mustache, who came accompanied by a surgeon to attend to our injuries; he cleaned the wound in my side, sewed it up, and applied some ointment and a fresh, clean bandage. Gradually, amid the vinous vapors, the men all fell asleep. Occasionally, El Zurdo or Saramago would moan out loud or there would be raucous snores from Copons, who was sleeping stretched out on a rug, as oblivious to his surroundings as he had been in the mud of the Flanders trenches.

Discomfort prevented me from sleeping. It was my first wound, and I would be lying if I denied that the pain from it filled me with a new and inexpressible pride. Now, with the passing of time, I bear other marks on both flesh and memory: that first wound is now only a near-imperceptible line on my skin, tiny compared with the wound I suffered at Rocroi or the one inflicted on me by Angélica de Alquézar's dagger. But sometimes I run my fingers over it and remember, as if it were yesterday, that night at Barra de Sanlúcar, the fighting on board the *Niklaasbergen*, and El Bravo's blood staining the king's gold red.

Nor can I forget Captain Alatriste as I saw him in the early hours of that morning when pain kept me from sleep. He was sitting on a stool, apart from everyone else, his back against the wall, watching the gray dawn creep in through the window, while he drank his wine slowly and methodically, as I had so often seen him do before, until his eyes became like opaque glass and his head sank slowly onto his chest, and sleep—a lethargy not unlike death—overwhelmed both body and mind. And I had shared his life for long enough to know that, even in his dreams, Diego Alatriste would continue to move through the personal wilderness that was his life, silent, solitary, and selfish, oblivious of everything except the clear-sighted indifference of one who knows the narrow line that separates being alive from being dead, of one who kills in order to preserve his life's breath and to keep himself, too, in hot meals. One who is reluctant to obey the rules of that strange game: the old ritual in which men like him have been immersed since the world began. Such things as hatred, passionate beliefs, and flags had nothing to do with it. It would doubtless have been more bearable if, instead of the bitter clarity that filled his every act and thought, Captain Alatriste had enjoyed the magnificent gifts of stupidity, fanaticism, or malice, because only the stupid, the fanatical, and the malicious live lives free from ghosts or from remorse.

EPILOGUE

The sergeant of the Spanish guard cut an imposing figure in his red-and-yellow uniform, and he eyed me with some irritation as I walked through the palace gates with don Francisco de Quevedo and Captain Alatriste. He was the same burly, mustachioed fellow with whom I had had words days before outside those very walls, and he was doubtless surprised to see me there in my new doublet, with my hair combed, and looking handsomer than Narcissus himself, while don Francisco showed him the document authorizing us to attend the royal reception being held in honor of the municipal council and commercial tribunal of Seville to celebrate the arrival of the treasure fleet.

Other guests were arriving too: wealthy merchants accompanied by spouses decked out in jewels, mantillas, and fans; minor aristocrats who had probably pawned their few remaining valuables in order to buy new clothes especially for the occasion; clerics in cassock and cloak; and representatives of the local guilds. Almost everyone was staring openmouthed this way and that, overwhelmed and impressed by the splendid appearance of the Spanish, Burgundian, and German guards, and as if half afraid that, at any moment, someone would demand to know what they were doing there and throw them out in the street. All the guests knew that they would see the king and queen only for an instant and from a distance, that their contribution would consist of little more than doffing their hats and bowing low to Their August Majesties as they passed; however, the mere fact of being present at such an event and being able to stroll like grandees in all their finery in the gardens of that former Moorish palace and talk about it afterward, this was the very acme of the ambitions cultivated by even the most plebeian of Spaniards. And when, the following day, this fourth Philip proposed, perhaps, that the municipal council should approve the imposition of a new charge or an extraordinary tax on the newly arrived treasure, he did so in the knowledge that Seville would still have enough of a taste of syrup in its mouth to sweeten that bitter pill—for the deadliest thrusts are always those that pierce the purse—and would, therefore, loosen their purse strings without too much complaint.

"There's Guadalmedina," said don Francisco.

The count, who was chatting to some ladies, saw us from afar, excused himself with a gracious bow, and came to meet us, oozing politeness and wearing his very best smile.

"By God, Alatriste, you've no idea how pleased I am to see you."

He greeted Quevedo with his usual bonhomie, complimented me on my new doublet, and gave the captain a gentle, friendly pat on the arm.

"There's someone else who's very pleased to see you too," he added.

He was dressed as elegantly as ever, in pale blue with silver braiding and with a magnificent pheasant feather in his hat. His courtly appearance was in marked contrast to that of Quevedo, who was dressed all in black, with the cross of St. James on his breast, and of my master, dressed entirely in browns and blacks, in an old but clean and scrupulously brushed doublet, canvas breeches, and boots, and with a gleaming sword hanging from his newly polished belt. His only new items of clothing were his hat—a broad-brimmed felt affair with a red feather in it—the starched white Walloon collar, which he wore open, as befitted a soldier, and the dagger bought for ten escudos to replace the one he had broken during his encounter with Gualterio Malatesta: a magnificent blade nearly two spans long and bearing the marks of the swordsmith Juan de Orta.

"He didn't want to come," said don Francisco, indicating the captain.

"I imagined he wouldn't," replied Guadalmedina. "However, there are some orders that must be obeyed." He winked familiarly. "Certainly by a veteran like you, Alatriste. And that *is* an order."

The captain said nothing. He was looking awkwardly about him, occasionally tugging at his clothes as if he didn't know quite what to do with his hands. Beside him, Guadalmedina stood smiling to this person or that, waving to an acquaintance, sometimes nodding to the wife of a merchant or pettifogging lawyer, who then furiously fanned away her blushes.

"I should tell you, captain, that the parcel reached its addressee, and that everyone took great pleasure in it," he said, with a smile. Then he lowered his voice. "Well, to be honest, some took rather less pleasure in it than others. The Duque de Medina Sidonia very nearly died of grief. And when Olivares returns to Madrid, your friend the royal secretary Luis de Alquézar will certainly have some explaining to do."

Guadalmedina continued chuckling to himself, vastly amused, all the while waving and nodding and generally flaunting his impeccably courtly appearance.

"The count-duke is in the seventh heaven of delight," he went on, "happier than if Christ himself had struck Richelieu down with a thunderbolt. That is why he wanted you to be here today, to greet you, albeit from a distance, when he passes by with the king and queen. You can't deny that it's quite an honor to receive a personal invitation from the king's favorite."

"Our captain," said Quevedo, "feels that the greatest honor the count-duke could have bestowed on him would have been simply to forget the whole affair."

"He may be right," commented the count. "The favor of the great is often both more dangerous and more paltry than their disfavor. I can only say that it's very fortunate that you're a soldier, Alatriste, because you would make a disastrous courtier. I wonder sometimes if my profession isn't harder than yours."

"To each his own," replied the captain.

"Quite. But returning to the matter at hand, I'll have you know that yesterday the king himself asked Olivares to tell him the story. I was there, and the count-duke painted a very vivid picture. As you know, Our Catholic Majesty is not one to show his feelings, but I'll be hanged if I didn't see him blink several times while he listened to the account, and for him, that's the very height of emotion."

"Will this translate into anything tangible?" asked Quevedo, ever practical.

"If you're referring to something that jingles and has a head and a tail, I doubt it. When it comes to cheese paring, if Olivares pares it fine, then His Majesty pares it finer still. They consider that the work was paid for at the time, and very generously too."

"True enough," said Alatriste.

"Well, you would know," said the count with a shrug. "Today is, shall we say, by way of an honorific coda. The king's curiosity was aroused when he was reminded of your involvement in that incident two years ago with the Prince of Wales at the Corral del Príncipe. And so he has a fancy to see you in the flesh." The count paused significantly. "The other night, at Triana, it was far too dark."

He fell silent again, studying Alatriste's impassive face.

"Did you hear what I said?"

My master held his gaze, but did not respond, as if the count had spoken of something that he felt neither a need nor a desire to remember, something in which he preferred not to be implicated. After a moment, the count looked away, slowly shaking his head and smiling to himself, in an amused, understanding manner. Then his eye fell on me.

"They say the boy acquitted himself well," he said, changing the subject. "And that he even brought away with him a nice little souvenir."

"Yes, he acquitted himself very well indeed," agreed Alatriste, making me blush with pride.

"Regarding this afternoon, you know the protocol," Guadalmedina said, indicating the large doors that opened out onto the garden. "Their Majesties will enter through there, the yokels will bow, and then the king and queen will leave through that door over there. It'll be over in a flash. As for you, Alatriste, all you have to do is doff your hat and, for once in your wretched life, bow that stubborn soldier's head of yours. The king—who will, as usual, be gazing somewhere at the horizon—will merely glance at you for a moment. Olivares will do the same. You nod, and that's that."

"What an honor," said Quevedo sarcastically. And then, so softly that we had to lean closer to hear, he recited these lines:

> *"See them all decked out in purple,*
> *Hands beringed with glittering gems?*
> *Inside, they're naught but putrefaction,*
> *Made of mud and earth and worms."*

Guadalmedina—very much the courtier that afternoon— started back. He looked around, gesturing to Quevedo to restrain himself.

"Really, don Francisco, a little decorum, please. This is hardly the time or the place. Besides, there are people who would cut off their right hand for one glance from the king." He turned to the captain and, adopting a persuasive tone, said, "Anyway, it's no bad thing that Olivares should remember you and invite you here. You have a number of enemies in Madrid, and it's quite a coup to be able to count the king's favorite among your friends. It's high time you shook off the poverty that's been dogging you like a shadow.

And as you yourself once said to don Gaspar—and in my presence too—one never knows."

"It's true," replied Alatriste. "One never knows."

There was a roll of drums on the far side of the courtyard, followed by a short blast on a trumpet, whereat all conversation stopped and fans ceased fluttering; a few hats were rapidly doffed, and everyone turned expectantly in the direction of the fountains, the neat hedges, and the pleasant rose gardens. On the far side of the courtyard, the king and queen and their cortège had just emerged from a room full of lavish hangings and tapestries.

"I must go and join them," said Guadalmedina. "I'll see you later, Alatriste, and if you can manage it, try to smile a little when the count-duke looks at you. No, on second thought, don't. A smile from you usually heralds an attack!"

He left, and we stayed where we were, on the very edge of the white path bisecting the garden, while people to either side of us moved away, eyes fixed on the slowly advancing procession. Ahead came two officers and four archers from the royal guard, and behind them the cream of the royal entourage, gentlemen and ladies-in-waiting—the former dressed in fine costumes adorned with diamonds and gold chains, and wearing court swords with gilded hilts; the latter wearing shawls, plumed hats, jewels, lace, and lavish dresses.

"There she is," whispered Quevedo.

There was no need for him to say any more, because I, struck dumb and rooted to the spot, had already seen her. Amongst the queen's maids of honor was Angélica de Alquézar, her golden ringlets brushing the delicate, near-transparent shawl drawn tight about her shoulders. She was as lovely as ever, with, at her waist, the interesting addition of a small jewel-encrusted silver pistol, which looked as if it could fire real bullets, and which she wore like an ornament on the scarlet watered satin of her skirt. A Neapolitan fan hung from her wrist, but her head was unadorned, apart from a delicate mother-of-pearl comb.

Then she saw me. Her blue eyes, which had, until then, been staring blankly ahead, suddenly focused on me as if she had sensed my presence or as if, by dint of some strange witchcraft, she had been expecting to find me on that precise spot. She gave me a lingering look, without glancing away or appearing in the least discomfited. And just as she was about to walk past me, which would mean, of course, that she could only maintain eye contact by turning her head, she smiled. And what a glorious smile it was, as bright as the sun gilding the battlements of the Reales Alcázares. Then she was gone, moving off along the path, and I was left standing there like a gaping fool, having entirely surrendered my three faculties—memory, understanding, and will—to her love, and thinking that I would gladly have returned again and again to the Alameda de Hércules or to the *Niklaasbergen*, ready to offer up my life, if only she would smile at me like that one more time. And so fast were my heart and pulse beating that I felt a sudden pang, a sudden warm dampness under the bandage, where my wound had just reopened.

"Ah, my boy," murmured don Francisco de Quevedo, placing an affectionate hand on my shoulder. "So it is and so it will always be: you will die a thousand times and yet your griefs will never kill you."

I sighed, incapable of saying a word. And I heard the poet softly reciting:

> *"The beautiful creature from behind her bars*
> *Promises that she's mine, only mine."*

The king and queen, in their slow, stiff progress, had, by then, almost drawn level with us. The young, blond Philip, strongly built and very erect, his gaze fixed, as ever, on some point in the middle distance, was dressed in blue velvet trimmed with black and silver, and around his neck, on a black ribbon and gold chain, he wore the badge of the Order of the Golden Fleece. The queen, doña Isabel de Borbón, was wearing a silver-gray dress with orange taffeta cuffs, and a bejeweled and feathered hat that set off her sweet, youthful face. Unlike her husband, she smiled charmingly at everyone, and it was a delight to see that beautiful French-born Spanish queen, the daughter, sister, and wife of kings, whose cheerful nature brightened the sober Spanish court for two decades and aroused certain sighs and passions about which I will perhaps tell you on another occasion. She also refused outright to live in El Escorial—that dark, somber, austere palace built by her husband's grandfather—although in one of life's little ironies, from which no one is exempt, the poor thing was finally obliged to take up permanent residence there, when she was buried alongside the other queens of Spain.

But on that festive afternoon in Seville, such things were all a long way off. The king and queen looked so young and elegant, and as they passed, all present removed their hats and bowed before Their Royal Majesties. Accompanying them was the imposing, burly figure of the Conde-Duque de Olivares, the very image of power in his black clothes, with that mighty back of his which, like Atlas, bore the awful weight of the vast monarchy of Old and New Spain, an impossible duty that, years later, don Francisco de Quevedo summed up in three lines:

> *How much easier it is, O Spain,*
> *For everyone to steal from you alone*
> *what you alone stole from everyone.*

Don Gaspar de Guzmán, Conde-Duque de Olivares and minister to our king, wore a broad Walloon collar and, embroidered on his breast, the cross of Calatrava; the fierce points of his vast mustache rose up almost as far as his wary, penetrating eyes, which shifted constantly, restlessly, back and forth—identifying, recording, recognizing. The king and queen stopped only rarely and always at the count-duke's suggestion; and when this happened, the king or the queen, or both at once, would gaze upon some fortunate person who for whatever reason—because of services performed or through influential contacts—was deemed deserving of that honor. In such cases, the women curtsied low to the floor, and the men bowed from the waist, their hats having already been doffed, of course; and then, after the gift of this moment of contemplation and silence, the king and queen would continue their solemn march. Behind them came certain select Spanish nobles and grandees, amongst them the Conde de Guadalmedina; as he approached us, Alatriste and Quevedo, along with everyone else, removed their hats, and the count dropped a few words into the ear of the count-duke, who bestowed on our group one of his fierce looks, as merciless as an indictment. The count-duke, in turn, whispered into the ear of the king, who stopped walking, brought his gaze down from the heights, and fixed it on us. While the count-duke was still murmuring into his ear, the king, his prognathous bottom lip protruding, rested his faded blue eyes on Captain Alatriste.

"They're talking about you," muttered Quevedo.

I glanced at the captain. He remained very upright, his hat in one hand and his other hand resting on the hilt of his sword, with his stern, mustachioed profile and serene, soldierly head looking straight at the king, at the monarch whose name he had shouted out on battlefields and for whose gold he had risked life and limb only three nights before. I saw that the captain seemed unimpressed and unabashed. All his awkwardness over the formal nature of the event had vanished, and there remained only his frank, dignified gaze, which held that of the king with the equanimity of one who owes nothing and expects nothing. I remembered the moment when the old Cartagena regiment mutinied at Breda and I was tempted to join the rebels, and how, when the ensigns were leaving the ranks in order not to be tainted by the revolt, Alatriste had grabbed me by the scruff of the neck and forced me to leave with them, uttering the words "Your king is your king."

And it was there, in the courtyard of the Reales Alcázares in Seville, that I finally began to understand the meaning of that singular dogma, which I had failed to understand at the time: the loyalty professed by Captain Alatriste was not to the fair-haired young man standing before him, not to His Catholic Majesty, not to the one true religion, or to the idea that either one of them represented on Earth, but to that one personal rule, chosen for want of anything better, and which was all that remained from the shipwreck of more generalized, more enthusiastic ideas that had dissolved with the loss of innocence and youth. Regardless of what the rule was—right or wrong, logical or illogical, just or unjust, justifiable or not—it was the rule that mattered to men like Diego Alatriste as a way of imposing some kind of order, or structure, on the apparent chaos of life. And thus, paradoxically, my master respectfully doffed his hat before his king not out of resignation or discipline but out of despair. After all, since there were no old gods in whom one could trust, no great words that could be bandied about during combat, it was a salve to everyone's honor—or, at least, better than nothing at all—to have a king for whom one could fight and before whom one could doff one's hat, even if one did not believe in him. And so Captain Alatriste held firmly to that principle, just as, had he given his loyalty to someone else, he might have pushed his way through that very same throng and knifed the king to death, without a thought for the consequences.

At that point, something unusual happened to interrupt my thoughts. The Conde-Duque de Olivares concluded his short report, and the monarch's usually impassive eyes now took on an expression of curiosity and remained fixed on the captain. Then our fourth Philip gave the very slightest of approving nods and, slowly raising his hand to his august breast, removed the gold chain he was wearing and handed it to the count-duke. The latter, smiling thoughtfully, weighed it in his hand for a moment and then, to the general amazement of all those present, came toward us.

"His Majesty would like you to accept this chain," he said.

He said this in the stern, arrogant tone so typical of him, piercing the captain with the two hard, black points of his eyes, a smile still visible beneath his fierce mustache.

"Gold from the Indies," he added with evident irony.

Alatriste turned pale. He stood stock-still and stared at the count-duke uncomprehendingly. Olivares was still proffering him the chain in his outstretched palm.

"Well, don't keep me waiting all day," Olivares snapped.

The captain seemed finally to come to. And once he had recovered his composure, he at last took the chain, and, stammering out a few words of gratitude, looked again at the king. The latter continued to observe the captain with some curiosity, and meanwhile Olivares returned to his monarch's side; Guadalmedina stood, beaming, amongst the other astonished courtiers; and the cortège prepared to move on. Then Captain Alatriste bowed his head respectfully; the king again, almost imperceptibly, nodded, and the procession set off.

Proud of my master, I looked defiantly around me at all those inquisitive faces, staring in astonishment at the captain, wondering who the devil this fortunate man was, to whom the count-duke himself had presented a gift from the king. Don Francisco de Quevedo was chuckling delightedly to himself and clicking his fingers, muttering about a need to wet both his whistle and his words at Becerra's inn, where he had to set down some lines that had just occurred to him:

> *"If what I have I do not fear to lose,*
> *Nor yet desire to have what I do not,*
> *I'm safe from Fortune's wheel whate'er I choose,*
> *Let plaintiff or defendant be my lot."*

He recited these lines to us for our pleasure, as gleefully as he always did when he found a good rhyme, a good fight, or a good mug of wine.

> *"So to the last, dear Alatriste, keep*
> *Alone, alone, until the final sleep."*

As for the captain, he remained standing amongst the other guests, not budging, his hat still grasped in his hand, watching the royal cortège process through the Alcázar gardens. And to my surprise, I saw a cloud pass over his face, as if what had just happened had, suddenly and symbolically, bound him far more tightly than he wished to be bound. The less a man owes, the freer he is, and according to the worldview of my master—capable of killing for a doubloon or a word—there were things never written or spoken that he considered to be as binding as a friendship, a discipline, or an oath. And while, beside me, don Francisco de Quevedo continued improvising lines from his new sonnet, I knew, or sensed, that the king's gift of a gold chain weighed on Captain Alatriste as heavily as if it were made of iron.

EXTRACTS FROM

SOME FINE POETRY

WRITTEN BY VARIOUS WITS OF

THIS CITY OF SEVILLE

Printed in the seventeenth century, without a printer's mark,
and preserved in the "Conde de Guadalmedina"
section of the Archive and Library of
the Duques de Nuevo Extremo (Seville).

ATTRIBUTED TO DON FRANCISCO DE QUEVEDO

The last evening and end of the ruffian Nicasio Ganzúa,
who died in Seville from a very bad sore throat
brought on by the rope.

FIRST BALLAD

In old Seville town, in its dark, lofty prison
The cream of the thieves are now gathered together.
They have come to this place for a grand celebration,
A banquet in aid of Nicasio Ganzúa,
For, at dawn, he'll be issued his very last passport.
And it's thus only right, in His Majesty's prison
For a solemn event to be given due weight;
But because it's the king who is giving the orders
No time must be lost—*tempus fugit*, my friends.
Here they come, brothers all of the criminal class,
Yes, those who are paid by the sum of their sword
    thrusts
And all of them dressed in the deepest of mourning,
Though armed to the teeth with glistening steel
(the jailer meanwhile has his itchy palm greased
with the silvery glitter of pieces of eight).
How they praise to the skies the condemnèd man,
Though their praises are not of a sacred kind,

See them sit round a table——the flower of ruffians——

For no honest rogue would ever dare miss

This wake for a man, for a hero illustrious.

How peacock-proud are these would-be nobles

(To be sure, in this gathering, no women are found)

With their hats pulled down low o'er their faces, like
    grandees,

As they drink down whole mugs of the reddest
    of wines

And toast, with huzzahs, the health of Saint Glug,

For to men of the world he's their patron saint.

All drink to the fame of the bravest of comrades

Who, to judge by the barrel of wine they imbibe,

Must indeed be a man most worthy of honor.

At the fore, is the handsome young Ginés el Lindo

Who, they say, is a practicing doctor of fencing,

Even though he's a queer and strums the guitar.

Nearby, Saramago, that fine Portuguese,

Who's always prepared to spout some philosophy;

For sure, he's a doctor *in utriusque*

And wields with a flourish both a pen and a sword.

Another fine rogue can be seen paying court——

from the town of Chipiona and sharp as a tack——

by name, El Bravo de los Galeones.

Then, Guzmán Ramírez, a man of few words,

Grabs a new deck of cards and is ready to play

With Rojo Carmona, his companion at table,
Who's known as a notable trickster to boot.
Many others there are in the thievery line,
Who love to distraction the pockets of others;
A newcomer there is, Diego Alatriste,
Who has come like a brother to be with Ganzúa.
And sitting beside him there's Íñigo Balboa,
A young man who showed at the great Siege of Breda
His courage in fighting—no coward was he.
While they're singing their songs and playing at cards,
While they carry on drinking the wine red as blood,
They are keeping a courteous eye on Ganzúa,
For that is the least decent people can do—
Come when they're needed, give care without stint,
For this kind of misfortune may one day be theirs.

SECOND BALLAD

They were deep in their game and their serious
    drinking
When in came the law so to read out the sentence
And all for the card-playing prisoner's sake.
But no interest he showed in these sonorous words,
Though his precious life's blood depended on them;
More concerned was he then with the scoring of
    points.
When the scribe and the guard were about to depart,

A monk Augustinian offered confession,

Which was straightway declined by Nicasio Ganzúa.

Thus he turned down the chance to sing out at
    vespers

The tune that he never had warbled at prime.

When the monk and the officers finally left,

And Ganzúa was carefully playing his hand,

He found at the end that he held a trump card

And so won the game and collected his winnings.

Then, dealing again, he smoothed his mustache,

And in tones low and grave he addressed his
    confreres:

"I am helpless, my friends, I am stuck in this prison,

Till my neck is caressed by the rope in the morning

With a love so intense it will certainly kill me,

For I'll never escape its tight'ning embrace.

So allow me, my friends, a list of farewells,

My last will and testament, mark every word!

Were it not for the stool pigeon who sang out too
    loudly

I'd be free, and not stupidly facing my death.

I ask you, friends all, give that slimiest of squealers

A good length of steel through the throat—make
    him bleed—

For to leave him the freedom to wag his long tongue

Is a curse and a plague and as deadly as sin.

Item Two: If you please, give a fistful of wishes

To the one who betrayed me—that traitorous
  jeweler—
Hit him hard in the chops when you give him my
  greetings,
For he certainly played me the vilest of tricks—
Thus make sure he will always remember my name.
Item Three: Stick your knives several times in that
  catchpole,
That turd, Mojarrilla, who handled me roughly
When I was arrested. And as for the judge
With his hand-me-down robe and his high noble ways,
Just give him the same, make him bleed for his pains.
And lastly, my whore, Maripizca,
Of clean blood and habits; my friends, look to her,
For though she's no child, proper "ladies" like her
Should not be alone when they walk down the street.
I close on this hour, on this date, in this place,
This the very last will of the ruffian Ganzúa."
Every heart there was moved and everyone stood
And did swear and did promise, as trusty friends
  should,
To execute, faithfully, all of his wishes.

THIRD BALLAD

Ganzúa, awaiting his execution,
Was dressed in the finest of clothes,

He had never before looked so handsome as then
On the night all his friends watched with him.
He was wearing a doublet of fine purple cloth
Whose full sleeves were slashed *à la mode,*
And green canvas breeches that were held up in style
By a belt that was four inches wide,
And shoes for a light Sunday promenade,
Adorned with two bright scarlet bows,
Each shoe with a silvery buckle that glittered
Against the deep black of the leather.
Early next morning, to enter the square,
He changed to a simple serge gown
As befitting a man who was soon to be led
To the scaffold's bare, high wooden hill—
Quite unlike the brave judges who put on their
    gowns
But stay safe and sound in their court.
He rode from the prison upon a gray mule,
Town crier stepping before
And carrying a cross and municipal rod
While he listed the prisoner's crimes.
Handsome Ganzúa rode on without falter—
No trace of last night's carousing—
And greeted with courtly politeness and grace
All those he had known, great and small.
He looked quite serene, like a priest in procession,
So that one almost envied his fate.

No stumble he made as he climbed up the steps,
Though one step was broken and gaping.
And when he was standing at last on the boards
He turned to the crowd and spoke thus:
"Death is of little importance, my friends,
But since by the king it arrives,
Let no one deny the evident truth
That mine is an honorable one."
All nodded and gravely accepted his words,
His whore and executors too.
And they thought it was equally proper and right
That his dear Maripizca had hired
A chorus of blind men to sing for his soul.
A sermon then followed their prayers,
And he recited the Creed with no hint of a tremor,
For it's always a dreadful and shameful dishonor
When infamous ruffians break down and blubber.
The fell executioner stepped up behind
And placing the noose 'round the prisoner's neck,
Said these words: "O, my brother, I ask your
    forgiveness,"
Then quickly he tightened the noose until death.
Our brave Ganzúa did not flinch or grimace,
For death, to him, was as naught,
But with quiet indifference he bore himself
As though he were sunk in thought.

FROM THE SAME

Advice Addressed to Captain Diego Alatriste

SONNET

If what I have I do not fear to lose,
Nor yet desire to have what I do not,
I'm safe from Fortune's wheel whate'er I choose,
Let plaintiff or defendant be my lot.

For if I joy not in another's pain
And worldly wealth brings me no hint of pleasure,
Grim death may come and take me without strain;
I'll not resist or ask for lesser measure.

And you, who even now know not the chains
With which this age imprisons a heart,
Diego—free from pleasures and from pains—
Keep, thus, far hence the prick of passion's dart;

So to the last, dear Alatriste, keep
Alone, alone, until the final sleep.

1. THE CORRAL DE LA CRUZ

Diego Alatriste was in a devil of a hurry. A new play was about to be performed at the Corral de la Cruz, and there he was on the Cuesta de la Vega, dueling with some fellow whose name he didn't even know. The play was by Tirso de Molina, and any first performance of a play by Tirso was a great occasion in Madrid. The whole city, it seemed, was either crammed into the theater or else forming a line outside in the street, and no one in that line would have thought it unreasonable to knife his neighbor if it meant getting a seat or even standing room. There was, however, neither rhyme nor reason to what he was doing now, namely, getting involved in a minor skirmish following a chance collision on a street corner. Such conflicts were, of course, a regular enough occurrence in the Madrid of the day, where it was as common to unsheathe one's sword as to cross oneself.

"Why don't you look where you're going, sir!"

"Why don't you, my man—are you blind?"

"God's teeth."

"God's and anyone else's."

And it was that disrespectful "my man"—for the other fellow was young and quick to anger—that had made a fight inevitable. "You, sir," Alatriste said, stroking his mustache, "can call me 'my man' or even 'boy' all you like, but only with sword and dagger in hand on the Cuesta de la Vega, which is, after all, just a step away—always assuming, of course, that you're gentleman enough to spare me the time."

The other man did apparently have time to spare, or was, at the least, unprepared to modify his language. And so there they were, overlooking the Manzanares River, on the top of a hill to which they had walked side by side like two comrades, without saying a word and without unsheathing the swords or daggers that were now clashing loudly—*cling, clang*—and glinting in the afternoon sun.

After an initial cautious circling of blades, Alatriste was startled into full attention by the first serious thrust, which he parried with some difficulty. He was more irritated with himself than with his opponent, irritated with his own irritation. This was not a good state of mind to be in; any swordfight, when life and health are at stake, requires both a cool head and a steady hand. If you lack either, there is a risk that your irritation—or whatever other emotion you happen to be feeling—might slip from your body, along with your soul, through some previously unnoticed buttonhole in your doublet.

But what could he do? He had left the Inn of the Turk in that same black mood, following an argument with Caridad la Lebrijana. The argument had erupted as soon as she returned home from mass and had involved smashed crockery, slammed doors, and a consequent delay in setting off for the theater. The chance encounter on the corner of Calle del Arcabuz and Calle de Toledo—which would ordinarily have been resolved with common sense and reasonable words—had instead channeled all his ill humor into this duel.

Anyway, it was too late to turn back now. The other man was in deadly earnest and, all honor to him, very good with a blade and agile as a deer. He seemed to Alatriste, from his manner of fighting, to have a soldier's technique: a wide stance, a quick hand, and many a riposte and counter-riposte. He would unleash fierce attacks, intent on wounding, give stabbing thrusts, then withdraw as if to cut and reverse, always watching for the moment when he might lunge forward on his left foot and hook the hilt of his enemy's blade with his dagger. It was an old trick, but effective if the person performing it had a good eye and an even better hand. Alatriste, however, was an older and more battle-hardened fighter, and so he kept moving in a semicircle in the direction of his opponent's left hand, thus thwarting his intentions and wearing him out. He also took the opportunity to study his opponent, who was a good-looking young man in his twenties. Despite his city clothes—short suede boots, an over-doublet of fine cloth, and the brown cape that he had placed on the ground along with his hat so as to be able to move more freely—he had, at least to the eye of an expert, a soldierly air about him: confident, brave, tight-lipped, and certainly no braggart, but concentrating on the job at hand. He was perhaps from a good family. The captain ignored a feint and made a circling movement to the right so that the sun was in his adversary's eyes. He silently cursed himself. By now, the first act of *The Garden of Juan Fernández* would be in full swing.

He decided to finish the business, although not so hastily that it might work against him. Besides, there was no point in complicating his life further by killing a man in broad daylight and on a Sunday. His opponent made a lunge, which Alatriste parried, making as if to deliver a straightforward blow, but instead shifting to the right, lowering his sword to protect his own chest and, in passing, dealing the other man an ugly cut to the head with his dagger. A bystander might have described this as both unorthodox and somewhat underhanded, but there were no bystanders. Besides, María de Castro would already be on stage, and it was still a fair walk to the Corral de la Cruz. This was no time for niceties. More importantly, the strategy had worked. The young man turned pale and fell to his knees, bright red blood gushing from his temple. He had dropped his dagger and was resting all his weight on his sword, which buckled slightly beneath him. Alatriste sheathed his own sword, then went over and disarmed the wounded man by gently kicking the blade from under him. Then he held him up so that he wouldn't fall, took a clean handkerchief from the sleeve of his doublet, and bandaged the gash in the man's head as best he could.

"Will you be all right on your own?" he asked.

The young man looked at him, confused, but did not reply. Alatriste snorted impatiently.

"I have things to do," he said.

The man nodded weakly. He made as if to get up, and Alatriste helped him to his feet, letting him lean on his shoulder. The blood was still flowing beneath the improvised bandage, but the man was young and strong. The bleeding would soon stop.

"I'll send help," added Alatriste.

He couldn't wait to be gone. He looked at the tower of the Alcázar Real that rose up above the walls, then back toward the long Segovia Bridge. No constables—that was one good thing—and no bluebottles either. No one. The whole of Madrid was watching Tirso's play, and there he was, wasting time. One way to solve the problem, he thought impatiently, would be to slip a real to some errand boy or footboy, of the sort usually to be found loitering near the city gate, waiting for travelers. They could then take the stranger back to his inn—or indeed to Hell or wherever else he might choose to go. He helped the wounded man sit down on a large boulder that had once formed part of the city wall. Then he restored to him hat, cape, sword, and dagger.

"Can I do anything more for you?"

The other man's breathing was somewhat labored, and his face was still drained of color. He looked at Alatriste for a long while, as if he found it hard to make out his features.

"Tell me your name," he murmured at last in a hoarse voice.

Alatriste was brushing dust from his boots with his hat.

"My name is my affair," he replied coldly, putting his hat back on. "And I don't give a damn about yours."